DATE DUE			

ADDRESS:
Rimbaud   Mallarmé   Butor

Liliane and Cyril Welch

ADDRESS:
Rimbaud   Mallarmé   Butor

SONO NIS PRESS

VICTORIA BRITISH COLUMBIA

1979

Copyright © 1979 by Liliane and Cyril Welch

Canadian Cataloguing in Publication Data

Welch, Liliane, 1937-
    Address

    Includes index.
    ISBN 0-919462-80-4

    1. Rimbaud, Arthur, 1854-1891. 2. Mallarmé,
Stéphane, 1842-1898. 3. Butor, Michel, 1926-
Mobile. I. Welch, Cyril. II. Title.
PQ296.W44   840'.9   C79-091201-5

Published by
SONO NIS PRESS
Victoria, British Columbia

Designed and printed in Canada by
MORRISS PRINTING COMPANY LTD.
Victoria, British Columbia

When two go together, one sees before the other
So that the best may come to be.
Alone, one might see, But one's sight is shorter
and one's discernment limited.

Iliad, X, 225-7

CONTENTS

PREFATORY NOTE

This book has been published with the help of a grant from the Humanities Research Council of Canada, using funds provided by the Social Sciences and Humanities Research Council of Canada. Work began on the project in the fall of 1974, with further generous aid from the Canada Council (Sabbatical Leave Fellowship) and the Marjorie Young Bell Faculty Fund.

Bibliographical information has been held to a minimum in the text itself (see, however, the Bibliographies appended to the end of the book). For the works central to the critique, the following abbreviations have been used in conjunction with page numbers:

R = Arthur Rimbaud, *Oeuvres Complètes*, Ed. de la Pléiade (Paris, 1972).

M = Stéphane Mallarmé, *Oeuvres Complètes*, Ed. de la Pléiade (Paris, 1961).

F = French edition of Michel Butor's *Mobile* (Paris: Gallimard, 1962).

E = English edition of *Mobile*, translated by Richard Howard (New York: Simon and Shuster, 1963). Much of the task in preparing the English translation lay in retrieving the original English text which the author had composed for his work. Thus the English offers a generally reliable rendition of the original, although we have occasionally preferred our own translations. Except for some cramping in the lay-out (the original is fourteen pages longer), slight incongruencies in alphabetical order (North Carolina appears under "C," etc.), and the missing map of the U.S.A., the form of the translation also remains true to the original.

Permission to quote "Caroline du Nord" from the original *Mobile* (© Edition Gallimard) and "North Carolina" from the English translation of *Mobile* (© George Borchardt, Inc.) is gratefully acknowledged.

INTRODUCTION

I

The 19th century was a time of mounting pressure. The sharpest minds of that age foresaw clearly that the changes then occurring would bring not only some progress in the fulfilment of typical human desires, but also and more emphatically a sorrowful end to the validity of established interpretations of the human condition. Some of these changes, notably the shift to organized industry on the level of economics and the rise of democracy on the level of politics, did offer new interpretations of sorts to fill the gap. But besides being unclear and at odds with one another (e.g., industrialization demands heightened social awareness and democratisation leads to increased insistence on individuality), the main thrust of these interpretations was negative: for acceptance they leaned heavily on the generally acknowledged need to reject as inadequate their predecessors. Thus, the latter were replaced by a stop-gap rather than an affirmative view of the human condition.

In part the restriction to refutation and the avoidance of construction on the level of interpretation were intentional and essential. For the changes occurring during this time implied that all constructive effort should be directed toward future practical tasks. In contrast, interpretive effort could only appear as leading to constraints on concrete construction in economics and politics. In short, positive effort should be confined to building railroads; interpretive effort should endorse such enterprises and ward off those who might call them into question. Progress was plain in its intent; ideology was evil. Only the great minds saw that progress was itself an interpretation and not a natural law; that the interpretation was not only weak but essentially negative; that, as Nietzsche put it, nihilism stood at the door.

Are we today in a more favorable position to understand the changes which have occurred, to interpret the new face of the human condition? The pressure mounted until the boiler exploded. Historians dispute the exact time and place of the explosion, but the World War was at least a visible manifestation and World War II eliminated any further doubts. Since those events we no longer live under obvious pressure of interpretation. The most pressing problems are always those of the day: unemployment, inflation, or pollution on the public level; divorce, abortion, inordinate debt, nervous exhaustion, or mental collapse in private life. With the boiler burst, the pressure released, and the pieces scattered in all directions, the gaping void in the human condition and the incapacity to respond to it, both dreaded by our most perceptive forefathers, have so much engulfed and disarmed us that we fail to understand both the fact and nature of the overall difficulty. We merely chase after one or the other of the scattered pieces. While in some sense the catastrophe is now history (Henry Adams predicted its date as 1921), hindsight has not proved overwhelmingly fruitful.

How are these recollections related to poetry? Reflective literature may explore the economic, political, and philosophical underpinnings associated with the pressure and the explosion, while analytic literature may describe the events themselves. Such exposition obviously cannot be the task of poetic literature. Still, the greatest poetry does elicit the heart of its age, often a troubled heart, and embodies a response to it. While expository undertakings may lead us to the innermost edge of the problem, they leave us helpless to do anything *with* it even if they do aid us to know what we are up *against*. Poetic literature, on the other hand, can create a place to stand and a way to respond in the face of prevailing and threatening forces. It *can* work this way, as something of a global if only momentary catharsis; however, it is not *obliged* to do so, for other functions of poetry do exist. But this one function does account in part for the durability of poetic literature in contrast to the high mortality rate of expository work. For the adequate description of an age varies with the changing perspectives of later time, while the need to respond to the heart of the matter, to move from peripheral considerations to the central ones, remains constant.

A poetic response to an age contains already an interpretation of it. A poem, an epic, a novel involves more, *is* more than this, since it also fashions an event for those who concretely hear, sing, or read the work. But this event embodies a way of making sense out of the whole of what is happening. For instance, Plato clearly understood Homer's work as not only telling entertaining tales but also as interpreting the human condition as essentially transient, forever variable; this interpretation stood in bitter conflict with the one offered by the philosopher and his followers. Interpretation in poetry is clearly creative in two related ways. First, it becomes evident along the way, *ad hoc*;

rather than being a conclusion of a process of inference based on prior evidence, the interpretation emerges as a premiss through which we experience all else. Second, it is essentially a way of affirming; although the things that happen in the course of human experience might not be accepted at face value, at least the battle with them is honored. Thus the interpretation always appears spontaneous in the face of circumstances, unlike a logical premiss contrived beforehand and applicable only tentatively.

One task of literary criticism is to elicit reflectively the interpretation, understood as creative, in given instances of literature. We propose to do this within our work. Specifically, we wish to understand some selected works as embodied responses, creatively interpretive, to the exigencies of our own time.

II

Why this particular string of French poets—Rimbaud, Mallarmé, and Butor? These happen to be especially interesting writers, and the work of each can stand entirely on its own. What, then, do we gain by considering them not only individually but as a sequence? Two things. For one, we can come to understand the identity of the exigency in differing ages, the continuity of the last and the present centuries, the same issue before and after the explosion. For another, the responses embodied in the works of these three poets exemplify three fundamental paths along which such response is possible: the path of immediacy ("life" in the concrete), the path of intellection ("ideation" involving the withdrawal from life), and the path of history ("heritage" as the ideation fashioning the forms of everyday life).

Arthur Rimbaud was born in 1854 and wrote up through the early 1870's. He published himself *Une Saison en enfer* (1873), while his *Illuminations* waited until 1886 to be published, apparently without his authorization. Both of these works represent the human condition as very vivid, very strange, very exacting, and above all very immediate, devoid of any mediation besides that of the poetic voice itself.

Stéphane Mallarmé was born in 1842, began writing in the early 1860's, and continued developing his work until well into the last decade of the century. His is a distinctively reflective poetry; his poems and his commentaries embody a response to a world increasingly hostile to the thoughtful remove from immediacy which had long before been considered as an essential possibility if not necessity for human kind. Thus his work often strikes unwary readers as intentionally obscure, although it has exercised a decided influence on those who were able to tune in on the problematic to which the work addresses itself. In any case, Mallarmé's poems articulate a mediation rather than an immediacy.

Michel Butor was born in 1926. During the 1950's, just when the United States was settling into unmitigated consumerism (an after-War complacence with peace), and while the French intellectuals were still pondering the stimulating and influential philosophical works of the War and post-War era, Butor published a series of poetic works addressed to the contemporary problematic of man in search of time and place: in search of his heritage. Most notable: *L'Emploi du temps* (1956; set in England), *La Modification* (1957; developments on the train from Paris to Rome), and *Le Génie du lieu* (1958; reflections on places in Spain, Turkey, Greece, Italy, and Egypt). In the fall of 1959, and then again in 1962, he assumed the role of visiting professor in the United States (first at Bryn Mawr, then the summer at Middlebury, and later at Buffalo). *Mobile*, an articulation of the "génie" of the United States, was first published in 1962. From then on the problematic of heritage appeared most localizable in America. In a French radio interview early in 1967 Butor remarked:

In the whole of America, in the entire idea of the "new world," there is a kind of extraordinary risk. Here a sort of crisis of humanity is in the making—not only for the people who are there, of course, but also for everybody else, everywhere.

In the spring of 1975 Butor accepted a Chair at the University of Geneva.*

Rimbaud and Mallarmé now stand in the hall of literary fame. But why choose Butor among our contemporaries? We certainly have no intention of usurping the role of future historians of literature. In answer to the question, then, we can only reply that Butor's work, especially his *Mobile*, is indeed contemporary, that it responds effectively to the problematic of heritage today, and that it is strongly, if only implicitly cognizant of

---

* The first novel referred to in this paragraph is translated as *Passing Time*, the second as *Change of Heart*; for information on the translation of *Mobile*, see "Prefatory Note." The quotation is translated from Charbonnier's *Entretiens avec Michel Butor*, p. 199.

the fundamental issues to which the works of Rimbaud and Mallarmé answer. In considering *Mobile*, we bring into critical awareness a work which, besides being worthwhile in itself, also recollects a lineage, an historical line of development, the elucidation of which is crucial for us today.

III

On the surface, then, the plan seems clear enough. We link up three poets and elucidate two or three of their poems (in the final case only one work). In analyzing each piece we both assume that, and show how it embodies a response to contemporary issues. In each of the three Chapters we first take stock of an exigency, then analyze a poem showing how it forms a powerful response, and from there on out we alternate between various reflective and further poetic interpretations of the exigency and the manner of meeting or avoiding it. Finally, the reflection gathers momentum in the course of the analyses. The three exigencies emerge as a unit as we see that the works of the three poets recall the same basic, historically evolved human situation.

Several facets of this plan suggest some more fundamental questions of methodology. *First*, we analyze only a handful of poems (let us call *Mobile* a poem, although it does fall outside every usual classification). Obviously, then, our own work does not make any claim to being quantitatively exhaustive. Should we not have branched out into other poems within the entire corpus of each writer? *Second*, our analyses present a dialogue between the poems and the exigencies of the human condition itself, while mediating the discussion by bringing in additional voices from the traditions which interpret these exigencies in differing ways. Our own work is then *not* a dialogue with those other literary critics who have also talked about the three poets under consideration. Would not such an additional dialogue have added another dimension to our own critique? And *third*, we claim that a heritage speaks to us in the works of all three poets, yet our critique does *not* provide an independent historical account of the eras in which the works arose. Might it not be necessary to establish the historical context of works prior to understanding them?

Such questions may appear innocent enough. However, each one leads into fundamental considerations both about how to approach literary works and about the human condition itself;

or—if asked only rhetorically—it avoids these considerations entirely. For we can decide whether extensive analyses contribute to intensive understanding of works, *only* after we discover how art works work in the first place. Similarly, whether and how much one improves one's consideration of art works by including a chorus of fragmented opinions orchestrated by oneself, is best decided on the basis of an understanding of the difficulties inherent in appreciating the works themselves. And we can determine the need for historical spade-work only after we consider how heritage enters into our experience at all. At least these three questions must lie at the foundation of any methodology which distinguishes itself from bald assertion of method.

Although in the course of our own work we do not *assert* any method at all, we do indeed follow a way (*hodos*), one which slowly brings into view answers to methodological questions. These answers may be outlined in advance but not, in the present case at least, with the intent of "proving" them. A work in aesthetics might possibly demonstrate its principles and thereby "prove" a methodology of art criticism, but a work such as ours can only prove its methodology by helping works do their work. In the actual "application," a method must above all prove itself at the end of the labor, the test being whether its principles allow the matter itself to come to light. There is, of course, some division of labor here, authors doing their share and readers doing theirs. In outline then we bring forward the following:

First of all, a work of art takes us into itself: a poem, a painting, or a concerto *is itself* only insofar as we participate in it. Even though there are evident enticements to enter a work, we do not always join in with ease. Once inside, however, a whole world, a space and a time, unfolds itself, surrounds us, changes the countenances of things, and transforms even ourselves. The whole "point" of a poem, for instance, lies in the entry; *what* reveals itself to us once we are inside tends to take care of itself; *that* we enter poses the difficulty. The critic's *basic* task is to aid and abet entry. And for all the differences among works by differing authors, basically they all rehearse the same *event*: an encompassing configuration which re-configures our otherwise familiar ways of being, thereby changing the countenances of things and transforming the participants. True, the critic must heed and recall what is configured, what changes and what transformations occur. For being unique, every work is an occasion in which uniqueness occurs. But both this sameness

xvi

among all works and the uniqueness of any one work, focus us on one work at a time. *Works are essentially single*: at any given time, one is enough and more than enough. The critic's task is then fundamentally distorted by analogy to any science. A geologist, for instance, makes and analyzes multiple borings to form a sort of grid picturing vast subterranean realities: no one boring, as no one datum for any scientist, "means" anything at all, let alone a "conclusion." For the scientist, only the grid, the picture formed from multiple probings counts. Thus the artistic and the scientific enterprise are sharply distinct: the one forms an event in which we participate, while the other forms a context in which we "square off" against a specified circumstance in order to "case it out" and make use of the determinations made about it. If we take the scientific attitude over into the realm of poems or other art works, we first of all (and, for the poems themselves this is fatal) reduce them from events, or works, to *objects*. We then do justice to these objects only by myriad borings and the formation of a general picture. Such an approach seems all the more self-evident since even to those who approach art works without any interest in or reliance on critics the works often appear first of all as objects, as strange things to be figured out. The helpful critic, on the other hand encourages an inside view and hearing of the *work* and understands all too well the inadequacies of remaining outside with an *object*, either left cold or driven to forming a grid of determination.*

Secondly, a true dialogue among human beings is a rare and beautiful thing. It presupposes that we concentrate neither on the listener nor on the speaker, neither on ourselves nor on our interlocutor, but on a *tertium quid*. Art works, such as the poems we ourselves have selected for critique, are especially notable in that they provide a "third factor" allowing us to talk to one another. We hear each other, and have something to say to one another, only if we are all *there*, present within an event where the configuration of the situation, the countenances of things, and our own being, emerge from the penumbra. One surely destroys a dialogue between writer and reader by trying to shore it up with fragments, always out of context, from other

* The distinction between art object and art work is a fundamental one. It may also be found, for instance, in John M. Anderson's *The Realm of Art*, in John Dewey's *Art as Experience*, in R. G. Collingwood's *The Principles of Art*, and in Robert Henri's pieces collected under the title *The Art Spirit*. These authors vary, of course, in the way they draw the distinction.

critics. Again, neither art works nor art criticism resembles the scientific enterprise the way geology does: in the construction of a grid referring to objects we might well have to call upon and sometimes contradict the determinations of others. In the case of literary and art criticism, such determinations are either totally irrelevant or not really determinations at all but rather isolated voices of *other* dialogues. In either case they risk distracting us from the primary dialogue in progress. Besides, a genuine dialogue directed to a *tertium quid* allows for an unofficial chorus of both like-minded and contrary-minded voices. Once inside, no longer lingering on the outside, we often say about another interlocutor at a previous time, "Ah, yes, *now* I see what he meant!" Appropriately pruned, we might even write this comment down into our text as a footnote. But no dialogue can be constructed out of or even enhanced by such fragments. A good critic creates a dialogue including the reader and directed toward the work; he enters into dialogues with other critics *qua* reader, not *qua* writer.

Finally, heritage (as we argue in Chapter Three) crowds in upon us as the settledness of aspirations and achievements in which we live. It seems to be a destiny of human beings that they come to terms with these crowding forces, and also a fact of our daily lives that we generally do not do so. When we do, we take up a position within the given aspirations and achievements, find them forming themselves in definite patterns, and find ourselves able to respond to them; when we do not, we either drift along within the general current or fight it as an evil fate. Being themselves responses to settled forces, art works can, and the poems we analyze do, provide the entry requisite for coming to terms with our heritage. Yet matters are not always easy. Works which have themselves become parts of our heritage not only crystallize it in themselves, they also appear as objects of the past which are opaque *because* they are past. Thus arises the historicist's claim that to understand a text we must first go back and reconstruct the circumstances (both personal and impersonal) in which the work arose. However, historical inquiry, being itself a response to heritage, can reconstruct only what appears in the crystallization or the lack of it: for instance, accounts can be inspired, drifting, or resentful, and in each case those materials will be reconstructed which appeared in that light or shadow. The dependence of histories on the event of heritage reveals the circularity of the historicist's argument.

Whatever the difficulties of entering, the handful of poems we analyze in this work are more originary than any history can possibly be. As critics we must cross the threshold into heritage and leave the rest to historians. In our present age of historicism, one negative task of responsible criticism is to avoid the temptation of confusing heritage with history, a confusion encouraged by the supposed need to decide in advance what is "subjective" and what is "objective" (the *event* of the art work *vs.* the *determinations* of historical inquiry into this event).

IV

Each one of these principles of method recalls a definite interpretation of the human condition, according to which at each moment two contrary possibilities pose themselves to us: to ride along on the situation in which we find ourselves, carried by it and remaining at an indifferent distance from its inner occurrences, *or* to enter into the situation, in some sense carry it, and move up close to the things emerging in it. This view of the human condition differs markedly from at least two others. It does not hold that man must free himself from the immanent context of appearances and attain to a vision of transcendent reality (as the founders of our Western intellectual tradition seem to have proposed), nor does it claim that man must reconstruct the immanent context to improve human control over appearances (as many representatives of the modern tradition have argued). The first view ran itself out several centuries ago, and the second, although still alive in some respects, has posed more problems than it has solved. The third interpretation of the human condition asks a fundamental question which the other two bypassed: What is the human condition like (in its "immanence," so to speak) so that transcendence *out* of it or, alternatively, reconstruction and mastery *of* it, could ever arise as live issues? Does not the first question marking human being ask whether and how we can enter *into* the time, place and tasks through which we normally only drift (as both the previous traditions admitted)?

All the while, art works have seemed to accept the third interpretation, or at least the question lying at its foundation, and accordingly received from our intellectual traditions an at most lukewarm, often hostile treatment. It was Martin Heidegger's work, most notably his *Being and Time* (1927), which provided the first systematic restatement of the human condition allowing a central place in human experience for art works. Not that philosophers in the older traditions did not somehow appreciate them: Aristotle certainly did, if only obliquely; Kant in his own way; and Hegel, Nietzsche, and Bergson more emphatically. But even for these thinkers art works remained under a peculiar probation, since the basic destiny of man was not yet understood as what we have called "entry." And of course there have been various independent efforts to work out a third interpretation.* However, in retrospect, we can see how Heidegger's work provides foundations sufficiently broad not only to allow for radically new assessments of nearly every domain of human concern, but also to understand both the power and the shortcomings of our traditions. Of course, the exact significance of Heidegger's work still escapes complete grasp. But in the last several decades a massive body of literature has grown up which, aside from internal differences and variations, forms a unity: each piece promotes the view that human destiny is "finite," i.e., one of entering (neither abandoning nor expanding). It is in this tradition that our own work takes its stand.

More specifically, or course, ours is a work in literary criticism. And in his quest for a new vision of the human condition the critic asks first and foremost: How are we to read the literature preceding us? In the modern tradition such thinkers as Bacon and Descartes answered this question with enviable simplicity: Do not read them at all! The new vision, however, holds in principle that to be human means to be wrapped into a finite situation comprising given times, places, and tasks: one dimension of our situation is our heritage. This determination both raises the question as unavoidable and provides a clue to answering it. In his *Truth and Method* (1960), Hans-Georg Gadamer, himself an early student of Heidegger's, argues that the tension between a text (from the past) and the present (in which we read it) belongs essentially to the experience of reading, so that proper reading and helpful exegesis must play precisely on this tension rather than hoping to dispel it. In what Gadamer calls the "hermeneutical" experience we momentarily "fuse" the structure of "pre-judgements" constituting the present with the structure of "pre-judgements" emergent in the work and somehow typifying the past. We err both if we think we have

* A very short list of such efforts would include Martin Buber's *Ich und Du* (1923), Gabriel Marcel's *Positions et approches concrètes du mystère ontologique* (1933) and Henry Bugbee's *Inward Morning* (1958). See also the Annotated Bibliography.

simply lept into the past or if we aspire to reduce the text to our own present. By reconsidering the human condition itself, Gadamer works out a third way, one which justifies the contention that the other two err. "There is no more an isolated horizon of the present," he says when speaking of the basic human condition itself, "than there are historical horizons which one would have to strive to obtain." For traditions already crowd in upon us, cluttering our present with pre-judgements: as human beings, we must both live *in* the present initially formed by this crowd, but also work *through* it for the sake of an encounter at the moment. In our own work we call this event of encounter the emergence of selfhood and thinghood. *One* way of meeting our destiny is to "test" our present structure of "pre-judgements," i.e., to work through it for the sake of emergence, by reading a work from our tradition. For in such reading we are confronted with an embodiment of tradition both alien and familiar to us: alien because it formed itself in another age with other configurations, familiar because it belongs to the stream of tradition making us what we are today. Gadamer's other works clarify that here he not only speaks to the "epistemological" foundations of historiography, but also endeavours to save a deteriorating pedagogical situation.

Many of the leading literary critics in Europe today were quick to assimilate the new vision of the human condition originally born back in the 1920's. Some, like Hans Robert Jauss, e.g., in his *Literatur als Provokation* (1970), also explicitly acknowledge their indebtedness to Gadamer and provide accounts not only of works of literature, but also of the principles of literary criticism. Others simply proceed to the task of interpretation: Jean-Pierre Richard in a very poetic and phenomenological fashion, Georges Poulet by concentrating on the themes of space and time in works, Hugo Friedrich in a reflective-historical manner, and so on (see our Annotated Bibliography). What all such critics have in common is tersely stated by Jean Starobinski in his *L'Oeil vivant* (1961):

The work questions me. Before talking on my behalf, I must lend my voice to this strange power which challenges me; otherwise, however docile I may be, I always risk preferring to this power the reassuring tunes which I myself invent. It is not easy to keep the eyes open to welcome the look which seeks us out. We must no doubt affirm not only for criticism but also for all enterprises of knowledge: 'Look so that you may be looked at!'

V

In the last analysis, a work such as a poem must itself address us. The work of literary criticism, on the other hand, can only aid and abet this address. And it fails if in any manner it claims to supplant the work it talks about, to tell the reader "all about it." For then it fosters the view that its own mode of discourse has its power and purpose independent of the work to which it addresses itself. Perhaps in principle any *kind* of approach can show and avow its dependence on the address, and so contribute to it in its own manner. There are many ways leading to the event, and precisely as many ways of detracting from it. For each way also allows us to stop short. An historical approach can stop with its abstract determinations. A psychological approach can stop with its own conception of consciousness. A reflective approach can stop with its own ideas. A thematic approach can get lost in its own themes. A poetic approach can become intoxicated in its own song. A structural approach can become consumed by its own constructions. On the other hand, if we complete any approach we arrive: in some sense we then leave the approach behind.

What addresses us in an art work? The work itself, of course. We are taken into it, and so find ourselves facing things within a reconfiguration of the human situation. So what addresses us *in* the works is our origins. Being original the work itself reveals these origins. The critic has to be original in this sense, too. But no critic can rightly lay claim to any originality of his own: he must let the originality of the works shine through. At most, the origins might "belong" to these. If the critic's approach appears new, its newness remains an incidental feature and becomes an issue in itself only from an outside standpoint. In any case, our own work does not aim to promote any conventional view of literature or literary criticism. Nor does it try to prove the validity of an innovated view. It simply proposes to cut a path, one among others and equally susceptible to clutter. Yet, with the courage to approach matters directly one may sometimes find oneself uncovering the truly great ways incessantly trivialized by tired convention and self-absorbed innovation.

Chapter One

RIMBAUD AND CITY LIFE

1. THE QUESTION

We live largely today in cities. But where is this? Where are we? and Where... today?

Cities are primarily places for business. Hence they are unlivable. One city is plagued by filth-producing industry, rendering the primordial act of breathing an unpleasant, even a difficult task. Another has successfully avoided heavy industry and is then plagued by hoards of fume-producing automobiles conveying avalanches of office workers and delivery boys to and fro throughout the 24-hour day. Thus, for all the facilities increasingly available, cities appear overcrowded. Those who still feel "at home" are the pickpockets, shady entrepreneurs, advertisers, beings who basically reject the city as a home and understand it as an uninhabitable, exploitable jungle. The complaint that the cities are overcrowded is commensurate with the complaint that no human beings live there: each avoids the others, knows only those who dwell miles away by car although handy enough by telephone. In gasping for breath and avoiding traffic, we have no time, no place, for others.

That cities are unlivable, no places to live, is evident in the efforts to counteract the ills: anti-pollution laws, pedestrian-only zones, and increased law-enforcement; private electronic air-cleaners, ear-plugs, tranquillizers, straight whisky, and weekly appointments with medical practitioners and psychoanalysts. These measures all aim at reducing the unlivability of the space, they are not at all designed to construct a viable place. They accept as their starting point, and undo only slightly, an unlivable situation whose meaning lies chiefly in commercial transaction, mass production and transport of goods, concomitant with mass organization and transport of persons. The one-time centers of cities are either abandoned to the fate of slums or built up into office buildings. Cities tend to become spaces through which one passes or where one transacts business. Woe to the man who cannot afford an abode outside the city: his ears, his nostrils, his eyes will sting him into insensibility or insanity.

During the last centuries Western history has been marked by

1

a movement away from the land and into the cities. The location of life at the outset of this strange movement is evident to us in the village, remnants of which still linger on in Europe, although it is practically unrecognizable in North America. A village is a place to live, an organization of multiple human interests around a point of departure: a departure into the morning of the land, away from the evening of organization. A village encompasses both ends of movement in an evidently viable manner, the home and the field.

To us nowadays a village appears very nearly as an art work. For here each human construction yields to the founding base of the construction. The roads and paths are finite: they run from thing to thing, from trough to well to stable door to refuse heap to field's edge, to brook's bank. Each stretch constitutes a response to something local, thus differing sharply from the modern highways running through or around a town, indifferent to all settlements, and avoiding all places of self-contained repose. Many details of village architecture suggest the same finitude as do the paths: windows are pierced often only afterwards in accordance with the internal exigencies of one particular peasant's life or in gradual response to the exigencies of the weather. In contrast, modern buildings are conceived as totalities in advance, not as responses to the local situation. Subsequent alterations often merely indicate earlier mistakes in calculation.

Today a village is often little more than a shell, a museum piece for the wanderer who can see in it a configuration that took shape within hearing of a convergence. Walking through such a village, we sense the effects of city life. With electricity and inside plumbing, with the rationalization of farming and the importation of cheap factory goods, deliberate human activity and daily rebirth recede and those who stay in such circumstances often sit in melancholy at their windows looking at life pass by, hiding their shame behind thin curtains.

Although the stream from the land toward the cities is a commonplace today, we are not witnessing a simple relocation, for the plausible-sounding location in the city is strangely lacking. The stream does flow, but with only a formal, non-supportive goal called "city." If this flow has any supportive power, it lies in the movement itself. Not a cathedral, but rather a railway, today one's private automobile, "locates" human concern and effort: the conveyance which contains intrinsically no reference,

2

and receives a goal only arbitrarily, according to the choices and whims of the moment.

A "return to the land," of the sort long advocated by people terrified by the stream into the cities, is obliquely feasible in terms of a weekend house, bird-watching or boating, hunting or fishing: all modes of recovery from and, more tellingly, recovery *for* city life. The land here is a relief, at most a nostalgia. Welcome as it might be for such uses, it does not offer a solution to the perplexities, the emptiness, the destruction of city life.

The question is: How can the present movement from the land into the cities configure a place to live? And this despite the fact that the movement initially denies the finitude requisite for configuration? The question must be distinguished from concerns for relief or reduction of ills. If the question does not endure throughout an effort to understand what a city is, what its movement already offers, we scurry on to solutions which always presume that we understand already the where of the city and need only confine or protect it. In this last instance, we surrender to the forces destroying the city's own potentiality.

The problematic of the migration from country into cities will receive an additional focus if we consider Karl Marx's systematic answer to the question. For Marx, industry was developed by a capitalism which now suffocates its own progeny but will eventually die a natural or violent death and leave industry in its purity of form as the contextual condition of human well being. The flow from the land toward the cities is here given an economic interpretation. Thus the problem relocates itself: even if the ex-peasant, the new city-dweller, manages to eke out of his employment a bare living, his work has no purpose beyond merely making a living. Whatever the worker or his employer makes is no longer his, but passes from the assembly line onto the market in mocking indifference to him. The movement has no point of consummation, it is alienated from the processes of labor and represents to the worker an endless dissipation of energies. In the modern large-scale co-operative effort, the substance, sustenance, or guiding star can consequently only be society itself. Society must become the reference of the worker, he must work for it and must feel included in it. As long as he works for another man, for the capitalist, he is alienated from the only possible consummation of his work, and society itself remains divided into two classes of unequal numbers, each warring against the other. According to Marx, this unstable interim condition of capitalism (city life in essence) shall eventually dissolve, society shall heal itself, and men and women will find their substance—when capitalists (who initially supplied the entrepreneurial spirit requisite for organizing human effort into industry) will disappear, when men and women will no longer become the wielders of other people's labor power. The requisite entrepreneurs can then be generated out of the already existing industry, and they will be paid employees like the rest.

Without agreeing or disagreeing with Marx's economic interpretation, let us note its basic structure. Man is, becomes, discovers what he is within or with regard to what he makes, whether with his hands or thoughts, be the result a cabinet, a civil law, or a philosophical treatise. So stated, the basic structure hardly diverges from the ancient Greek version. Yet nowadays human effort, where socially integrated in a distinctively modern manner, is partial and organizational. Both the time of labor and that of private consumption evidence only endless movement. Thus the question: In this industrial society, wherein resides the completing moment, the consummation of the effort? Marx's answer stems from the consideration of a question posed in the face of the structure: What basically does industrial labor make? He answers this question, and so also the first one: society itself, mankind as a whole. For, he argues, man is the agent, the labor power, inaugurating the operation of modern industry. Within the sphere of industry itself there may be no "end" in sight, no consummating purpose. But if we look behind the endless movement, rather than ahead, we discover the agency which serves as a clue to understanding the location of substance.

Today total economic interdependence constitutes the basis of the modern categorical imperative. But does such a dependence, such built-in collectivity, recommend itself to our affirmation? No doubt we do well to affirm it, for rejection might eventually entail self-destructive maladjustment. Yet does this collectivity of the human context recommend *itself* within the frantic transpassings of modern industry? Clearly not. In itself, such collectivity, such dependence, experienced most poignantly during the rush-hour traffic, is repellent. Precisely today's large cities display a marked lack of "fellow feeling," a definite and calculated effort to seal oneself off from the rest of mankind, a prevalent, perhaps subdued hostility of the individual for the masses. Marx's analysis, like any other memorable one,

4

traces the lines of force to propose neither a solution, nor an experience of consummation, but a need, a lack, a possibility, ... a question.

Once again: How is affirmation possible within and of nonfinite movement? This question undercuts the Marxian economic-political analysis recommending affirmation of society as the substance of modern industrial labor. It also undercuts the individual solution of fleeing the city during one's free time. Finally, it undercuts the group effort to counteract the evils of industrial society, its pollution, crime, and other shortcomings. Plainly, these latter counteractions remain problematics of survival. They by-pass the central issue: How can the city be experienced as configuring a moment of consummation? This simple and generally forgotten question asks not how we might survive, but how we can live well, how the city, as the apogee of industrial society, can appear and be blessed.

2. THE PROSE POEM *"VILLES"*

Even the question of "how" presupposes that the revival is *possible*. We must therefore ask it with this possibility in view. Any genuine question must issue from, remain within hearing of, the very thing called into question, the very thing calling *for* the question and so calling upon us to pose and answer it. One way to remain within hearing is to consider carefully works which do configure the experience of city life as consummated.

In Arthur Rimbaud's *Illuminations* (probable date of writing: 1873-1875), several prose poems explicitly state the experience of the city in the mode of revival. We may consider the first of the two entitled *"Villes"* (*R*, 135). (See the following facing pages; the translation besides anticipating the commentary, also stands in "exploded" form, conforming to the groupings revealed by the commentary.)

How do these 23 statements configure an experience of cities? The images are wild and fantastic, a condescending critic would say; chaotic or mad, says the unfriendly one. Yet these effects are no doubt intended by the configuration. The first statement reads:

(1)   These are your cities!

The opening announces and declares, in the mode of wonder, perhaps even defiance, a "general" phenomenon, "cities" not as

VILLES

Ce sont des villes! C'est un peuple pour qui se sont montés ces Alleghanys et ces Libans de rêve! Des chalets de cristal et de bois qui se meuvent sur des rails et des poulies invisibles. Les vieux cratères ceints de colosses et de palmiers de cuivre rugissent mélodieusement dans les feux. Des fêtes amoureuses sonnent sur les canaux pendus derrière les chalets. La chasse des carillons crie dans les gorges. Des corporations de chanteurs géants accourent dans des vêtements et des oriflammes éclatants comme la lumière des cimes. Sur les plates-formes, au milieu des gouffres, les Rolands sonnent leur bravoure. Sur les passerelles de l'abîme et les toits des auberges, l'ardeur du ciel pavoise les mâts. L'écroulement des apothéoses rejoint les champs des hauteurs où les centauresses séraphiques évoluent parmi les avalanches. Au-dessus du niveau des plus hautes crêtes, une mer troublée par la naissance éternelle de Vénus, chargée de flottes orphéoniques, et de la rumeur des perles et des conques précieuses, la mer s'assombrit parfois avec des éclats mortels. Sur les versants, des moissons de fleurs grandes comme nos armes et nos coupes, mugissent. Des cortèges de Mabs en robes rousses, opalines, montent des ravines. Là-haut, les pieds dans la cascade et les ronces, les cerfs tettent Diane. Les Bacchantes des banlieues sanglotent et la lune brûle et hurle. Vénus entre dans les cavernes des forgerons et des ermites. Des groupes de beffrois chantent les idées des peuples. Des châteaux bâtis en os sort la musique inconnue. Toutes les légendes évoluent et les élans se ruent dans les bourgs. Le paradis des orages s'effondre. Les sauvages dansent sans cesse la fête de la nuit. Et, une heure, je suis descendu dans le mouvement d'un boulevard de Bagdad où des compagnies ont chanté la joie du travail nouveau, sous une brise épaisse, circulant sans pouvoir éluder les fabuleux fantômes des monts où l'on a dû se retrouver.

Quels bons bras, quelle belle heure me rendront cette région d'où viennent mes sommeils et mes moindres mouvements?

CITIES

These are your cities!
Here's a people for whom these Alleghenies and Lebanons of dream rose themselves! Cabins of crystal and of wood that move themselves upon invisible rails and pulleys. The old craters, belted with collossi and with palms of copper, roar melodiously among the fires.
Festivals of love sound over the canals suspended behind the cabins. The hunt of chimes rings out in the gorges. Corporations of giant singers rush up in garments and banners glittering as the light of the peaks.
On the platforms, amidst the chasms, the Rolands sound their valor. On the footbridges of the abyss and the roofs of hostels, the blaze of the heavens beflags the masts. The collapse of apotheoses rejoins the fields of the heights where seraphic centauresses evolve among the avalanches. Up above the level of the highest ridges a sea troubled by the eternal birth of Venus, loaded with orpheonic fleets and with murmuring of precious pearls and conches: this sea at times grows dark with deadly flashes. On the slopes, harvests of flowers, large as our arms and our goblets, bellow. Processions of Mabs, in russet and opaline gowns, climb ravines. Up there, their feet in the cascade and the brambles, the stags suckle Diana. The Bacchantes of the suburbs sob and the moon burns and bays. Venus enters into the caverns of forgers and hermits.
Groups of belfries sing the ideas of peoples. From castles built of bone issues the unfamiliar music. All the legends evolve and the elks fling themselves through the towns. The paradise of storms caves in. The savages dance ceaselessly the festival of the night.
And, one hour, I descended into the movement of a boulevard in Bagdad where companies sang the joy of the new labor, in a heavy breeze, on the move without the power to elude the fabulous phantoms of the hills where we all had to find our bearings.

What sturdy arms, what happy hour, will restore to me this region whence come my slumbers and my least movements?

individual but as several. Only in the 22nd statement do we hear of *a* city, Bagdad, a nearly legendary one standing in uneasy conjunction with the bulk of the configuration. And only in the two last statements does the articulation receive an apparent and, again, uneasy grounding in a narrator. Accepting in good faith the poem's claim to configure cities in the mode of severality rather than individuality or personality, how are we to discern a workable structure shaping the experience? Only a detailed consideration of what the poem evokes can lead to such a discernment. However, we may take as a clue precisely the most puzzling and challenging feature of the poem: the central statements 8 through 16 recall legendary figures, from Roland to Venus, to configure what is distinctively modern. Postulating at least this much order, even though still in the mode of puzzlement, we may proceed to discern a rhythmic structure in the remaining statements.

After the initial announcement, the subsequent three statements fulfil the promise. What is to be discerned in a city? The second statement answers:

> (2)   Here's a people for whom these Alleghenies and Lebanons of dream rose themselves!

Most remarkable in a city are its people. To be sure. But what kind of people? Special, peculiar ones "for whom" mountain ranges, the Allegheny Mountains in the Eastern United States and the Lebanon Mountains along the Eastern Mediterranean, jutted themselves out of the flat crust of the earth, heavenward. From the standpoint of a village dweller, whether in the gentle Ardennes or in the towering Alps, the statement is fully sacrilegious and oddly backwards. The mountains of a village constitute the focal point "for which" the village people are there. Decisions in a village bend the people toward the exigencies of nature. Decisions in a city, however, bend nature to the exigencies of men. In a village we *see* even distant mountains. In a city, in Lausanne or Rome or Denver, we *fight* the mountains: if we see them, we do so according to their possible use for amusement or for profit. For the city mind the mountains are there for it, not it for them. Thus old-time village mountain climbers often complain that for their younger city counterparts the mountains are merely indexes of their own prowess and reputation. And scientific considerations about mountains direct their research and results to oil and mineral deposits, waterways, dangerous faults—items of keen interest to modern industry. Although a geologist would likely never ground the significance of his investigation in the possibility of industrial advantage, industrial concerns nonetheless initiate and finance, directly or indirectly, the research.

Correlative to a people's vision of the human circumstance is a manifestation of human response. Such manifestation, in the form of a construction, is evoked by the next, essentially vocative statement:

(3) Cabins of crystal and of wood that move themselves upon invisible rails and pulleys.

From the myriad varieties of human construction, "cabins of crystal and of wood" are selected. These are not simple houses of glass and plaster. Moreover, they move themselves. Finally, these self-moving, specially made constructions are essentially part of a network, although one "knows" this participation only abstractly since the directing rails and the empowering pulleys are unseen. We may think of railway cars or funicular cars or the cabin conveyances in fun parks, steel factories, or mountain resorts. Taken separately, the words of the statement each have a clear reference, but the statement as a unit fits any number of constructs of human conveyance within a network. Not a stable palace or mansion, nor a transcendence-exuding church steeple, nor a point of consummation like a table of bread and wine: yet the positive framework of the choice clearly reveals the mode of human response most forcefully demanded by modern city life.

A people and the manifest human response coalesce around a third thing: the place of work. Only the penultimate statement of the poem explicitly refers to "the new labor," the watchword of the theoreticians of industrial society. Yet the fourth statement locates the experience of this new labor without naming it:

(4) The old craters, belted with colossi and with palms of copper, roar melodiously among the fires.

A people, *some* cabins, *the* craters. Aged, these craters are belted with oversized images of men and with living nature in mineral form. The metallurgical industry, at one time in the mountains on the edges of society, is now transformed into the hearth of human labor. In the process of this transformation, men emerge as staggering colossi of supercraftsmen, and living nature is transmuted into its mineral content. The sound of this place, these old craters, is not of the wind or of the birds in the trees: it is of the high furnaces roaring in their fires. The melody reveals the basic strain of urban life.

The initial four statements first announce and then build the stagings of cities:

> These are your cities! Here's a people for whom these Alleghenies and these Lebanons rose themselves! Cabins of crystal and of wood that move themselves upon invisible rails and pulleys. The old craters, belted with colossi and with palms of copper, roar melodiously in the fires....

These lines first stage an inside view of cities; the play itself then follows. What is achieved by this initial and crucial staging? We have seen *how* it comes into being: strange-sounding claims turn out to be accurate descriptions. Not for the peasant and not in the geologist's official report, but in concrete human experience, for those involved in city life, mountain ranges come to be there for city people. Yet this is not public doctrine. Particularly nowadays, when the victory of the cities over the country is uncontested, we forget the revolutions which have occurred. Our cities are comprised mainly of department stores and service industries lodged in skyscrapers and employing, besides maintenance and sales personnel, mainly pencil pushers, desk workers, computer programmers. Yet "heavy" industries remain the supportive basis of these symbiotic shops and light industries. Such basic industries are the points of contact with those mountain ranges and minerals, within the incessant movement of this revolved relationship with nature. The poem succinctly states the contact and reinstates the city in the peculiar and exciting character of this contact.

How is an inside view achieved? Oblivion is the recurrent point of departure. The "insides" of oblivion vary from the blindness of immediate absorption in the trivial routines of one's job, to the euphoria or despair of groundless afterwork. One's job may have an "inside," but no view; one's "free time" may include a view, but has lost its "insides." In the shattering of oblivion which the poem is now preparing, we return to the *source* of both work and afterwork, to the network's point of contact with the elements.

The Greek polis was built explicitly to open onto the four elements of earth, air, fire, and water: rock, wind, sun, and sea. The modern city is based on cement, steel, and oil. However, the

10

latter-day point of contact differs from ancient ones not primarily in its reference, but more fundamentally in its conception of the human role. Today we do not bend ourselves to the elements, we break them down, literally pulverize them (as in cement and concrete) and even disintegrate them (as in nuclear power); so that in their formlessness they become receptive to the new form we wish to give the pulp. Whereas our forefathers accepted the stone in principle and then chipped it down to the measure of man, we today smash the stone into powder and build up a habitation to any measure we please.

An inside view affords discernment of the outside, of what faces and founds human organization. Such a view, however, is not "normal"; it is extra-ordinary. For it shatters our ordinary images of things, it reverses our perceptions during immediate absorption in daily tasks and during afterhours of fatigue and recovery. This reversal surfaces in the syntax of the poem. In "*Villes*" elements are juxtaposed which contravene the signification structuring the course of movement and which undermine the "common sense" of afterhours complacency: the mountains have jutted heavenward for us, the crystal dwellings move themselves, and high furnaces are surrounded by giant statues of men and by trees of metal. Yet the descriptive claims themselves are "true," i.e., accurate. For they are measured on an event of truth. The prevalent modes of oblivion are dissolved at the point of contact for the sake of emergence of that with which the contact is made. The descriptions of a poem "fit" not because they reflect prevalent features within the ordinary significations of life, but because they shatter the oblivion of ordinary signification with its very own components, opening it (the signification) out upon its source and turning us toward this source. Whereas accurate observations about *things* and about *persons* form two quite distinct groups, the truth which dissolves the oblivious signification of ordinary experience is a unitary event, an opening onto things and simultaneously an opening of ourselves.

Thus the sensuousness of the prose poem. The inside view effects a point of contact where the things of cities loom up. Just as rock, wind, sun, and sea surge into view from the ancient Greek town of Lato on the island of Crete or from the sanctuary of Delphi on the mountainous mainland; so gravel pits, oil wells, high furnaces, and power dams may constitute a point of contact for us today. They *may* do so if the signification has first

11

undergone a reversal, if the oblivion has been shattered with its own tools.

The chief implement of urban oblivion of things is mass production, i.e. the utter indifference of things, the lack of material differences accentuated by the proliferation of generic differences. Our urban environment is ugly not because of its filth, but because it offers only *kinds* of mass produced things. Each is one of a kind, having a definite lifetime, depreciating according to a mathematical formula, and being replaced by the calendar rather than by direct exigency: this necessary pattern of modern production extends into all dimensions of modern life. Yet "*Villes*" takes into its articulation precisely this realm of indifference. Mountains in essence serving the people, myriads of mobile constructions strangely propelled, and varying industrial machinery, locate colossal undertakings upon a "nature" that at one time asserted her own self-subsistence and capricious violence. The poem allows for a sensuality by revealing things as they *are*, urbanly, in the context of massive production of otherwise indifferent things.

The expressiveness of the prose poem enters immediately with the sensuousness, even though the explicit voice of a narrator only enters in the last two statements. For in the reconstruction of the human role *we* are thrown back into the point of contact with things: *we* are propelled out of the oblivion of our everyday absorption within, and our periodic retreat from, labor.

The chief character of urban self-oblivion is collectivity, the utter indifference of people, the lack of individuality. Urban life is impersonal because uncountable numbers of people share everything in common. Yet the poem engages precisely this collectivity. The mood of "*Villes*" is definitely not one of lyrical individuality. Neither, however, is it the political mood of collective solidarity. How, then, does the poem extract a human stance out of urban collectivity? Statements 2 and 4 suggest an answer. Although the mountain ranges come into being as serving the purposes of this urban breed, this "people" turns directly toward the elements with *all* its might. Whereas a glance at the mountains yields the comment, "They are just there for us," a glance at the people reveals "colossi and palms of copper" surrounding what used to be a source of fire but is now among the fires, i.e., parts within an "ever-living fire" (Heracleitus, Diels fragment 30). In other words, the inside view into which the poem pulls us and wherein our stance is radically

12

transformed, opens *us* out onto the elements forever other than, supportive of, human organization. The inside view is a view to the outside: and it is *we* who see.

The first four statements of "*Villes*" set the stage for the play that follows immediately in the next three statements. The fifth reads:

(5)   Festivals of love sound over the canals suspended behind the cabins.

The pattern of signification, once again, is strange. Yet one item is familiar: we are sent up to, or around behind, the crystal cabins already presented. Here we find canals. But these are "suspended"—in the same way a bridge is suspended over water. The imagery is reversed. The traditional attitude accepts nature as inevitably given in fixed form, and human interests are adjusted to it. The new, as yet unacknowledged attitude accepts initially only the human interest and adjusts nature to this. Ideally, a modern canal goes exactly where we direct it, we "suspend" the water where we wish over the land. Yet this wilfulness is only a background. The image of this statement is ultimately auditory rather than visual: we are asked to hear a festival "sounding over" those canals suspended behind the mobile cabins of crystal and of wood; throughout the poem such "auditions" dominate the "visions." But why festivals "of love"? Festivals pertain to the moment of released and renewed contact with the source of human effort, they celebrate human labor in the face of its ground. But modern effort is in-grown. Being intra-humanly based, it contrasts neatly with the nature-based effort of the ancient Greeks and the God-based efforts of Christian Rome. Modern celebration, to all appearances, commemorates man only, collective human effort as such and nothing more. Thus the festival heard over the waters is one of love, of human bonds.

Yet the articulation of in-grown human effort receives a strange and reversed directionality. The poem continues and cumulatively accentuates what the fifth statement commences. The sixth statement reads:

(6)   The hunt of chimes rings out in the gorges.

Although "*Villes*" brings modern cities to the fore, it recurrently takes us to the contrary of cities. We begin to realize that cities *are* this movement. This modern movement, far from being

13

directed toward a traditionally conceived nature or toward any transcendent source of nature, heads rather toward "elements": in the mood, we may provisionally suspect, of modern chemistry. That a hunt should "ring out in the gorges" comes as no surprise; that chimes, carillons, should do so, does not tax our imagination: in Europe each separately is not uncommon. But what "rings out in the gorges" is "the hunt of chimes." Chimes are on the hunt or chimes are being hunted: the language here does not allow for a clear distinction between the objective and the subjective genitives. However, whether as hunting or as hunted, the chimes are said to belong to the hunt. Normally, though, chimes belong to a church steeple or a bell tower, and they ring out to announce a festival, a celebration. Chimes traditionally gather a people together around an edifice in the center of a village or town, in celebration of what transcends the people (on the occasion of baptism, marriage, death, and so on). The statement of the poem here reverses the direction: hunting or hunted, the chimes move away from the center of the people and into the gorges. Urban life is essentially a collective hunt, a chase, which receives its own celebration when it is properly acknowledged as a movement away from the center, not just on weekends and to a refuge, but at all times out into the wild.

The seventh statement, the last of the three carved out for critical consideration as a unit, appears to answer the question: What is the distinctively human role within an organization that issues no longer from a consecration of a center but rather from a preparation for an advance upon essentially alien elements, elements so far accorded identity only in terms of human purposes? The "answer" opens this question rather than closes it:

> (7) Corporations of giant singers rush up in garments and banners glittering as the light of the peaks.

Not just singers, but giant ones, and these not as solitary, e.g., Faustian individuals, but as incorporated into one body. A "corporation," in French, can only mean (as it does in old English) a body of men plying a common trade (a "guild," except that this refers to a common payment of dues rather than to the formation of a common body). And these singers do not stand complacently as a chorus looking onto the action. They rush up, as a collective body, in garments and banners reflecting the pure bright light of mountain peaks. The "banners" are the oriflammes, the gold-flaming flags traditionally (in France from the 12th to the 15th centuries) marking the solidarity of those engaged militarily in a quest or a defense of the sacred. Much of the imagery of "*Villes*" is war-like. Yet if there is anything *sacred* here is is the movement itself. It can lie neither in a quest, since this would imply a return to the center, nor in a defense, since this would in turn imply that the center is a "substance" while the periphery is "property" and what lies beyond is mere "accident" to be warded off. If the sacred *is* the movement itself, then men and women, in rushing up as a body and in war-like fashion, quite properly sing. Together the three statements do indeed articulate the same directionality of human response:

> Festivals of love sound over the canals suspended behind the cabins. The hunt of chimes rings out in the gorges. Corporations of giant singers rush up in garments and banners glittering as the light of the peaks.

Evidently, the singers sing what otherwise only sounds over the canals and rings out in the gorges: loving and hunting. They are the giants who accept urban life in its "truth," who are "in the know" as to the life-directing exigencies of the city. Thus their song continues throughout the configuration of cities.

Yet the central bulk of the prose poem, statements 8 through 16, does not focus on familiar urban phenomena. It rather speaks of events from our literary heritage. The subject is doubly strange, since city life not only differs from the life sung by such literature, it contravenes it explicitly whenever the two, city life and our essentially rural heritage, come into direct encounter. By and large we avoid such encounter. We moderns often assign literature to a realm of culture; flirting with "cultivation," we hope to escape the urban realities pressing in upon us: a weekend culture to fill our weekend house. If by some mistake the two do in fact meet, the bizarre signification of the literature is branded as mere superstition, the product of an overworking yet basically timid imagination. In the poem "*Villes*," however, our literary heritage enters neither as culture nor as a competitor of urban life: it enters as a description of our cities. How is this possible?

The rapid succession of images forces us to recall the gist of each literary reference, which then undergoes a sudden transformation rather than a development. The fleeting movement of the images thus reflects already the movements of city life. Statement 8 reads:

(8)   On the platforms, amidst the chasms, the Rolands sound their valor.

Charlemagne's historical commander Roland is the hero-be-come-legend of the 12th century *Chanson de Roland*: the man who sounds his appeal for help not when he needs it, but only when the pending defeat indicates too late that he needed it, therefore more as an announcement of the end than as a plea for aid. But now the one "inimitable" Roland has been multiplied into a phalanx of heros who "come in his name." They form a definite type and stand in a definite place: *the* Rolands are on *the* platforms "placed" in chasms. The location is partly rural and partly urban: from countryside to loading dock, from the singularity of Roland to the plurality of heros still sounding their valor in this movement. The next statement has a similar purport:

(9)   On the footbridges of the abyss and the roofs of hostels, the blaze of the heavens beflags the masts.

A *passerelle* (a footbridge over a river, a gangway to a ship, a "bridge" on a ship) is a place for movement on foot: here over "the abyss," a gorge or a chasm. An *auberge* (a hostel or inn) affords temporary sojourn, one moves into and out of it, receiving sustenance (food and shelter) only in passing. On, i.e. above these locations of movement an event transpasses: "masts" (whether ship masts or telephone, nowadays television poles) are "beflagged" by the blaze of the heavens, presumably the play of light of the noonday sun. All but one of these images are rural: wild and tame, in any case "passing" and glorified by the presence of the sun. Only the beflagging depicts a human act, one marking human organization and commensurate with the banners and Rolands of the previous statements (7 and 8). This image of beflagging is again war-like, suggesting the extremes (the end, but perhaps also the beginning) of battle. And it dominates, from above, the image of the land, whether wild (as the abyss) or tame (as the hostel), drawing it into the configuration of the city. Indeed, in the city a war rages not between two parties within the city, but between the new human organization and the old nature. The city is not a "new" thing that simply supplants the old, it is the battleplace itself. Statement 2 initiated a paradox which continues through the entire poem: a man-centered activity has no center, it is activity essentially moving us out upon the elements on the periphery. In

16

brief, the forbidden fruit of the city life is self-sufficiency. In our oblivious naïveté we often believe that a city should be a purely human, self-contained organization and that only by error does it remain dependent on the elements:

> (10)   The collapse of apotheoses rejoins the fields of the heights where seraphic centauresses evolve among the avalanches.

In the city the deifications of man collapse. *A Roland is no longer possible.* But in collapsing they rejoin the fields: they do not recede into the gloom of defeat but rather these new Rolands belong on the high plateaus where they are illuminated by the light of the noonday sun. On these fields of the heights, presumably battlefields, creatures "evolve." Besides having the English sense of "development," the French word carries the military meaning of troop maneuvering, shifting of places, rearrangement of battle positions. These creatures from the heights are partly human and partly natural: centaurs have long been interpreted as marking man's awareness of his bifurcation. Man belongs to the pristine realm of earthly creaturehood, being at times totally absorbed into his vital functions. But he also belongs to a realm transcending the pristine one: he is responsible *for* earthly existence. These bifurcated creatures, in feminine form, remain after the collapse of man's deifications. Yet they are still seraphic, i.e., angelic and so transcendent beings. For they accept the battleground, the *place* where the old has fallen: they move "among the avalanches."

Attention dwells not long on any one moment. The next statement returns us to the sea:

> (11)   On above the highest level of the ridges, a sea troubled by the eternal birth of Venus, loaded with orpheonic fleets and murmuring of precious pearls and conches: this sea at times grows dark with deadly flashes.

Our ordinary perceptions are reversed: the sea rises above, does not extend below, the mountain ridges. As the significance of the whole scene is turned "inside out," the insides reveal themselves. The sea becomes wild through the birth of Venus, an eternally recurring phenomenon: our attention is drawn to the source of the birth, not to her subsequent amorous adventures. As a source, the sea is loaded or charged with ships, presumably battleships: yet singers directly in the service of Orpheus "man" them ("*orphéonique*" was a neologism at the time of Rimbaud;

17

no doubt the poem intends to lay emphasis on the root meaning rather than on "choral groups"). While the source of Venus is the sea, the sea also carries fleets of Orpheus, a man (not a god or goddess) who, by means of his singing, hopes (in vain) to recover his beloved. At the bottom of this sea, finally, lie precious pearls and conches, luxuries in the pursuit of which even city people engage. The three images of love, song, and search constitute the "insides" of the scene of the sea. With its "insides" revealed, the scene "darkens" with a "light" that spells death. The "inside" significance of the mythic birth of Venus, the legendary venture of Orpheus, and the daily pursuit of riches discloses itself in mortality. This finitude of ours "flashes" out to us only "at times." Yet, when it does flash it darkens the scene of human sojourn, revealing the darkness already there. Here as elsewhere, the imagery preserves rather than destroys the pristine ground of our rural literary heritage for urban life.

Four images follow in rapid succession, taking us around the mountain in a movement essentially urban even though rurally directed.

> (12)   On the slopes, harvests of flowers, large as our arms and our goblets, bellow.

Just as we are settling into a comforting pastoral scene, we are told that the flowers (the harvest of them) bellow, i.e., pierce the air with an animal cry. The meaning of the idyllic scene "comes back": flowers are there, just as the mountains are there, for us. We experience flowers in a city-like way in and through our use of them, but first of all in gathering them. This gathering transcends *our* optic. The harvest reveals *their* speech, albeit an animal speech: the way we hear them. Ensconced in our country house on the weekends, we may not like this description, but it suggests the essence of our urban life. As does the next:

> (13)   Processions of Mabs, in russet and opaline gowns, climb ravines.

Queen Mab of Celtic legend is pluralized for the same reason Roland was. She rules over our dreams. But the dreams are not inclosures, escapes from reality: they take us to what we in our waking hours avoid and "forget." Rightly and pristinely understood, Queen Mab aids us to "climb ravines" in splendor. Pluralized, garbed rustically and translucently, she is shown setting the correct example. Precisely in violating the traditional imagery, the statement preserves the pristine meaning. Then:

> (14) Up there, their feet in the cascade and the brambles, the stags suckle Diana.

This huntress, and goddess of the hunt, is familiarly thought of as hunting down, killing her prey. However, this view is not even justified by the corpus of legend telling of her acts: Diana *cares* for, takes care of, what she hunts. Although a virgin forever chaste, she suckles stags (unlike the English, the French *teter* works only one way: the stags take Diana's breast). As the references to Venus and Orpheus develop, to some slight extent, the "festivals of love" in statement 5, so the reference to Diana says something about the "hunt of chimes" in statement 6. Then:

> (15) The Bacchantes of the suburbs sob, and the moon burns and bays.

We know the priestesses of Bacchus for "bacchantic" abandon, their reabsorption into nature in revel and through wine. Again, orgy marks the *end* of movement. Modern priestesses on the fringes of cities (an all too evident class of modern beings) pass into such final ecstasy for good reason: the *beginning* out of which they move is described quite accurately as a sobbing correlative to a strange and violent appearance of the moon. Normally the moon appears to us as cool and quiet, cast against the more prevalent background of the burning and baying of daylight urban life. To us city dwellers, the cool and the quiet of the moon is expressive of ourselves as we would wish to be. In itself, the moon gathers the burning and baying of the day: it occasions the sobbing of the bacchantic priestesses of the suburbs long before it incites us to the ecstasies of absorption in the nighttime nature. As always, the imagery is not so clever as it is simply true.—And finally the goddess of love reappears:

> (16) Venus enters into the caverns of forgers and hermits.

The passionate goddess—Aphrodite in Greek legend, wife of the comically ugly yet famously skillful forger Hephaistos—appears at her humble beginnings rather than in the more "interesting" moments of her subsequent promiscuity.

To articulate an inside view of cities while incorporating our literary heritage would seem to be impossible. Yet, in statements 8 through 16, *"Villes"* directs these essentially rural and legen-

19

dary elements back into city life, largely by catching each element at its inception rather than at its completion. In this way, ancient figures appear commensurate with modern phenomena.

But why should we be concerned at all with the literary heritage? It is admittedly rural rather than urban and therefore seems best relegated to the romantic who flees the cities and does not accept or understand them. Would it not be "more productive" to forsake such references and face the multitude of contemporary urban phenomena in their own terms?

The chief exigency of man is to return to things. During the busy and idle hours of our daily jobs we drift about, recalling, projecting and hopefully filling recurrent needs. We plot the interval conveniently as a temporal sequence. Rural life brings its own moments of return: the morning's cockcrow, the noonday's meal, the evening's fireside. By contrast, urban life manifests itself as frozen oblivion, for it holds no built-in moment of return. Facing city life solely in its own terms, we are frozen into an "eternal" interval of organized social movement. Perhaps on weekends we abandon this urban interval: *we* return to things, but modern life is not returned to things; on the contrary, our return requires that we forget the week. Thus the ordinary as well as the romantic responses accept and perpetrate an alienation. Unlike these perpetrators, *"Villes"* (and, as we shall see later, *"Métropolitain"*) articulates a return to things which also brings our cities, and not merely an isolated or collective personality, into contact with things. To affect this return, the poem can accept neither urban life (frozen oblivion) nor rural life (now a thing of the past) in its own terms. Nevertheless it does affirm them poetically: the one because that is where we live, the other because it marks the possibility of a return.

Although a return can be articulated without explicit reference to our heritage, a genuine return requires at the very least an implicit incorporation of it. For the situation in which we live *is* by virtue of our heritage. The Greek, Roman and Celtic legacies form the basis, still today, of Western life. Even if we forget this heritage, it certainly does not forget us. In a sense, it is all we have. Cities are but out-growths of Rolands and centauresses, Venus and Diana and Mabs: materialization of definite concepts of valor, of transcendence, of love, of pursuit, and of imagination. An articulation of cities that by-passes this heritage by-passes the heart of cities as well.

20

It is clear by now in what manner "*Villes*" incorporates the "past." The sequence of statements gathers a multiplicity of familiar historical "points," converting each into a point of contact with things themselves. Although the references are explicit, none is articulated in duration (only Venus enters so much as twice). Each remains an autonomous point converted directly into a contact. No sooner does one appear than it becomes transparent to "these Alleghenies and Lebanons" which are only "there" for the purposes of "the people" and yet demand our entire attention.

But does the conversion of signification do justice to the myths of our heritage? In pondering this question we should recall that these myths characteristically show human being emerging out of its contrary, out of a teeming nature. Man belongs to nature not irrevocably, but as a child belongs to his mother, namely as growing out of her. His belongingness is alternately forgotten and recalled as he proceeds to arrange a life at some remove from his source. Typically, then, we read and hear these myths in the first instance exclusively for the "arrangements": the battles of Charlemagne, wars with centaurs, the recurrent peregrinations of Venus away from her earthy husband into the arms of lovers, the actual dreams induced by Queen Mab, the vengeful feats of Diana, and the orgiastic rites of the priestesses of Bacchus. All the while, though, these "stories" are told to indicate an origin in the craters, gorges, mountain peaks, chasms, abysses, the sea: in teeming, non-human, unpredictable, unarranged, ever-surging nature. Thus the statements in "*Villes*" while converting the significations of these myths do not distort them, they fulfil their founding significance.

Furthermore, does the style of contact with things engendered in the poem reflect accurately the human exigencies present in modern cities? In pondering this question, too, we should recall that Western myths recommend to man that he cultivate his remove from nature. This recommendation is made consistent with the periodic and even devastating reminder of nature, e.g., through the power of sex and the inevitability of death. Perhaps we may here rightly suspect a connection between that strange phenomenon called Western Civilization and its seemingly contrary ancient and rural origins. Although Roland and Venus are very earth-bound, we are not at all advised to return to the simplicity of earthy existence. Chinese and Indian civilization, at their heights, accepted the human arrangement as the point of departure, and growth always required developing roots back into the nature essentially abandoned and forgotten in societal organization. From the start, the Western recommendation has been to fly above the earth. This counsel was consistently followed. The philosophical idealisms of the nineteenth century legated to us a structure for understanding not so much how (although this is the pretension) as *that* the Alleghenies and the Lebanons rose themselves up for man. In the West and increasingly in the westernized East, human kind has developed an organization which soars above the highest peaks, low enough to profit the navigation but hopefully high enough to avoid collisions. This organization reaches its palpable apogee in modern cities, where indifference to origins blooms and children are unaware that milk comes from cows rather than cartons. Thus the poem's alterations of the stories (pluralization of Roland and Mab, the humble actions of Diana and Venus, and so on) reflect quite aptly the "altered" contemporary condition of man. For today we are thoroughly ensconced within human organization and a relevant "recommendation" sends us toward the roots of the city without forsaking our abode therein.

The following five statements (17 through 21) somewhat relieve the tension at the "edges" of cities by portraying the inside scene as a composed whole. First:

(17)   Groups of belfries sing the ideas of peoples.

The earlier reference to "the people" (in statement 2) is here resumed, although now the reference is multiple. In French a belfry is a watchtower, originally a mobile one for attack in the siege of a city, later the permanent tower of a town employed for detecting the approach of an enemy. The "ideas," the prejudices of the masses as well as the cumulative insights of developing technology, speak from these towers in the form of song. Modern ideas are promulgated, perhaps generated, from elements of urban construction, not from great individuals (an individual Roland) and not even directly from the people. Today we need only think of radio and television. Next:

(18)   From castles built of bone issues the unfamiliar music.

Presumably this "music" accompanies the singing of the ideas of peoples. It is, however, unfamiliar, unknown. The "peoples"

22

understand this music as little as the modern city dweller understands the context of his prejudices or even his insights: an intelligent and learned engineer only knows the elements or ideas directly pertinent to his tasks, he does not understand the master plan into which his bridge must fit. The music then issues from "castles built of bone," from central constructions, imposing in their presence but concealing more than revealing. City dwelling gives the sensation that the rhythm is set by all those multiple buildings with no one visibly responsible for it. Then:

> (19) All the legends evolve and the elks fling themselves through the towns.

Legends (all of them, including those recalled by the previous statements of the poem) "evolve," again in the French sense of assuming battle formation, arranging for an encounter, and thus making themselves heard. This "evolution" is said to mark urban life, presumably in tune with the music accompanying the song of ideas. Simultaneously we witness a correlative "mark" of city life: a flinging through the "*bourgs*," the walled towns designed to ward off troubles. The "flingers" are "*les élans*": either "elks" or "yearnings" (the French does not resolve the ambiguity). Elks would normally be kept out of a walled town. They represent the possibility of an insurgence of wild nature in keeping with much of the poem, especially with Diana suckling her stags (one dictionary defines an *élan* as "a large *stag* of the north country"). Yearnings, on the other hand, also characterize town life, the longing to escape petty entanglements and return to the earth or even into the real cities. The two meanings thus cross: nature surging toward man and man surging toward nature. This elemental movement, occurring at a moment when all legends are assembling for a "show down," leads us into an event with negative force:

> (20) The paradise of storms caves in.

Cities themselves require that all active, formative, and directed organizational forces be sucked into and anchored within the walls, even though they "evolve" in the face of the elements outside. One of the constant sensations of modern life has been the collapse of paradise, the loss of any human power that could acknowledge transcendent power. Statement 10 already reads: "The collapse of apotheoses rejoins the fields of the heights...."

23

The insistence on grasping everything in human terms makes "paradise," the hovering domain of transcendent meaning, "cave in." This paradise is then aptly viewed as one "of storms," i.e., no longer of bliss but of raging aspiration now cleansed of unrealistic hopes. We pride ourselves on this purification. The final statement in this connection reads:

(21)   The savages dance ceaselessly in the festival of the night.

Other than the general reference to "people" (in statements 2 and 17), "*Villes*" speaks now for the first time about individuals unrelated to legends. They are dancing, presumably to the song and music already heard, and in concert with the troop movements and flingings already seen. The poem construes as a dance of wild men the 24-hour-per-day bustle of the modern city, where "time is money" and money is everything because it marks the success of strictly human organization. These men are wild because, for all their "culture" and "civilization," they are continually "on the prowl" and "in search of prey." Yet the savagery of city dwellers surfaces as a dance, a ceaseless dancing of the festival of the night. The difference between day and night, a difference very prominent in a rural community, vanishes in the urban setting. Rather than sleeping for the sake of a daytime labor in the fields, we today engage in daytime transactions in order to finance our nighttime activities. This familiar historical development of urban life becomes often distressingly perceivable in towns which are just assuming the shape of cities, where the oldtimers can still remember when the streets were quiet at nine o'clock, and where the current carrousers and careeners are still conspicuously tumultuous and disruptive of the sleep of others. —Together, the five statements read:

> Groups of belfries sing the ideas of people. From the castles built of bone issues the unfamiliar music. All the legends evolve and the elks fling themselves through the towns. The paradise of storms caves in. The savages dance ceaselessly the festival of the night.

Statements 1 through 4 create an inside view of cities, concentrating us on the constructions of man. Now these five statements bring the human disposition into the definite focus of mass revelry. This focus comes late, for it refers back to the inside view of statements 1 through 4, to the panorama of modern phenomena described in statements 5 through 7, and to the influx of our heritage in the nine statements preceding the revelry. The orgy is distinctively modern, although perhaps analogous to the Dionysian ecstasy entailing reabsorption into the forces of nature. Today all forces are humanly conceived; they demand an urban rather than a rural participation.

How are we to read and understand the remaining two statements? The penultimate directly continues the text:

> (22)   And, one hour, I descended into the movement of a boulevard in Bagdad where companies sang the joy of the new labor, in a heavy breeze, on the move without the power to elude the fabulous phantoms of the hills where we all had to find our bearings.

This final statement of the paragraph is startling. For the first time, an "I"-narrator appears. For the first time events unfold in the past rather than in the present. And for the first time the poem suggests an imperative that touches upon, calls upon ourselves. Each of these three features deserves careful consideration.

1. "And, one hour, I descended. . . ." Abruptly we are plunged into silence. The revels of urban life subside. For there steps forth not the perceived, the tumultuous panorama, but rather the perceiver, the witness. This witness remembers descending. The "I" (the narrator), a latecomer in the poetic articulation, is outside the action, in the stillness of recollection.

An "I"-narrator always carries an articulation. Ordinary discourse leaves often intentionally vague *who* this "I" is. A favorite device is to claim that someone *else* said what is now simply repeated for the information of the hearer. However ambiguous poetic discourse may be, it cannot be evasive. In the case of "*Villes*" the "I" is essentially a witness. It enters in the mode of recollection, although what has been recollected takes the form of a presence, as any genuine recollection does. Thus the contrast between the clamor of the recollected (statements 1 through 21) and the silence of the "I" who enters: a witness speaks, but in speaking lets what he is witnessing speak for itself. If the things themselves are to speak, the witness is, in speaking, silent.

Furthermore, the "I" fitting urban life is essentially but a part receiving its being from its participation. An ancient maxim claims that our realized selves *are* that to which we bear witness. Empedocles wrote: "All according to what is present does the understanding of man take shape" (Diels fragment 106); and

25

Aristotle, from whom we have this fragment, writes in the same work (*On the Soul*) that "the soul is, in a way, all things" it experiences. Only for a brief interlude in the West did the notion occur (to the rationalists and then, by way of reaction, to the romantics) that the self of man could be scooped out of the onslaught of things and accorded a separate status. In modern city life the frenetic absorption into the course of events forms the starting point, even for the army of urban prophets, the psychotherapists who provide and cultivate a "subjective" retreat from the all too demanding "objective" city: one more weekend house. In contrast to rationalist, romantic, and also psychological interpretations of selfhood, the self of "*Villes*" manifests itself in the willingness to descend, to enter by going down into the city as a witness, in recollection, to the clamorous presence of human forces in amorous conflict with undefined, essentially undefinable "natural" forces.

Finally, *what* the "I" witnesses passes under peaceful review in its entirety: " ... where companies were singing the joy of the new labor, in a heavy breeze, on the move without the power to elude the fabulous phantoms of the hills. ..." From the perspective of a self recollecting a descent into the cities, the song recorded earlier (explicitly in statements 7 and 17) has sung "the joy of the new labor," the exultation possible for human effort in the modern context. Man's response in this new situation is, as it ever has been, one of labor, the fashioning of materials into forms integral to human habitation. Yet we do not hear or see the singers of these songs at the moment of their power. They are "circulating" or "circling" (*circuler* describes the movement of traffic, pedestrian or other, people "going about their business"; policemen shout "*circulez!*" when dispersing a crowd that has gathered around an accident). However, in "moving about" as traffic, these city dwellers have been trying to *elude* "the fabulous phantoms of the hills," all those historical powers constituting cities and their source of joy. And these singers lack the strength even to avoid encountering these 'phantoms.'

2. The experience is recast, in recollection, into the past. What does this temporal recasting contribute to the presentation of cities? Every human situation, every construction, has a past: a situatedness, a constructedness. At any given moment ("one hour") we enter into circumstances on the basis of their established dimension. An astronaut setting foot on the moon is a strange sight because the instant of his foot's touch-down, and

the rock or sand which meets his foot, are empty, indeed alienated factors of the situation. We know that the years of research, the combined labors of thousands of men and women, the co-operation of hundreds of industries, here coalesce, re-establish themselves around a speck of time and space having (in the astronaut's case) no essential duration or place, a mere nothing surrounded by a plenitude of human organization: the foot may touch solid ground, but man cannot dwell here. But in a city we do in fact retain the possibility of a home. We recognize this possibility in the established character of the city: the movement that is itself a "fixed" feature of a city, the tradition glorifying (sometimes shaming) the human role in this movement, the heaviness (thickness) of the air, *and* the impotent desire to elude the very source of possible joy. Why this impotence? Anything strictly of the past appears futile: in itself, and *only* as past, it is without possibility, it is "finished." Our fellow human beings easily appear to us as trapped in a narrow track of futile movement. For once we do claim to understand someone or something, we are committed *a priori* (as Kant would say) to articulating the course of events as a structured sequence determined according to laws of efficient causation, and as excluding freedom. However, the point at issue is not how a scientist finds himself looking at data. It is how each of us, as city dwellers, experiences the city each day. At the instant of our entrance, the already-ness of the city comes most prominently to the fore. This is the moment of human impotence, even though all the "factors" are present for a participation yet to be enacted. It is necessarily a moment of descent.

The sustaining *presence* of cities presupposes a moment of entrance when the city is "present" only in the frustrated fixedness of its past. At this moment the one-time presence remains as the guiding light for the self who enters. Yet the presence is also absent: it is buried in the past each day as we arrive at work. Upon our arrival, the past becomes the arena of possibility, of the future. This future, like its correlate (the past) is not another time: it is the same time (the same establishment) which may come to itself. Here we can forestall the explication of the imperative in statement 22 and consider directly the final statement of the prose poem:

(23) What sturdy arms, what happy hour, will restore to me this region whence come my slumbers and my least movements?

The region of cities expressed so far in their presence needs to be restored to the self who has descended into the movements of *a* city, the unlikely, i.e., unrepresentative city of Bagdad. The restoration occurs in the future, it is a possibility embedded in the conditions where the singers are only hoping to elude the forces comprising their habitation. The restoration is the *happy* hour, contrasting with the hour of simple descent. Upon descending, the self hopes for "sturdy arms," arms adequate to restore the region now experienced in the mode of nostalgia as he or she is plunging into an actual city. Finally, the region is a double source: from it arise not only the movements in which the self may participate and through which the self is genuinely present, but also the rests, the slumbers requisite for the individual although not for "the people" as a whole, the savages who "dance ceaselessly the festival of the night."

If the all-supportive region must be "restored" to the self, we must understand that this future possibility pertains to the sense of presence already articulated in the twenty-one previous statements of the poem. The region has been lost to the self precisely at *any* hour of descent into *any* actual city, here into Bagdad. The poem is a recollection of this loss of presence, a loss correlative to the possibility of its restoration. It does not describe a fact, it confirms the possibility (the future) embedded in the established condition (the past) of modern living. By itself, urban living leaves us with a merely spurious present where we avoid genuine encounter. The poem confirms real presence as a congruence of "future" and "past" in the senses indicated.

3. But we have neglected the last phrase of statement 22: "... where we all had to find our bearings." The "hills" with their "fabulous phantoms" locate this "where." The imperative expressed in the past tense of *devoir* does not just implicate the "companies" of singers (the great men and women already established in our cities), but also the speaker, the self. (The French *l'on* is only imperfectly translated as the impersonal "one," since the English tends to single out, whereas the French carries a strong sense of generality: *all*.) The imperative says: each must "refind" himself, i.e. find his bearings, find out where he or she is. This "must" occurs in the past. Any bearings, we *have* found were measured against the place which "others" impotently desire to elude: high places locating all those ghosts from the past, from Roland to Venus. Today we still live with the imperative to come to terms with, to find ourselves in regard to, the kind of presence that has been confirmed in the poem.

28

3. MODERN AFFIRMATION

Discovering where we live demands that we affirm the location, our own being located there, the elements we encounter there, and the structure (path) of this encounter. The poem *"Villes"* leads us into the location of cities and thereby sets the conditions for a discovery which is simultaneously an affirmation. We have discussed the poem from the standpoint of the discovery. The affirmation is built into this discovery already, chiefly by the conversion of significations. But the poem also invites us to consider, in a reflective manner, the problematics of modern (city-bound) affirmation. Why is it so difficult, in our epoch, to affirm city life, to find sustenance in the urban context of contemporary life? This question may be posed simultaneously with the question: Why is it so difficult to go along with the articulation of *"Villes"*?

The difficulty lies in the essential discontinuity between the *context* of human effort ("the new labor") and the *moment* of confluent meaning (the restoration of this "region" to the self). The configuration of modern cities contains no intersection of meanings at which the individual is reminded of and aided in an affirmation of the moment. A European village will likely be dominated by a church steeple reminding the inhabitants of the possibility of moving from the context of their efforts into moments of clarity (in regard to their own destiny), of transparency of their context (of intra-village life) to the earth (divine creation); in short, village life structures itself already with a view to the possibility of affirmation. Furthermore, the reminder might even be supplemented by further aid, the village priest. Cities essentially lack this continuity of context and moment.

The faith of Periclean Athens was that a properly constructed polis would lead to a momentary affirmation. The faith of Imperial Rome was that perfect organization, as an active process, would already suffice for affirmation. The faith of Christian Rome (and Medieval Paris) was that submission of oneself to divine "judgement" or "decision" would allow for the emergence of unique personality. The faith of the Enlightenment (also that of the Founding Fathers of America) was that modern science and popular government would, through public education, lead progressively to an ever greater number of people able to assert their individuality in private sub-contexts contained within a larger context of equality and liberty for all. And the inscrutable Orientals seem all the while to have smiled at every pretension to a humanly devised movement between context and moment. Such a sketch of world history suggests that discontinuity of the context of human effort with the moment of confluence poses a difficulty peculiar to our modern epoch. Today the steeple is, by the nature of the case, missing. A city may be overflowing with monuments recalling special events leading up to the present configuration, but these monuments have no future. Even a cathedral (Notre Dame in Paris, Saint Paul's in New York) has only a past. If a cathedral has any *live* significance for us, it stands apart, and we with it, from the city in which it is only nominally located.

The prominent art works of our tradition have also worked on the basis of a continuity between context and moment. Homer's *Iliad* develops a series of moments on the basis of an affirmation of heroic style of life, particularly in warfare. Sophocles' *Oedipus* moves us, without essential disruption, from the affirmation of a context of kingship into an affirmation of a single moment of individual responsibility. The classic Greek temples affirm the everyday affairs of religion and business continuously with any given moment of intersection of land and wind, sun and sea. Shakespeare's *Hamlet* and Goethe's *Faust* do include moments of desperation and scepticism in the face of the context of human effort, but they still base the development of affirmable moments upon those contexts (royalty and science, respectively). The paintings of Van Gogh often reveal a desperate struggle with the possibility of continuous affirmation: his earlier ones (e.g., paintings of weavers at work, and then also of bridges) affirm the context of modern life as the basis of an affirmation of moments; his later works progressively abandon the context and aspire to a purity of moment without any roots in the context. The paintings of Monet also vary, perhaps more in the mood of benign bewilderment than in the mood of despair: from the playful light of lilly ponds and cathedral façades to the earnest of railway trains traversing bridges in the countryside or dominating the vaultings of a station. A purity of moment on the one hand (where the context is incidental), and on the other hand a development of a moment out of a contemporary context. —In these cases we "work along" within a continuity of affirmation, or at least within the problematic of continuity. As is well known, though, distinctively modern works require that we "work along" within discontinuity. We

30

cannot be asked to move from an affirmation of the Korean or the Vietnam wars toward an affirmation of moments within these contexts. Neither can we be asked to move from a prior affirmation of any form of government toward an affirmation of a moment of decision. Neither from nobility (or any upper class) nor from science. But, then, how is any affirmation at all possible?

Modern art works have generally embodied a provisional answer to this trying question: For they tend to declare that anything whatsoever can, without reference to its context, serve to inaugurate a moment. Whereas artists and poets of our tradition had to conceive of a whole (war, kingship, science) and only then develop a moment out of the chosen whole, modern artists and poets generally ignore such contextual considerations and delve directly into moments. When their works do consider the context, bitter criticism predominates. Of course, and as in any epoch, many works of this type are not very satisfying or convincing except as indications of a need and therefore as remembrances of a possibility.

Rimbaud's *"Villes"* follows the modern pattern. Somehow (the "how" remains questionable) a moment is formed out of an array of possible moments, an array which leads *back* to an affirmation of the whole (urban life: cities) without relying upon a prior affirmation of it. Cities are not described independent of moments. Each statement is itself a possible moment, each begins immediately with the *moment* of mountain chains arising solely for the people rather than with a *context* of coal mining or lumber camps. The poem is first of all an accumulation, not a whole. Yet the affirmation leads from each moment in the array toward the whole, as the configuration gathers momentum and finally asserts its accumulated force: first in the fading of the whole ("And, one hour, I descended . . .") and then in the anticipation of its return (" . . . what happy hour will restore to me this region . . .?").

We have reviewed the technique of configuration in Rimbaud's poem in order to see (as critics), but more importantly to hear an articulation of moments allowing for a cumulative affirmation of cities, the place where we live. To understand and to participate in the affirmation we must first ask what emerges within cities, identical with what emerges in the poem, and then also what constitutes the oblivion out of which things emerge. Although these two questions have an ideational purport, the

31

ideas are certainly not set out in the poem for our reflection. Yet the poem accurately reflects city life, if not as we initially or predominantly *think* of it, nonetheless as we do in fact experience it, i.e., move within its structure. In other words, even though the configuration of "*Villes*" contains no self-reflection, no reflective point of convergence, it does embody a powerful experience of oblivion and emergence allowing for a free convergence, the reader who "hears" cities so configured enacts his or her own convergence at his or her time and place. As critics asking What about the emergence? and What about the oblivion? we may become clear *why* discontinuity is necessary in modern affirmation.

Nature emerges, but a very peculiar and modern nature. What stands opposed to man, and yet allows and requires man to live in the opposition, is conceived as a *blank*. Its form derives from "the people," from human organization, whether in blast furnaces or in air conditioners. Modern urban life strips all elements in nature of their living form and reconstitutes them according to the will, needs, whims, desires, and plans of man. Even as a blank, nature may "declare war" against us, but we determine everything about this war (time, place, weapons)—everything except the outcome, since this always remains to be seen.

Older literature often refers to nature as "she." Nature was then living form, a power in itself and one to which man responded. Man found himself at home in responding to power acknowledged as not his own. Aristotle provides a philosophical statement of this ancient view (*Physics*, 199a16): "technique in part completes what nature is unable to finish, in part imitates her." That is, man responds to things while drawing upon those things in their being (a being essentially providing for human habitation); thus his responses must conform to, become transparent to what presents itself as having power, life, and form of its own. For the Greeks and for Western man until about the year 1600, nature clearly supported man already prior to man's formative response to her. The nature emerging in technique ("art," as it is usually translated) emerges in her own right, not in man's.

Sometime later in the halting development of Western civilization, nature became mere stuff for human construction and consumption, an "it." Kant's analysis of the modern effort to understand the new nature formulates this "it"-character. In his

32

Critique of Pure Reason (second edition in 1787; B 163 ff.) passing comments reveal the strange "nature" posing problems for both physicists and philosophers of the modern age: materially, i.e., from the standpoint of what we actually *face*, nature is "the sum total of appearances" (*der Inbegriff aller Erscheinungen*); formally, i.e., from the standpoint of how we *conceive* of nature, it is "the lawfulness (*Gesetzmässigkeit*) of appearances in space and time." Kant's *Prolegomena* (§15) states this even more explicitly: "Nature is the existence of things insofar as this existence is determined according to universal laws." Scholars may ponder and dispute these formulations, but modern life bears witness that we today see in nature only what stands within or with regard to human organization. For this human organization clears a way for us through and up to the otherness called "nature."

What does "*Villes*" add to the modern mode of experiencing nature? Normally we like to think that we can safely move within our organization, experiencing only "appearances" in a predetermined "lawfulness." The poem, however, places us at the *edge* of organization, at moments of encounter. The factor called "nature" remains blank, while human response is brought directly up to this blank. Mountains, craters, waterways, gorges, chasms, the sea, ravines, stags, and caverns are *there* despite the fact that this there-ness (Kant's "existence," *Dasein*) is seen through the eyes of the people, surrounded by human constructions. In fact, things are there *because* of, on the basis of human responses configured (significations converted) in ways retaining human organization as the center while yet affirming also the periphery, namely the blank nature on the verge of organization. In this affirmation we acknowledge that the blank nature on the periphery forever defies complete organization. The defiance arises from the infinity of time: there is always a tomorrow, and we shall then wake to new appearances. The acceptance of this ceaseless defiance is essential to our location on the edge: it marks the valor of modern Rolands and the dance of modern wildmen.

Only on the edge of modern organization, in the face of nature as a blank, is an affirmation possible which includes the human context. For in the midst of the modern organization we are simply buoyed along: the context of life is a refuge, a place to which we shrink. In the midst of pure, settled, left-over organization the context of life becomes a negation, the waiting room of a train station. We can cherish this waiting room for its warmth, but we cannot affirm it, since in it the construction is not functional, in it *we* are not functioning. Only when we are traveling on trains are we partaking of the function. And only in building, in designing, or in poetically re-articulating the trains are we on the edge of this functional construction where affirmation is fully and genuinely possible.

In fact, at the heart (paradoxically: the edge) of genuine scientific research we experience nature as the blank correlative to human organization. Scientific research involves a continuous process of revival and encounter: we engage in years of organizing it (the "results" of previous research) around a moment. This effort is called an experiment, a contrived experience: everything with life and power is ours, and we *wait* to see what will happen in the encounter, namely whether the organization will become disturbed at that moment. We "know" the blank in a provisionally final way when the preconceived organization remains in tact, unruffled, "lawful" in the encounter. However, the "objectivity" associated with the scientific temperament requires that we only report what happened and, in predicting what will happen, remain open at each new moment for a possible disturbance within the presumed "conceptual framework," whereupon adjustments are made in good cheer and in good faith. Modern science is organized operation. The best scientist is an operator forever on the edge of operation, backed by an immense conceptual framework and open to each moment of encounter with blank nature: he is the modern adventurer, rivaled only by the engineer who employs accumulated know-how and gigantic machinery to clear a roadway through jungles, over vast and difficult terrain—a *straight* road which, although requiring *during* its construction an arduous attention to the givens of the land, does not bend to nature in the least, and allows for ceaseless transportation between cities.

Rimbaud's poem confronts us with the style of emergence possible in, relevant to, modern urban life. In order to affirm city life and what it offers we must acknowledge this kind of emergence. What, now, about the *oblivion* to which this emergence is correlative?

We experience oblivion as entrapment within human organization, within a configuration which is simply configured and no longer configuring. We may distinguish three sorts of this oblivion.

First, there is the indifferent oblivion of daily routines of shopping or of going to work, when these are mere unchallenging repetitions. Although this oblivion may be *felt* in a personal way, it is above all collective. For the routines do not belong to us, they belong to the city, making life there possible. This oblivion, as also the remaining two kinds, is *functional*. Since an individual here does not merely forget something, he cannot overcome oblivion simply by remembering what has been forgotten. We hardly have to remember anything at all to function quite well, whether shopping or typing. Recollecting what is happening in this oblivion only enhances, in the first instance, the feeling of entrapment.

A second sort of oblivion is experienced near the edge of human organization. This adventurous oblivion characterizes, say, the businessman who concentrates his energies on steering a course up to junctures where unforeseen and unforeseeable factors demand response (the extension of production or of the market, the rationalization of these processes, or whatever). The challenge here is to encompass and eventually swallow the opposing factors, to master circumstances often of one's own making. Although such ambition requires great powers of concentration and rare ability, it remains a mode of oblivion in the crucial sense of the word. For this effort aims at securing organization. The businessman-adventurer may himself be in the front lines, on the very edge of organization, in the face of blank elements—just as is the scientist at his best. But no businessman, and no scientist, no strictly modern man organizes or reorganizes the context of human interests with a view to fitting it in with nature, bending it to the elements, serving creation. The organization coming into view as an active process is still one of functional oblivion, no matter how demanding it might be in terms of concentration, skill, and "memory." The functionality of this mode of oblivion has been abstracted and cultivated, streamlined and accelerated: it has evolved into modern operation.

The urban context in which we live is alternately one of indifferent oblivion and adventurous oblivion. The first arises in any human context, the second is a fixed character only of modern urban life, even though isolated individuals may have incarnated it in earlier epochs.

There is, however, a third sort, even more distinctive and revelatory (when faced) of our epoch: the oblivion of *theory*.

Again we must understand this oblivion as perfectly functional: it works, it is not a mistake in the usual sense of the word, it is even in some sense necessary although its proponents seldom see either its significance or its limitations. The mainstream of academic "social science," e.g., history, sociology, and economics manifest this third kind. These disciplines study *human* organization from varying perspectives and provide theories supplemented by facts about this organization. The theories vary from academic to academic, with intermittent renegades (particularly on the question as to whether and how man is basically passive or basically active). But the mainstream of these theories reflects the chief exigency of the "insides" of modern cities: how a network is held together, configured, as a dynamic whole tending to extend its area of influence. Contrary to the beliefs of their proponents, these studies are not "value free" or even simply "objective" reportages. For the "final reports" inevitably constitute a recommendation. In stating how a network of forces (say, a particular society) achieves a degree of cohesion and internal consistency, a study recommends that we, its beneficiaries, learn something about how to keep human organization together into a viable whole. One human possibility is implicitly, sometimes even explicitly, denied, and rightly so for modern urban living: the possibility of adjusting human responses at every moment to the exigencies of non-human forces. Only the alienated "oddballs" in a modern city espouse such adjustment.

The mainstream of contemporary theories about the human condition is best called formalism. Any academic discipline which structures and supports the oblivion essential to both the indifference (passivity) and the adventure (activity) of human enterprise is formalistic.

We may review one instructive event in the history of economics. In this field, Marx's *Capital* (1867 to 1894) was the first exhaustive effort to survey, analyze, and understand the historical development and in-built propensities of urban organization. This exploration of entrepreneurial capitalism aimed at tracing the modern economic lines of force back to roots. As Plato and Aristotle, Kant and Hegel, so also Marx sought these roots in the craftsman's encounter with materials, initially in labor and subsequently in reflection. According to Marx *values* accrue to the human situation at the moment of intersection of labor and nature; capitalistic enterprise, the latest producer of such values (here called commodities), functions on the basis of a new kind of labor in which men and women, even children, work not as individuals but as "moments" of one large (collective) supercraftsman (*der Gesamt-Arbeiter*). This thesis stands against many contravening appearances and is meant to prevent us from being "fooled" by them. For instance, while the capitalist may appear to generate values graciously by his own organization, Marx argues that labor-power really generates them and does so on the basis of a human organization which precedes the capitalist. Although the entrepreneur variously aids the outgrowths of industry, he does not constitute its ground or root. Rather, labor is the source of value. Thus this view is known as the "labor theory of value." Concretely, a piece of wood, in passing through a process of production, increases in value only because labor transforms it into a baseball bat or a chair; apart from swindle, the dollar-price of the article *expresses* relative value within society, it is not *equivalent* to value. Man, not money, is the "form" of socially useful, hence socially valuable material (the functionality of the bat or the chair).

Modern economists are not likely to defend the pre-Marxian view that the capitalist, whether as industrialist, banker or merchant, creates and founds value. The mainstream also accepts the complicated lines of force Marx brought to light. It rejects, however, the "labor theory of value" on the grounds that the distinction between price and value is unworkable. Prices, but not values, can be seen to form a system with *internal* criteria of cogency and consistency, and also of recommendations for economic policy. Thus the very basis of Marx's analysis is abandoned. The denial of it follows not so much from the "red" scare as from the omnipresent "root" scare, although the academic justification of the denial refers us to the undeniable "practicality" of formal price systems. As one otherwise sympathetic British professor of economics (Joan Robinson) writes: " . . . no point of substance in Marx's argument depends upon the labor theory of value. Voltaire remarked that it is possible to kill a flock of sheep by witchcraft if you give them plenty of arsenic at the same time. The sheep, in this figure, may well stand for the complacent apologists of capitalism; Marx's penetrating insight and bitter hatred of oppression supply the arsenic, while the labor theory of value provides the incantations." To the formalist, every statement of a substance for city

37

life appears as a private incantation, while every basis supposedly uncovered reflects merely personal projection, and every thoughtful argument intending to justify a statement of a discovery is essentially an elaboration of the "insides" of the operation.

The young student of modern "social science" notices the effect of formalism in the fact that every path within his chosen discipline leads him only toward further interlaced paths within the same domain. At most the student can trace out a path leading him into other fields. Inter-disciplinary studies are encouraged in exactly the same way, and for the same reasons, that business corporations assume international proportions and scientific investigations aspire toward principles of unification. The student probably begins his travels hoping some basis will loom into view: the soul, nature, God, or at least a sound moral maxim to guide human conduct. And occasionally a competent maverick professor will in fact bate his pupils in this direction. In linguistics, for instance, a good deal of interest has recently been aroused in affirming a creativity of the individual soul as underlying the manifold of human linguistic ability. This effort, called Cartesian linguistics, is correctly criticized as being reactionary rather than avant-garde. In such cases the extra-formal basis is postulated at the outset and is not at all proven.

But back to modern affirmation. At all times and places the cracking of oblivion has required an act or a leap of faith or of will. During the Christian epoch the *need* for and reminder of this event was built into the manifest forms of life: a church steeple in the center of a village, to resume our example. Our epoch, that of the city, denies any intrinsic relation between the context of life and the moment of emergence. Our form of oblivion rejects, *a priori*, the need, and so easily "refutes," *a posteriori*, any supposed reminders (such as the "labor theory of value" or the "creativity of the soul"). Modern life essentially provides no avenue from context to moment, only a highway leading out of the city toward the weekend cabin, a movement remaining well within the bounds of oblivion.

Thus the discontinuity. Dwelling in cities, we find affirmation genuinely feasible only if we begin already with what offers itself at the moment. Affirming what we encounter at a given time and place, we may possibly affirm the *context* in which that moment was possible. However, there is a hitch, for city life has already pre-figured what offers itself. If we are ever to affirm the context of our life, we must acknowledge the city-likeness of each and every thing. This likeness does not lead to an affirmation, but each thing affirmed has this likeness. For we see the new nature, the *blank* nature, through the context of our life. Otherwise the "blank" is *nothing* but a blank, and we pass it over. City life can be compared to a glass with refractory properties necessary for any experience at all, even more so for a discernment of things within the experience.

The affirmation of *"Villes"* accurately reflects the discontinuity of emergence and oblivion in each of its converted significations. We may recur momentarily to the image of Mabs scrambling up the ravines (statement 13). Mab is familiar in her function of informing our dreams. Dreams have always been, and continue to be, understood as enigmatic revelations of otherwise unnoticed supports of our individual and/or collective involvements. In modern urban life Mab would have to point the way to the raw edges of the city. In the poem, however, there are many Mabs, and they go to the edges themselves: they set the example for us. Why be so explicit? Without this ruthless conversion (from a hovering fairy to colorful scramblers) the phenomena of dreams would, as all moments of city life, fall under the craft of modern formalism: these contextual indications of a point of contact would be reinterpreted as elements strictly within the context. As is well known, modern interpreters of dreams see in them chiefly an expression of the dreamer, of his or her generally unfulfilled personal desires to crawl back into internal safety or into phantastic but still internal pleasure. On the formalist view, the signification of dreams can never constitute a path of affirmation. Generally the interpretation leads to a negation: the dream indicates a fear, a retreat in the face of something which the dreamer should learn to overcome. Rimbaud's poem, in undoing both the familiar form of Mab and the modern formalism of the interpretation of her works, preserves the source of dreams as the point of contact of human organization with nature. To effect this undoing Mab must become Mabs setting the example in a way befitting urban life.

Still, why choose Mab from the wealth of possible subjects? This legend has a special bearing upon the character of poetry itself. For several centuries now, poets and critics have been discussing the roles of dream and reality in poetry. Since the advent of formalism, the results of science appear to constitute or at least point to reality, while the works of poets seem to compensate for the ennui of science by providing instructive or amusing dream worlds. Yet only to the flippant reader can *"Villes"* appear as *simply* a dream, i.e., a balloon of fantasy blown up by the puffing personality of the poet to a size allowing for the peregrinations of an idle posterity in search of distraction. For the poem reveals city life itself as a dream, and reveals this only because it, the poem, also bursts the bubble at every moment, not by negating this "dream" but by bringing us up to its outer skin. No matter how wretched or comfortable, boring or exciting, city life is a balloon life, a dream life in waiting for reality.

The terminological confusion of dream and reality, and their effective function in the process of affirmation, may be unravelled if we agree to a distinction between human construction and the point of focus during the construction. In village life the reality is obviously the mountains, the gorges, and ravines, while the network of societal concerns (local politics and the like) constitutes the dream world that must give way, each day, to the reality. Even on Sundays the peasants are told to transcend the dream for the sake of creation and its creator. However, in city life economic facts alone still do not deserve the name reality. These facts are *real* enough, and they even withstand investigation simply in their interrelations and with only a private and personal basis outside their interconnection. But to admit that the givens of city life are real (and demanding), does not require us to conclude that they constitute the realness, the reality of city life.

The mountain ranges "of dream" and the scramblings "of Mabs" form the "region" where both "slumbers" and "movements" are possible once it is restored as an urban oblivion opening up on the emergence of things. The affirmation bears upon both the oblivion and the emergence, but works "discontinuously," i.e., from the exacting contact back to the familiar context.

4. THE PROSE POEM *"MÉTROPOLITAIN"*

A great poet is not a philosopher, he does not pave a thoughtful path from one set of givens toward a vision of what supports the givens. Rather the great poet configures a complex of phenomena to form a context of human concern which "vibrates" with the conflict of oblivion and emergence. Rimbaud's complex of phenomena bear upon cities, the apogee of modern life. He consistently assumes the task of studying and thinking this complex—thinking it transitively, since his poems evidence *in* themselves no thought *about* cities, no extracted thoughts, but rather ones directly configuring the phenomena. The works of Charles Baudelaire, greatly admired by Rimbaud, introduced the task: they move us into urban phenomena, generally Parisian. "You gave me your filth," Baudelaire says to Paris, "and I made gold out of it" *(Tu m'as donné ta boue et j'en ai fait de l'or).* Yet the previous line of this posthumously published preface indicates the manner of Baudelaire's achievement. It is piece meal: "For I have, from each thing, extracted the quintessence."

Rimbaud's works start already from urban life *as a whole.* His poems work on this mode of life until it yields its truth as a unitary event. The difficulty of this unique task becomes apparent when readers and critics try to "go along" with the poetic articulations. Rimbaud's works require that we acknowledge the inexorable, excruciatingly painful predicament of modern life. The configuration of this predicament, although so true to cities, baffles us so long as we search for something else in the work. For then we are compelled to conclude that the configuration is merely a wild dream, a composite of a wide variety of fantasies. Why we should bother reading, let alone preserving, such fantasies, no one can rightly say.

In *Les Illuminations* we find, besides the two entitled *"Villes"* and another called simply *"Ville,"* the poem *"Métropolitain"* (R, 143). (See following facing pages.) The adjectival title carries the sense of "what is metropolitan" or "what pertains to the metropolis" or, since the poem is so tightly structured into five intersecting vectors of force, "metropolitan confluence."

A metropolis, or "mother city," spawns outlying settlements and ties them to herself by manifest economic, political, or cultural bonds. The poem gathers the vectors of this process into five strophes (units of "swaying" rather than stanzas, units of "standing"). These strophes structure the process. They comprise a confluence of forces in which the polis, the city itself, is but one vector. In *"Villes"* cities appear as openings where the non-city, the blank nature of gorges, ravines, and chasms, forms the focus of the inner-city ("inside") view. In *"Métropolitain"* the flux of the non-city becomes thematic already in the structure of the poem.

We may provisionally note three structural features. (1) Each strophe terminates with a single word which apparently "stands"

41

MÉTROPOLITAIN

Du détroit d'indigo aux mers d'Ossian, sur le sable rose et orange qu'a lavé le ciel vineux, viennent de monter et de se croiser des boulevards de cristal habités incontinent par de jeunes familles pauvres qui s'alimentent chez les fruitiers. Rien de riche.—La ville!

Du désert de bitume fuient droit en déroute avec les nappes de brumes échelonnées en bandes affreuses au ciel qui se recourbe, se recule et descend formé de la plus sinistre fumée noire que puisse faire l'Océan en deuil, les casques, les roues, les barques, les croupes.—La bataille!

Lève la tête: ce pont de bois, arqué; les derniers potagers de Samarie; ces masques enluminés sous la lanterne fouettée par la nuit froide; l'ondine niaise à la robe bruyante, au bas de la rivière; ces crânes lumineux dans les plans de pois—et les autres fantasmagories—la campagne.

Des routes bordées de grilles et de murs, contenant à peine leurs bosquets, et les atroces fleurs qu'on appellerait coeurs et soeurs, Damas damnant de langueur,—possessions de féeriques aristocraties ultra-Rhénanes, Japonaises, Guaranies, propres encore à recevoir la musique des anciens—et il y a des auberges qui, pour toujours, n'ouvrent déjà plus—il y a des princesses, et, si tu n'es pas trop accablé, l'étude des astres—le ciel.

Le matin où avec Elle, vous vous débattîtes parmi les éclats de neige, les lèvres vertes, les glaces, les drapeaux noirs et les rayons bleus, et les parfums pourpres du soleil des pôles—ta force.

METROPOLITAN

From the strait of indigo to the seas of Ossian, on the pink and orange sand washed by the wine-stained heaven, boulevards of crystal have just now risen and crossed themselves and are directly inhabited by families young but poor and fed by the fruit merchants. Nothing rich.—The city!

From the desert of asphalt flee straight in a rout (with sheets of fog stratified in frightening stripes across the heaven which curves itself back, draws itself back, and descends, formed by the most sinister black smoke that Ocean in mourning can produce) the helmets, the wheels, the barks, the croups.—The battle!

Raise your head: this bridge of wood, arched; these last gardens of Samaria; these masks, flushed under the lantern lashed by the cold night; silly Undine in her noisy gown, at the bottom of the river; these luminous skulls within the plans of peas—and the other phantasmagoria—the countryside.

Roads lined with gates and walls, hardly retaining their groves; and those atrocious flowers one might call hearts and sisters, Damascus damning in languor,—so many possessions of fairy-like aristocracies from beyond the Rhine, from Japan, from Guarania, still fit to receive the music of the ancients—and there are inns that never more shall open—there are princesses and, if you are not too overwhelmed, the study of the stars—the heaven.

The morning when, with Her, you both battled among the flashings of snow, the green lips, the ices, the black flags and blue beams, and the purple scents of the polar sun—your strength.

for what the strophe brings to light. The word (the city, the battle, the countryside, the heaven, your strength) is the *definiendum*, "what gets defined," and its preceding strophe is the *definiens*, "what does the defining." (2) The terminal words of the first two strophes (the city and the battle) stand apart from the *definiens* and are followed by exclamations. (3) The subsequent three strophes address us individually in the personal (*tu*) form.

The technique of "definition" is crucial. In naming the *definiendum* only after the *definiens* has "had its say," the strophe defines its vector according to a selection of events independently in force. If the order were reversed (if, for instance, the fourth strophe began, "Here, now, is the heaven...") we would imagine the thing to ourselves as something already familiar. As a result, we would then assess the "description" to discern how it accords with our preconceptions. In other words, the normal procedure tends to reduce the definition to ourselves and to preclude any "induction" into the events themselves. Beginning with a familiar word rather than with the eventful "thing" itself, our definitions will likely be "nominal" rather than "real," in the Scholastic sense of this distinction: they will tell us how to use a word, they will not take us to the thing. The "definitions" in "*Métropolitain*" are necessarily *real* definitions, since they take us directly into the "metropolitan confluence." Poetic discourse, as distinct from much expository effort, is of necessity real rather than nominal, it incites the *thought* and experience of a subject before naming it.

In "*Villes*" the opening statement does in fact present the *definiendum*: "These are your cities!" Yet in this case the following twenty-two statements univocally create and maintain an inside view of the thing: they place us within cities, we see and hear outwards. For all its variety, the poem structures a single perspective that takes us to the outer *edges* of cities. In this respect, "*Métropolitain*" effects a different experience of the polis: it intertwines its five vectors to place us at the *entrance* (also the exit) of the polis where these vectors of force coalesce with one another to catch us in their ultimate line of force.

In translation the first strophe reads:

> From the strait of indigo to the seas of Ossian, on the pink and orange sand washed by the wine-stained sky, boulevards of crystal have just now risen and crossed themselves and are directly inhabited by families young but poor and fed by the fruit merchants. Nothing rich. —The city!

The core of the event may be located in the fragment:

" ... boulevards of crystal have just now risen and crossed themselves ..." Here as before, we ask whether this event can lead to
the name with which it is subsequently christened. The place is
"boulevards of crystal." A city is essentially a place of movement
rather than repose. More, it is a place of windows: mercantilism.
Boulevards of crystal also suggest the quantity of these windows
which are viewed not according to their avowed purposes (to
attract attention, to display, to sell), but rather according to the
broad avenues of movement: we can perceive these (and other)
things *our* way rather than *their* way, here as crystal. However,
our way, the boulevards, are also acting: they "have just now
risen." This sense of "*venir de ...*," of being present in the mode
of just having done something, stands in decisive contrast to the
meandering and timeless paths of a village which are and always
were preceded by the land to which they are but responses. In a
city, the fact of human achievement is prominent. When a child
shows a bouquet of flowers to his or her mother, the significance
lies in the fact that he or she is the one, the source, who has
picked, arranged, and presented the bouquet. This source is to be
"seen" much more than the product. As for the boulevards of
crystal, they have also "just now" crossed themselves. They form,
then, a network of human movement and interest prior to what is
to the side of them (the merchants).

Once we follow the imagery of the core event, the remaining
qualifications follow as necessary and essential. The "just having
risen" of boulevards of crystal stretches first of all through space:
"From the strait of indigo to the seas of Ossian. ..." The second
reference is clear enough. Ossian is a legendary Irish warrior and
bard, his seas are the Gaelic Seas between Ireland and Scotland.
The first reference might fit any strait in the globe so long as it is
indeed a "narrows" yielding a strong sensation of blue. Yet the
association of indigo is definitely oriental (curiously, Rimbaud
did in fact travel, in 1876, from Singapore, where there is a "strait
of indigo," to Ireland; see *R*, 1003). However, the force of the
imagery, once related to the core, lies not in points on the globe: it
lies in the sense that these boulevards of crystal *span* the globe,
stretching from the blue of southern narrows to the cold and dark
of northern seas. A modern polis knows no center, it is essentially
a cosmo-polis. Since the 19th century, thinkers and poets have
remarked that modernity, the "collapse of apotheoses," entails
the realization of a world market (Marx), the unification of man
by means of communications (Tolstoi), world war (first with

45

arms and then with concepts) for the mastery of earth in the name of philosophical doctrines (Nietzsche), or what intellectual magazines call the "international homogenized consumer culture." The poem renders "visible" the "invisible" of the modern polis.

The spanning in space is brought back down to earth: the "boulevards of crystal" which have just risen and now "cross one another" to form a network stretching all the way "from the strait of indigo" to "Ossian's seas" are *grounded* "on the pink and orange sand washed by the wine-stained sky." The globe spanning network is founded both onto and underneath what the city otherwise bids us to ignore: the earth we stand on and the life-inciting sun. The two together provide the color and the wine, the blood, of life.

Finally, toward the end of the strophe, enter the inhabitants of the eventful placement of human networks. These people "move in" *in continenti tempore*: *after* the rising of the boulevards but *without* any break in the sequence, i.e., continuously with the event (the sense of the French *incontinent*). The core described comes first, the inhabitants take their bearings with regard to it. Thus they are "poor." City life being intrinsically all-demanding, any expectation from it is vain. Contrary to what the ex-peasant or small-town boy thinks upon entering the city, he will owe more to it than he will ever earn out of it. This economic experience is based on the original sequence described in the strophe, and not simply on the excessive greed of a small number of entrepreneurial capitalists. However, even though the families are poor, they are essentially young: they still have their life before them, unlike the villager whose life is always behind him. And it will be noticed that these families "get themselves fed" from merchants and not from the land. Both impoverished (indebted) and young (forwardly oriented), they have no time to go to the source: the middleman provides the necessary "alimentation" while these collectivities proceed directly to travel the boulevards of crystal.

The first vector contains an admission of its own insufficiency: "Nothing rich." The second strophe supplies one line of force so far missing:

> From the desert of asphalt flee straight in a rout (with sheets of fog
> stratified in frightening stripes across the heaven which curves itself
> back, draws itself back, and descends, formed by the most sinister

black smoke that Ocean in mourning can produce) the helmets, the wheels, the barks, the croups. —The battle!

Apart from the parenthetical interlude, the proportion reads as a second image superimposed on the first, "The battle!" upon "The city!" Although only one element of the subject, "the helmets," is explicitly war-like, the remaining ones, "... the wheels, the barks, the croups", all refer to human conveyances typical of both cities and battles. Wheels carry us over the land, barks over short stretches of water, and croups may carry second riders (the croup of a horse is that part directly behind the saddle). These three kinds of conveyances are in part protective, whereas the function of helmets lies solely in protection. Yet all four are fleeing in a straight line *and* in a rout.

In contrast to the idyll of the first strophe, the second vector superimposes a negative movement: a fleeing to save one's own skin. The cumulative effect of the imagery enhances the contradictory mood. The flight is straight and yet routed: clear in its direction yet both disbanded and without a pre-laid path (*dérouter* means to disintegrate a collectivity *and* to deprive of a road). Moreover the heaven above reflects further the mood: the sky *curves* back and prepares to strike *straight* down. In addition, everything that is fleeing straight is itself rounded, from helmets to croups. The power of the strophe lies partly in these combinations of visual images.

The place of the fleeing movement draws together the participants and the action. The opening phrase states the direction of the vector. While the boulevards of the first strophe stretch "from the strait of indigo to the seas of Ossian," the superimposed flight takes place "from the desert of asphalt" straight into nowhere. While boulevards are first seen in their invisible essence as lines of communication spanning the globe, they now appear as comprising a "desert of asphalt" from which human efforts move. Humans (left unnamed but still silently present) guide the machinery *away* from this desert, and do so as individuals in desperation (disbanded from their collectivities, i.e., not in "military formation"). This movement describes a battle in which we are momentarily defeated although not destroyed. The place of the battle is perfectly congruent with the place of the city. The flight is *away* from both.

What does the parenthetical interlude add to the experience of defeat in battle? (The parentheses are inserted only in the translation.) The machinery of battle, in fleeing, retreats *with* "sheets of fog stratified in frightening stripes across the heaven," while this heaven, besides moving, is "formed by the most sinister black smoke that Ocean in mourning can produce." The sky and the sea are seen, from the inside of the rout, as reflecting the events on land. The force of this reflection lies in its interruption and in its domination of the flight. Essential is this: the battle is darkened, not enlightened by the flight from the desert of asphalt. These boulevards may be as unsustaining as the desert and as uninspired as bitumen, but in flight from them, from the essential claims of urban life, the heavens themselves withdraw and strike out, no longer washing the pink and orange sands but leaving them as dry deserts. Furthermore, the seas which in essence locate the spanning of the globe with avenues of communication fill the heaven with the "most sinister black smoke" they can produce. Indeed, flight from the battle turns the sight of the cities into a desert of asphalt, abused sands of blackened boulevards.

The "giving up of the cities," correlative perhaps to an alleged "return to nature," does not merely lead to a degeneration of our modern abode, it also receives from nature herself a punishment. The sky is frighteningly clouded by the seas "in mourning": we cannot *see* anything, neither earth (country), air (sky), fire (sun), nor water (sea). Still, the poem does not construe the abandonment as pure non-being or cowardice. Although hardly "wise," the abandonment superimposes itself on the city as an inevitable moment of it, a moment where the desert of asphalt and the sea of darkness announce the necessity of the city. In a rout, much more than in a charge, we are aware of the frightful need to take stock of where we are.

The subsequent three strophes of the poem bid us to take stock. They address the reader as a friend and as an individual. They inform us again about the country, the heavens, and our own strength. The mood is one of composure, with no further exclamations. The third strophe reads:

Raise your head: this bridge of wood, arched; these last gardens of Samaria; these masks, flushed under the lantern lashed by the cold night; silly Undine in her noisy gown, at the bottom of the river; these luminous skulls within the plans of peas—and the other phantasmagoria—the countryside.

We are addressed individually at the moment of flight, *after* boulevards appear as the desert, when we cannot *see* owing to the blackening fog. Yet we are told to "raise the head." Obeying this simple exhortation we shall see what otherwise remains unseen. The fog is dispelled if only we pause and, in pausing, look up. We need not first secure the city, win the battle, or even turn around to face the forces that have routed us. A mere "looking up" causes the darkness to dissipate.

What then appears, what becomes visible? Not the spanning of the globe, the sand washed by the sun, poor people shopping. That paradisical point of departure will never more be the same, to it we shall never again return. Rather, we first focus onto a singular thing: this bridge. Instead of expanding, the field of vision increasingly contracts: this bridge is of wood, and it is arched. Not a reorganization into troops, but rather individual concentration on unique things arrests the flight. For organizational purposes, a bridge *is* its function of allowing us to escape, to cross to the other side, and it is *nothing but* this function. But once the flight is arrested, once we look up, the bridge looms: it is of wood, and it is arched.

In looking up we also see *these* gardens. In a *potager* one grows vegetables and occasionally fruits for one's own consumption, for one's own "pot" and not for sale: for their use value and not for their exchange value, as Marx would say. In days of mercantilism, such gardens are vanishing. The few remaining ones strike us as present in the mode of disappearing. Strange in themselves, they are seen in strange and vanishing places: in Samaria, a region, once an ancient city, in Palestine. Accepting our location in the realm of international commerce (a system interpreting each and every thing in terms of its exchange value), we behold these gardens not as true to the day, but as remnants of truths of yesterday, truths of another, perhaps a saddening kind today.

Then: "these masks, flushed under the lantern lashed by the cold night." Fishermen, perhaps, and at the time of painful nighttime work. Whoever these people are, they appear not at a moment of their ease, but in their humble roles. These are not the "wild men" of the cities who "dance ceaselessly the festival of the night" (statement 21 of "*Villes*"). Their roles place them in the face of the elements: the cold lashes the man-made light that in turn flushes the contorted faces. Addressed in an intimate manner as individuals, we see our fellows not as mere collectivities (the young but poor families) nor as users of instru-

49

ments (of the helmets, the wheels, the barks, the croups). They face the wind, the land, the water, the sun in its nighttime absence. Yet we know that what we perceive at this moment is necessarily masked: the frontage of this encounter with the elements protrudes, while the men and women as such withdraw behind this frontage.

Then: "silly Undine in her noisy gown, at the bottom of the river." In flight from the onslaught of the city, we are now asked to pause and to see an invisible power in the river. Undine, a water fairy, literally a "wave," of Germanic lore, needs and so lures a mortal mate to love in order to obtain a soul; she either kills in love or dies in love. As in "*Villes*," a willingness to see the invisible significance of rural myth marks the possibility of our acquiring a place to stand, to move, occasionally even to rest, in an otherwise frenzied and pointless urban life. To be sure, Undine is "silly," yet she is present in her noisy gown. We moderns can only take mythic creatures at their face value during our childhood. But their significance lies in our belonging to that which we do in fact face. The waters of modern power dams also claim us "in love"—alternately marking our mortality and draining themselves for our interim vitality. As our vital relationship with the land is evident in the vanishing of little gardens and their replacement by modern commercial agriculture, and as our dependence on the sun of the day is visible in the cold of the night, so debt to the waters of the earth is manifest in the rural myth of a water fairy in love with mortals.

Finally: "these luminous skulls within the plans of peas." When we look up, we first of all see not "rows" of vegetables. Rather, we see "plans," *schemes* for raising large quantities of specialized crops for the market. No human activity within modern organization is able to *support* the organization. Even farming is no longer a genuine rural enterprise, it has become industrialized. Out in the country we are struck more by human scheming and less by the peas, the oranges, the grapes. Yet, as we look up, we shall see not even these schemings directly. Rather, we see "luminous skulls" within them. These ghostly apparitions are the remnants of the living labor which went into the construction of the fields, and is now gone and dead. But when pausing in flight we *see* these skulls nonetheless.

All five images—the bridge, these gardens, these masks, Undine, and these skulls—suggest a presence of nature, one which is absenting itself. Even a bridge, wooden (therefore perishably "natural") and arched (therefore yielding to nature and slowing down the traffic), is a thing of the past. And masks (contorted faces) responding to the exigencies of nature with only a weak instrumental aid, are in principle superfluous in a fully mechanized society (where "masks" are interpreted as ways of defending one's ego in the presence of others rather than results of bending oneself to the elements). These and other "sights" are called "phantasmagoria": literally assemblies of appearances that ever rush upon us, ever fluctuate as we advance in the human sojourn. Taking our stand within urban life, we still find our bearings in reference to this vector called *la campagne*.

Although we North Americans translate this word by "countryside," it sends a European mind to something that barely exists in the New World. Our rural history was too short to create a *campagna* such as lies outside Rome and Naples. The word refers to the cultivated area around a center of human life: it "feeds" the center and so excludes both forested land and wasteland. Thus in the original sense an Italian *campagna* is already a metropolitan vector. However, the poem changes the direction of its force: we experience the countryside in flight from the city. And from the view of the land achieved when looking up, we see nature powerfully present although absenting itself. This change of direction preserves the *definiendum*. At the same time it reminds us of our non-rural destiny.

The fourth strophe appears to continue the catalogue of sights available to us individually once we pause in flight to look where we are:

> Roads lined with gates and walls, hardly retaining their groves; and those atrocious flowers one might call hearts and sisters, Damascus damning in languor—so many possessions of fairy-like aristocracies from beyond the Rhine, from Japan, from Guarania, still fit to receive the music of the ancients—and there are inns that never more shall open—there are princesses and, if you are not too overwhelmed, the study of the stars—the heaven.

The *definiendum* in this case is the correlate of the countryside, the heavens above, the sky: what earlier washed the "pink and orange sands" on which the "boulevards of crystal" had just risen, and what then was seen to "curve itself back, draw itself back, and descend," formed by black smoke. In its third and definitive appearance the reality of the heaven does not direct us "up above," since "the study of the stars" is explicitly classified as a mere option after the reality has been acknowledged in its overwhelming power. The "real" heaven somehow looms in the phantasmagoria rushing upon us between "roads" and "princesses." These, it will be noticed, take as their recurrent point of departure the countryside of the preceding strophe, in the mood of sheer absence. How do we here experience "the heaven"?

The *definiens* receives a unity of reference from an experience possible on the European Continent and on the British Isles, but impossible on North American soil. The description stems from the heritage formative of and so absently evident in the land of the Old World: the country estates of aristocratic families. Walking through the countryside of Europe or England we experience the etherealness of this land. These aristocratic estates no longer emit the "music of the spheres" but still do receive the music of old, even though *we* have to supply the orchestration. The aristocratic, essentially non-urban source of both countryside and city, evident to us as we pause in flight from battle, belongs to a fairy-like, far distant past: from beyond the Rhine (typically Middle European, ghostly), from Japan (the antipode of Europe), even from Guarania. This last "source" is the region of Paraguay once inhabited by the warrior-tribe of Guaranians: neither Western nor Eastern, this completely a-historical land is even more "of the past." Urban life is fundamentally historical, being the life of development. The unity of reference emergent in the *definiens* orients us to the past of this historical development, to what already *is*, and not to what *might* be in some imaginary heaven.

All three "aristocracies" possess, still today, this land. They are, we might say, "absentee" landlords. The opening phrases of the strophe describe *what* they possess, what composes the heaven, the "beyond" of the countryside. Not much: some roads lined with iron grilled gates, decaying walls which barely define the groves of trees behind; then also the flowers that spring up everywhere. Sheer absence.

But why the manifest negations commencing with the "atrociousness" of the flowers? If we pay no heed to the significance of the absentee ownership, of the "collapse of apotheoses," we can easily forget that these "flowers" springing from the decay seduce us away from the cities into a sterile romanticism. We *might* call them "hearts and sisters." They are dangerous because they lure us into seeing in absence a surrogate presence, a languishing heart or a virginal sister-soul, a sub-

52

jective *inner* "heaven," a weekend house built today by one's psychotherapist but erected in the nineteenth century by the minor, forgotten romantic poets. All the while Damascus, the place of this danger as well as the romantic source of damask, *damns*, i.e., lends no support to the escapist interpretation of heaven. The unity of these lines ("these atrocious *fleurs* that one might call *coeurs* and *soeurs*, Damascus damning in *langeur*) is achieved phonetically rather than semantically, thereby strengthening the suggestion of the deceitful dreaminess lurking along these roads.

This "heaven" vector is the strangest one of the five. As the other vectors, it is metropolitan in character. It structures, along with the others, the confluence of the mother-city, a city which is also a battle, a city from which we flee and, in fleeing, find ourselves addressed. Pausing, we look up, first to the sights of the countryside and now to those of the heaven.

Recalling its context, we can discern the direction of this vector. It is, to be sure, a "beyond" which "hangs over" the countryside, but a beyond turned *into* the countryside, and just as unattainable for mortals as the Heaven of the days before urban development and globe-spanning commercial enterprise. The countryside, although a vanishing factor, still holds meaning for us in the drawing power of its withdrawal. The heaven is essentially the absence that belongs to this withdrawal. It has now become, as in "*Villes*," our heritage: not as a vanished *time*, but as the *place* that is withdrawing. If we avoid the temptation to replace it by a surrogate presence, the absence, like the "blank nature" of modern urban enterprise, can still exercise a sustaining force upon city life. True, the "inns" or "hostels," which once promised always to open their doors to weary travelers, "never more shall open." But even though the doors remain closed, the ancient modes of reception nonetheless "hang over" everything we see. If we are to take our stand in the battle, in the city of our life, then the absence of heaven is essential to the pause in flight.

The fifth and last strophe resumes with special force the individual ("*tu*") address. It reads:

The morning when with Her, you both battled among the flashings of snow, the green lips, the ices, the black flags and blue beams, and the purple scents of the polar sun—your strength.

53

The self attains to its strength only after, i.e., on the basis of, the city as the battle and the countryside with its heaven. Rimbaud chose for "strength" the word *force*, not *pouvoir* (German *Kraft*, not *Macht*); *force* does not mean power over other things, but power expressing and manifesting a center of force *among* other things. Strength is expressive, not repressive or suppressive power. The self discovers itself as a metropolitan "vector" force, somehow in essential reference to the countryside with its heaven and the city as a battlefield.

As in "*Villes*," self-discovery is temporal. We know our strength in reference to the past. In "*Métropolitain*" the "historical past" expresses this new temporal dimension. On one specified morning, now recalled as such and presented in the mode of a tale, there occurred a specific battle in a specific setting. The recollection of this morning informs us individually of our true strength, our true being, in implicit contrast to an unspecified illusion. We are to understand this "information" in the mode of a presence suggesting to us our own possibility, our "future" in the entire poem's vector field. —These structural features pose avenues of further consideration.

First. Our strength reveals itself, according to the *definiens*, in retrospect upon a specified *morning* of battle. Why this time of day? Our forefathers learned affirmation in recollection. In the evening they pondered the polis as transparent to a living nature whose inner life supported the life of man: this is ancient Greek, Christian, and even early Renaissance doctrine. Today, however, nature is blank: it (no longer "she") manifests itself to us only in laws of behavior formulated by us into rules of operation (therefore, these laws are *our* laws as much as *its* laws). In the morning, we of today must face this terrifying blank, accept the challenges of organization. In the evening we likely sink back into our constructs, whereupon no enlightenment can occur, at most reorganization preparatory to the adventures of tomorrow.

Second. Our strength, we are told, reveals itself in our *battling* along side of Her (not, it is to be noticed, *against* her). This Her receives no further specification. However, feminine form typically suggests an opposition to success-oriented, masculine values. In feminine opposition to masculine aggression lies a reminder: every moment, although most apparently one of conquest, is or may be also one of care. Our strength, we are told, proves itself (*did* prove itself, if we only pause to recall it) in our

54

willingness to re-enter the battle otherwise (and since) foresaken. It proves itself when we struggle with this feminine force "at our side." Conquest, to be sure. For such is the nature of the modern metropolis. However, precisely in this conquest we normally take flight: seemingly the inhabitants of the city, we evacuate it each day. In pausing to "raise the head," we see things otherwise invisible: the countryside and the heavens. Nature may remain a blank, but it also draws us to itself, and thus another dimension of life is gathered, one in which the things on the periphery (the *only* things possible for city life) may be preserved as withdrawing. Preserving the withdrawal of things, we come into our strength, a strength realized only in conjunction with Her, with feminine care for things. So coupled, we may re-enter the battle, we may once again inhabit the city.

Third. The battling now takes place among specific flashings of snow, green lips, ices, black flags and blue beams, and purple scents of the sun of the poles: in each case *these* or *those*, not just some or any. We *do* find our strength among these things: neither in fleeing from the things of the city, nor in mastering those absenting themselves in the countryside, nor in languishing in the things essentially absent in the heaven, nor in giving up the battle and simply falling in love with things. But how can we understand the "among" if we cannot understand *what* these things are?

The last strophe does in fact name the things on this battlefield: snow, lips, ice, flags, beams of light, the sun at the north and south poles. They are recollected as having been present already "that morning." Then, at that instructive time, they were (and are now again) perceived through selfhood, i.e., at the moment of our strength. The things bear down as flashing, green, cold, black, blue, purple. In short, things on the battlefield appear sensuous at the moment of our strength, and their sensuousness is a measure of that strength. Why, at the moment of selfhood now recollected, should thinghood be so markedly sensuous?

To approach this crucial question, let us review the development as a whole. In *any* case we become our *selves* in facing up to *things* as these selves and these things meet (often only to avoid) one another within a *context*. The poem creates a context of overwhelming "metropolitan confluence." Idyllically, selves are but members of collectivities, families fed by the merchants (Strophe I). Hidden within or behind conveyances, these selves are also fleeing. Owing to the black smoke of battle, things hardly appear at all (Strophe II). Then, as the individual raises his head, he gradually comes to himself and things simultaneously appear, forcefully although precisely in the mode of vanishing (Strophe III). Finally, the individual learns his strength in reference back to a special moment of battle, femininely qualified (Strophe IV). And in *this* development, things are sensuous.

The essentially sensuous things of the fifth strophe are the *same* things that have already appeared, disappeared, and reappeared in various transmutations. The boulevards of crystal comprising the initial city vanish to reappear as the desert of asphalt from which hidden selves are de-routed (put to rout), and this unsustaining desert yields to the *routes* (roads) lined with recollections of absence. Similarly, the heaven thrice appears: as washing the idyllic sands, as formed of black smoke, and as the absence described in the *definiens* of the fourth strophe. Thus things are sensuous only when driven into variety, when appearing in the mode of variegation.

Selfhood in the metropolitan context lies in the recollected strength to face things as forever shifting their countenance. We are therefore not struck at the matinal moment by *what* things are, we are impressed *that* they are. This moment is trying. For the thatness of things tries our strength in their vary-able manner of appearance. Our strength proves itself in this battle as feminine acceptance of the givenness of things, an acceptance modifying the masculine effort to *determine* things in the processes of conquest. Selfhood emerges as we joyfully face things in *their* thatness, as we make *ours* the how-ness of their appearance. How things appear depends *generally* on whether we are contemplating the idyll of the city, fleeing from the terror of battle, or pausing to look at the things of the countryside and the heaven. Furthermore, their manner of appearance depends *specifically* on what we are undertaking as individual city dwellers. In any case we face an immediate sensuous *manner* rather than an ultimate *what*. In *this* femininely modified battle, thinghood emerges as the sensuousness of things.

Since Socrates, the mere suggestion that thinghood is essentially faced in terms of vary-ability, of vary-egated sensuousness, has been anathema. Yet once we accept the urban context of our life we necessarily renounce any ground outside human organization: nature becomes a blank up to which organization moves, but not on which it can be based. Of course, we may still hope to discern reassuringly stable *structures* within the urban context (although no investigation has yet been indubitably successful in its effort to do so). Things themselves, as we directly meet up with them anew each day, remain undecided by *any* inner-contextual pre-consideration. They present themselves either as things absenting themselves or as things absent, as countryside or as heaven. As distinct from passing things up (calculating, using, buying, selling, consuming them), we *contact* them only directly, i.e., through the five senses. Our strength, our selfhood, is tried and possibly proven in this context.

The German philosopher Kant first argued convincingly that the modern ambition to know things, to achieve organized power over them, necessitates a sharp distinction between appearances (phenomena) and the thing itself that appears (*das Ding an sich*). In Kant's terminology, we *know* appearances. However, any given moment of knowledge (when we are knowing and do not simply recoil into established organization) requires that we also *think* the thing itself. The thing forever on the edge of organization is called a "noumenon" (from the Greek, meaning "what gets thought"). Thus, even though nature is henceforth a blank known only as "the lawfulness of appearances in space and time," it is nonetheless the crucial point of contact at any moment (in French one says literally: "the morning *where* ..."). In Kant's own argument, the noumenal point of contact is crucial, for, in knowing, we move up to it and we must refer to it the manifold of appearances under investigation. Without the "thing in itself," without the noumenon at the edge of human organization, the manifold of appearances has no "objective" unity. That is, in abstraction from non-knowable but still thinkable "things" we could not refer our organization (conceptual framework) legitimately to the environment in which we wish to establish the organization, the rules of operation called knowledge. Without the noumenal reference of phenomenal things, the organization becomes a mere personal and private fantasy.

The eighteenth-century philosophical statement of the distinction between thing-as-in-itself and thing-as-appearing-to-us was the first unequivocal discovery of the exigency hitherto only implicit, indeed hidden within modern ambition. The ambition emerged already clearly around the year 1600, for example in Bacon's *New Organon*: "to establish and extend the power and dominion of the human race itself over the universe" (Book One, Aphorism 79). The necessary distinction between modes of facing a "universe" thusly "dominated" was formulated with a view mainly to the development of physics. The purport of the distinction, the exigency it entails, we all experience nowadays in urban life.

For us today, the exigency is chiefly to affirm the sensuousness of things as revelatory of these things themselves (as *thought*) and not only of ourselves. This affirmation is painful because it leaves things themselves as vary-able. Always intruding at the edge in their sheer thatness, things themselves will draw us toward themselves (into the gorges, up the ravines, over the chasms) and will forever be shifting their countenances. If our strength fails, we shall interpret the sensuousness as simply ours, in the same way a drug addict wallows in his sensations: no matter how beautiful, variable, strange, such sensations are not *of* anything. Unable to move on the periphery, in the face of the thatness of things, we recede into the balloon of prior human achievement. Sensuousness then gives way to mere sensuality, an incestuous play of one's own senses. Such sensuality disallows any affirmation of the context. It searches for a moment without a context, it denies the context, and is essentially a mode of negation.

"*Métropolitain*" simultaneously proposes and recalls a femininely modified battle "among the flashings of snow, the green lips, the ices, the black flags and blue beams, and the purple scents of the polar sun." The poem concretely achieves, for a moment, what we otherwise only talk about abstractly before and afterwards. It takes us into the confluence of five forces: the city and the battle as congruent (Strophes I and II), then the countryside and the heaven as locating the things forever on the edge of city life (Strophes III and IV), and finally our strength as a recollected, femininely modified ability to turn and "do battle" (Strophe V). At this moment of turning we discover our strength and the sensuousness of the things themselves which withdraw and draw us along, as the tails of meteors. Herein lies the possibility of modern affirmation.

5. A CONCLUDING THOUGHT

In principle, "*Villes*" and "*Métropolitain*" should speak to us already. They do not require the break-down into the "exploded views" we have devised. Thus we should beware of expositions from any quarter, and ask ourselves afterwards whether we cannot simply listen to the poem, forgetting the talkative elucidations. Any relevant exposition of a poetic work can only be an interim measure. In the end we must return to the original speech. If we can hear the speech already without the elucidation, at the beginning, so much the better.

In fact, however, Rimbaud's poems are not generally allowed to speak for themselves, or at least they are not heard well. As in so many situations, we hear mainly what we want to hear. In literary analysis this prior condition of volition is perhaps a necessary one. But then we must ask whether we *want* to hear what Rimbaud's poems have to say.

Nearly five years after Rimbaud's death in 1891, Mallarmé remarked (*M*, 514 and 1587: in a commentary requested by and printed in an American journal) that Rimbaud, in his quest for "new sensations" hitherto "not known," was convinced he could "encounter these in the bazaar of illusion peculiar to the heart of cities" (*les rencontrer en le bazar d'illusion des cités*). It is instructive to ponder these words not only because Mallarmé was himself a poet whose career ran parallel to that of Rimbaud, but also because his remark is a concession made at a distance. Mallarmé expresses not approval of a project he himself would care to undertake. He rather voices a scepticism about a conviction he finds strange.

Mallarmé recognizes Rimbaud's undertaking: to study and, more obviously, to bring into poetic articulation, the modern urban predicament. This study directs itself to the "bazaar of illusion." That is, we are not asked to take the city at face value, for its life offers at first only a marketplace of human misconceptions. We find this bazaar in the *cités*, in the heart of cities. And through the study we can encounter "sensations" that are new in the sense of "modern," not necessarily in the trivial sense of exciting (the French is *neuves*, not *nouvelles*). Finally, the study is difficult because the modern mode of sensation of things, although in force, is "not known."

We shall only be able to listen to the poems of great poets when we understand that these poems emanate from arduous and careful study, and that in any given case the study stems from a concern for what affects us all.

Yet city life insists that all human interest and effort fall into one of two classifications: either (a) it is a manner of moving within organization (shopping and the like) or (b) it is an extension, possibly a preparatory clarification, of operation (entrepreneurial work, whether in commerce or science). Since it would be pretentious and even demeaning to place poems in the second classification, urban life encourages us to place them in the first: while the mass of city dwellers prefer to mull through the streets shopping or to lie on the beach sunbathing, a few individuals (according to urban classification) betray a personal, subjective preference for reading and writing poems. City life, presently indeed a "bazaar of illusion," will never allow poems to issue from, instigate, and embody a *study* of its life. Yet Rimbaud's two poems (and many others: see also his early "*L'Orgie parisienne*") are just that: studies.

They direct themselves to illusions which not only conceal the truth of cities but, doubling this sin, deny that poems could ever study and embody this truth. They direct *us* through these illusions, preserving the urban form of oblivion while opening it out upon emergence.

CHAPTER TWO

MALLARMÉ AND FINITE TRANSCENDENCE

1. THE QUESTION

How can we nowadays take some one thing seriously? There is an easy answer to this question, one to which we too readily succumb. We concentrate upon a specified realm (our family life, our love life, our hobbies, our church activities) and expend the remainder of our energies as needs be: earning a living (one's job), fulfilling the expectations of others (one's duties), escaping from burdensome responsibilities of any sort (one's relaxing distractions). However, this easy answer recommends a doubtful criterion and presupposes a pernicious alienation. The criterion states that we must take our own things seriously and not those of others—for instance, not our employer's place of business or our spouse's sewing or bowling club. And all the while we presuppose that the public and the private domains require essentially different modes of response, since the first serves as a mere means for the second—as the highway and telephone systems dominating the landscape merely serve to deliver goods and information fueling a life elsewhere.

Yet only that can really be taken as our own to which we give ourselves, in which we find ourselves in this giving. The difference between grudging performance of one's routine tasks and the wholehearted doing of one's own "thing" lies not in a taking to oneself of the thing, but in our own belonging to it. Only the skill and the responsibility "belong" to us. We master procedures, not things, and our relation to things is one of devotion.

And only that human response is individual which redeems the entire context of one's efforts. The difference between being oneself (an individual) and simply falling in line with the general run of humanity lies not in the insistence upon carving out a private life: this effort precisely characterizes the general run. It lies rather in the development of a meaningful response to the public domain. Paradoxically, we stand our own as individuals to the extent that we can *carry* the human situation in which we live. For this situation provides the channels wherein we move, and precisely this movement must become individual.

Our scrutiny of the easy answer raises two questions. First, granted that we can take something seriously only if it is our own, how does this owning evolve correlative to being taken up into the thing, to being owned by (devoted to) it? Second, granted that we can take something seriously only if we stand apart as individuals from the otherwise devouring human context, how does this stand evolve correlative to carrying the human situation and not simply abandoning it?

Reformulating, we ask: How is *finite concern* possible? "Finite" means bounded, defined, gathered within limits; negatively, it means not dissipated, not roving, not aimless, not shifting. "Concern" is a human disposition toward things; it involves both responsiveness and responsibility. Finite concern entails, then, both a focus on things and an individuality of self, both a thinghood and a selfhood. And these are precisely the essential issues in the experience of taking some one thing seriously.

The question arises only because the human situation as such does not ensure finite concern. The development of this concern, or the notable lack thereof, comprises the eternal repetition of the human condition, as well as the recurrent need and relevance of telling its story. It is the fundamental question, although often unacknowledged, that hovers over all genuine philosophical works, many poetic works, and even some historical works.

Yet our age actually *defies* the question by directly or indirectly denying finitude. Although this defiance merits historical, sociological, and philosophical study in itself, here we shall simply exemplify it in three features of our age which we face when we raise the question: the effects of television, of psychoanalysis, and of modern science.

Television tends to disintegrate political focus. We view news and documentary coverage, live or compiled only hours before, on problems suffered by peoples in places having no concrete relation to the place where we directly assume our daily responsibilities. The problems of the people in Bangladesh must, of course, be "sensational" if they are to affect our own sympathies: bloody war, mass rape, and plague surpass the limits of our own experience. In general, the farther away from our own place, the greater must be the "sensation" if the problems are to be of interest to us, and the greater the sensation the less the concrete concern and the more abstract the sympathy. As a result of such disintegration we ignore our own polis and we lose the possibility of focusing on the concrete. The disintegration expresses itself most bizarrely in abstract charity: collecting clothes for people on the other side of the globe, rather than carrying them over to the other side of the tracks; "adopting" children from exotic regions of the world (i.e., submitting a monthly check to a distant organization) instead of taking care of our own orphans; financing hospitals in Africa, introducing a style of life totally alien to the inhabitants, when the United States provides very feeble medical care for its stricken classes proportional to its general wealth. This cosmopolitanism of passive sympathy weakens or even destroys the focus necessary for active and concrete concern. Television drags us out of our home and all over the globe, landing us nowhere. Even when otherwise informative, it is generally distractive rather than recollective in intent. We are asked to be "interested" in and "concerned" about everything, and we end up focusing ourselves on nothing at all.

Of the many effects of psychoanalysis, we select only one: the disintegration of what the Greeks called *philia*, "friendship" in the broad sense covering also the relationship possible between parents and children, between lovers as well as between peers. For genuine friendship requires a focus of concern explained away as specious by psychoanalytic theory. This view of human relations envisions and justifies each individual as an isolated personality receiving "in-put" from, and expressing itself in, the environment, particularly in regard to alien personalities. It follows that these others (father, mother, brother, sister; lovers or school chums or employers) represent either contrary ways of being (arousing suspicion of our own inadequacy) or competition in the field of expression (crowding us out of our own domain if we are not careful). In practice one is unable to take anybody else seriously. Thus, in its effort to explain certain general phenomena of social behavior, psychoanalytic theory undoes the possibility of focused human relations. The most bizarre instance of this undoing of *philia* is evident among those who have undergone psychoanalysis or received elementary training in it. In the absence of one who might otherwise be their friend, these amateurs analyze him or her as would be appropriate only for a general to analyze the enemy: dissecting motives, personal history, hang-ups, weaknesses, self-images, illusions, desires, and stupidities. Here the open warfare of village gossip has been stylized into sophisticated slander with little possibility for reconciliation.

At the roots of television (destruction of *polis*-focus) and of psychoanalysis (destruction of *philia*-focus) lie the historically more far-reaching transformations enacted in and by the development of industry. From this we extract its brain, namely science, and within this wide-ranging subject we select the effect modern science has had on our ability to focus on *things* in the strict sense. This strange effect manifests itself in the change of meaning of the word "idea." The originally Greek word was coined in the experience of a paradox. When focusing on a bird flying overhead, we bring to bear on the moment a complex of insight which also, and in principle, comes into play at other moments in regard to other birds. However, the Greeks were originally interested in the focus, and their theoretical discourse investigated how the complex necessarily contributed to the focus. Ancient thinkers argued that (and how) this complex accounts for keeping the focus on the bird *whole*, "in one piece"; the complex was therefore named *kath'olon*, a term misleadingly translated as "universal." Nowadays, however, we do not ask how the *kath'olon* helps us to take some one thing seriously, but rather how we can work out "universal" complexes of human operation, into which things merely "fit." Essentially alienated from any one thing, a modern scientific idea proves its relevance and power insofar as it accounts for a multiplicity of things. Consequently, training in modern universals teaches us how never to take seriously any given thing, but to see in it only what applies to other things as well: however identical or similar the instigating paradoxes, the modern interest moves exactly opposite to the ancient one. Modern concern for "nature" exemplifies the modern idea. Actively, such concern comes to the fore in efforts to preserve natural resources: general availability for future industrial exploitation. Passively, the concern surfaces in a sentimental love of animals and plants. In neither of these cases do we experience the kind of focus at work in learning to draw, or in a painting by Van Gogh.

Of course, the defiance (nihilism) built into our age by television, psychoanalysis, and (the root of it all) modern science does not prevent us absolutely from raising the question of finite concern—or from focusing on our own political context, on a friend, on things presenting themselves to us. But when we do ask about the possibility of finite concern, and also find ourselves actually concerned about some definite matters, we are in revolt against the prevailing powers and interpretations, be this revolt ever so inconspicuous to others and even unintentional on our part.

No historical situation can ever ensure finite concern. However, as already argued (in Chapter One, the section on "Modern Affirmation"), our present epoch lacks channels which can encourage focus. A thing of the past such as the Lord's Prayer invited one to be concerned in specific ways about a kingdom, about those who are at our mercy, about the earth and its sustenance. The Church manifestly guaranteed nothing whatsoever, least of all its own preservation, but the era of its reign (as well as other eras) did provide channels in which the question could be raised "officially." That these channels often proved useful for other (sometimes perverse) purposes as well, does not detract from the encouragement they afforded once an individual did ask how he could break away from the dreariness of everyday non-finite concerns and develop a special, individual, and focused concern for his context, for the human beings he worked with, and for the earth he cultivated.

We recall the contemporary denials of finite concern in order to clarify the difficulties facing any contemporary effort to raise the question hovering over the human condition in any age. These difficulties define the *materials* of our situation; they become *obstacles* only when we ignore them. Great art and poetry articulate such materials. We have already seen how Rimbaud's poems incorporate related materials to configure a viable experience of urban life. We shall presently examine some efforts to structure a distinctively modern convergence of meanings.

The question—How is finite concern possible?—has not, it will be noticed, been answered. Raising the question has led to a structure of prerequisites, i.e., some understanding of what we face if we wish to pursue the question. How can this structure be appreciated as a whole, as a unit?

Above all, the question asks us to distinguish between everyday concerns and finite concern. Everyday concern directs itself to *unfolding* a spatial and temporal arena of one's doings and undergoings in order to extend or secure, on a repetitive basis, the area of one's influence and efficacy. Finite concern, on the other hand, is a *development* wherein one finds oneself singled out as individual and as focusing on things, both of which (self and things) are already "there." Such development, unlike the previous unfolding, rather than directing itself toward anything, issues from what is already present although passed over in oblivion. The relationship between non-finite and finite concern remains puzzling, since the first, for all its oblivion, supplies the materials necessary for the second.

A simple example can illustrate the distinction between the unfolding of (everyday) and the development of (finite) concern. Imagine entering, early in the morning, a cheese shop (a *crème-rie*) in a French provincial town, in order to obtain provisions for the day's journey. Your stay in the town was simply a stop-over, and the provisions you intend to purchase will constitute the noon and evening meals during this day. A foreigner under-way, your concern is very "everyday," and you expect to "un-fold" this concern by passing through the cheese shop, by the cheeses, past the cheese lady. Now, what may happen? You of course expect the cheese lady to unfold *her* everyday concerns, notably to make a sale, part of a series of repeated transactions allowing her to extract a living out of an economic system of social desires and natural needs. For the sale, she need only in-form you of the relative qualities of cheeses and their prices, and this only when asked. By and large, the transaction is likely to come to a close in this manner and to pass into the ever-growing collection of immemorabilia. —But other things may happen, things of a continuing significance, even if eerie, as time goes on. For one, some slight indication of interest in local cheeses from you may unexpectedly enliven the cheese lady, and there might ensue an exchange of experiences centering around cheeses and even including the entire meals in which special varieties were central. For a moment your past concern for future travels, as well as her past worries about future solvency, evaporate, and in their stead appears a focus involving, to be sure, retrospections and prospections but above all a presence of articulation centered on the substance of the shop. The cheese lady not only sells cheeses, but *knows* them. She not only sells them to make a living, but concentrates on them with a contagious conviction that cheeses are in themselves important. A spell is cast, one so fragile that it may be broken simply by the arrival in the shop of another customer, one with whom the lady has an everyday re-lationship: then the mood is over, you choose your cheese, pay for it at the cash register, and make your exit as quickly as possible.

Such experiences are memorable because they suggest that

finite concern does develop within everyday concern and in fact supports, makes meaningful, the otherwise dreary course of affairs.

2. THE SONNET
"LE VIERGE, LE VIVACE ET LE BEL AUJOURD'HUI"

The question has so far been raised dialectically with a view to eliciting the prerequisites of an answer. Ultimately, however, the issue of the question, finite concern itself, can be upheld only in a transparency to what is of concern. Dialectic at best prepares for a traversal. The traversal itself occurs in another mode of articulation: the poetic.

Stéphane Mallarmé's *"Le vierge, le vivace, et le bel aujourd'-hui"* articulates what we have called finite concern. (See following facing pages.) The sonnet first appeared in 1885 and reappeared unchanged two years later in a collection of his poems (*M*, 67-68, 1485).

In a provisional manner, we may note three structural features evident in an initial reading of the sonnet. First, a story of sorts is being told: an invigorating matinal scene, on a frozen lake with the possibility of a "thaw"; a swan frozen into this lake due to his own earlier mistakes; the struggle of the swan to free himself; and finally the apparent failure of the otherwise hopeful enterprise, and pending death. Yet every moment of the story unfolds in strange, seemingly incompatible phrases which lend the tale a vibrative power. For each description suggests of its own accord that it might be evoking something beyond the sequence of events simply outlined.

Second, the last word of the sonnet, the second of the two explicit references to the swan, is capitalized in the text. At the very end of the poem the Swan becomes a symbol; the sonnet is a symbolist poem. Through this poetic device the articulation deliberately allows the images of the story to stand for other images marking the human condition as such. However, perhaps every poetic work can be read as at least implicitly structuring situations other than the one explicitly in view. Rimbaud's *"Villes"* and *"Métropolitain"* speak not simply to and about Charlesville or Paris, but to and about any situation of modern urban life. On the other hand a symbol (and let us stay with the one in Mallermé's sonnet) "adds" to the experience an explicit point of convergence. The Swan, rather than the lake or

SONNET

Le vierge, le vivace et le bel aujourd'hui
Va-t-il nous déchirer avec un coup d'aile ivre
Ce lac dur oublié que hante sous le givre
Le transparent glacier des vols qui n'ont pas fui!

Un cygne d'autrefois se souvient que c'est lui
Magnifique mais qui sans espoir se délivre
Pour n'avoir pas chanté la région où vivre
Quand du stérile hiver a resplendi l'ennui.

Tout son col secouera cette blanche agonie
Par l'espace infligé à l'oiseau qui le nie,
Mais non l'horreur du sol où le plumage est pris.

Fantôme qu'à ce lieu son pur éclat assigne,
Il s'immobilise au songe froid de mépris
Que vêt parmi l'exil inutile le Cygne.

SONNET

The virginal, the vivacious, the beautiful today
Shall it lacerate for us with a beat of elated wing
This forgotten hard lake haunted beneath the frost
By the transparent glacier of flights that flew not!

A swan of time ago recalls that it's he
Magnificent but who, without hope, is freeing himself
For not having sung the region where to live
When the ennui of sterile winter came blazing.

His whole neck will shake off this white agony
Inflicted by the space on the bird who denies it,
But not the horror of the ground where the plummage is caught.

Phantom destined to this place by his pure radiance,
He immobilizes himself in the cold dream of scorn
Worn amidst useless exile by the Swan.

the day, locates the gathering point of the image and also, being a symbol, the gathering point of the idea. Our exposition will consider in detail how this gathering works.

Finally, we may note the overall temporality of the sonnet. Just as the phrasing of the story and the symbolism of the idea, so also the timing contributes to the polyvalence of the articulation. It is chiefly timed as "today," yet immediately the experience transmutes into an expectation ("Shall it lacerate...") and later (in the first tercet) into a prediction ("... will shake off..."). As a whole, the present and the future revert to the past, in terms of guilt ("... flights that flew not!" and "For not having sung..."). The intersection of present, future, and past contribute decisively to make a moment, to converge a manifold of experience upon a definite time and place.

While considering in detail how the sonnet "works," we should remain open to how it addresses itself to the question of finite concern.

The first quatrain reads in translation (which lacks, of course, the sonorous quality and the evocatory power of the original):

> The virginal, the vivacious, the beautiful today
> Shall it lacerate for us with a beat of drunken wing
> This hard forgotten lake haunted beneath the frost
> By the transparent glacier of flights that flew not!

The opening verse sets the stage for the entire scene: it is today, not simply any day, but this day right now. This day is virginal, it has not been "used," it is "pastless," it does not carry within itself a sense of past decisions or of past mistakes. Today is also vivacious: it bespeaks life, doing, thinking, deciding, perceiving. And it is beautiful: affirmable and bright because seeming to promise fulfilment. One by one, these three qualifications of the opening scene are eroded and finally contradicted in the course of the story: the swan carries the burden of his failures to fly, he is dying, and he suffers pointless exile in a frozen and forgotten lake. Yet the sonnet tells of a single moment only: we do not experience two moments, the one described by the first verse and then another, later on. We must evidently leave open what this contradiction means.

The subsequent three verses of the quatrain initially take the form of a question, then shift into an imperative: shall it (this today, such as it is) break up the surface of the frozen lake?—it must! The concrete interest in this possibility becomes clear only in the second quatrain, which depicts the swan in his plight.

Immediately, however, *we* are asked to take an interest in the possibility: will today lacerate *for us* this frozen surface? In the French the "for us" is simply *"nous"* and the second verse momentarily reads, before we pass on to the third and fourth verses, "Shall it lacerate us"; only when the "hard forgotten lake" becomes the object of the possible laceration does the *"nous"* reveal itself as what grammarians call "the dative of interest." The passing ambiguity straps our interest to the event transpiring, while then loosening the bonds to give us free play in our reading. This minor instance of the tension in the images leads toward a convergence of the configuration on a single moment.

We view "this lake" as possibly breaking up. A lake, the natural abode for a swan, is here hard—first of all because it is frozen, but then also in the sense of being hard to bear, difficult. Recalling the symbolism of the sonnet, we may see in this characterization a statement of our own human condition.

The lake is haunted. Beneath the thin layer of difficulty, beneath the matinal frost which, on a clear day, may dissipate itself, there lies the formidable hardness, a glacier impenetrable by the brightest of suns. Precisely this haunts the (our) natural abode. However, the glacier is *of* "flights that flew not." *These* do the haunting, as the water in "the cup of water" rather than the cup itself quenches our thirst. As these flights haunt the abode they appear in the *form* of the glacier. Flights (itineraries: *vols*) and flying (moving away: *fuir*) are the way of life, the natural activity of swans. This natural activity, as acts which failed to complete themselves, has now congealed. It haunts the abode as obdurate cold. In haunting, however, it remains transparent, and the lake itself falls into forgetfulness. Thus, if we now see the abode, we perceive first of all that it has hitherto not been seen and that, if it has anything to offer, we initially look through and beyond it. Finally, somebody's past emerges as a failure. The today may be virginal, but he who faces the day is not.

The poem also specifies the manner of possible laceration: "with a beat of elated wing." The reference to "wing," along with "flights" and "flying," directs our vision forward to the swan. This personage, his wing, is *"ivre."* In the context of the opening verse, *ivre* has the sense of "enthusiastic." Subsequently, especially in the first tercet, the sense shifts toward "frenzied," although never quite so far as "debilitatedly drunk." In the face of the moment, at the break of dawn over the abode, the scene exudes a mood of great expectation marked by both a question and an imperative.

The first quatrain presents the elements of the entire image. It articulates a special moment: a place, a time, and a personage, i.e., a center of needful activity. The image (audibly presented in the original) stretches beyond the visual. The patterns striking the eye also structure a *concern* which, as it becomes increasingly focused, ultimately converges the entire configuration. The elements of the visual image tell the story of this concern: a break of day, an abode lit up by this moment, the entrapment, the character and then also the cause of the entrapment. Finally, the first strophe also states the kind of response initially plausible to realize the concern: "a beat of elated wing," a simple if nonetheless belated exercise of natural powers (by a bird).

The remaining verses unfold this concern not in terms of what happens at a later time, but rather in terms of what is actually happening within the scene already set. We are taken into the image, not on to another image.

The second quatrain evokes the personage, the center of the concern elliptically present (wing, flight, flying) in the first setting of the scene:

> A swan of time ago, recalls that it's he
> Magnificent but who, without hope, is freeing himself
> For not having sung the region where to live
> When the ennui of sterile winter came blazing.

This personage recalls himself. The French being reflexive, the swan appears as "coming to his senses." He thus counteracts the oblivion first of all affecting his abode, the already forgotten lake. Yet the oblivion is *his*. Moreover, it *has been* his "all along"; he and his oblivion have a decided past now entering into and making a moment. Recalling himself, he brings this self into the situation. *He*, and not another, is stuck. The third and fourth verses of the second quatrain advance a reason for this predicament. Meanwhile, however, the second verse stipulates a presence of the swan apart from his past sins.

He is and always has been magnificent. We recall that the "today" of the first quatrain appeared also virginal, vivacious, and beautiful. It is not uncommon to harbor a high opinion of oneself, but in this case the opinion corresponds to reality. The swan *is* magnificent. Nonetheless and notwithstanding, he also frees himself. Thus, magnificence does not at all preclude "being stuck." The poem never explicitly states the exact predicament. We read it as implicit in the thought that "he is magnificent but still has to free himself," just as we read the sense of being frozen into "lacerating the hard forgotten lake with a beat of elated wing." However, it appears strange that the swan indeed frees himself, that he does not merely try to do so, that in some sense he succeeds. Thus the imperative-question of the first quatrain seems to be realized, while we also know from the final tercet of the sonnet that the swan is destined, immobilized, exiled. Freedom realizes itself here in a paradoxical and complex way.

Moreover the qualification that the swan is "without hope," seems to contradict also the expectation promoted by the entire first quatrain. The inconsistency vanishes, however, if we take seriously the "dative of interest," the "for us" in the first statement of the scene. *We* look forward, as outsiders, to the future. Once on the inside we note that the personage in the predicament proceeds to free himself, but "without hope." Does this lack of hope signify despair, a crumbling of the self? Evidently not, since he proceeds and, according to the following tercet, succeeds at least in "shaking off agony." What, then, does the "without hope" signify?

The second half of this quatrain fully states a reason for the allusions of the imagery in the first half and thus indicates the explicit inclusion of ideation. The reason reads:

> For not having sung the region where to live
> When the ennui of sterile winter came blazing.

Upon first reading, these verses seem to explain simply why the swan is stuck in the ice: when the winter came, he did not fly away, as would be appropriate for a migratory bird. Indeed, this explanation fills out the visual image. But what does it explain? Evidently, the condition of being frozen in. Yet the poem does not explicitly state the predicament. Instead, we read: (1) the swan is coming to his senses, (2) he sees himself magnificent, (3) he is without hope, and (4) is he freeing himself. The reason explains explicitly some or all of these events. We ourselves fill in the elliptical visual image with the thought that the swan is frozen into the lake. Although this inference on our part belongs to our participation in the articulation, we cannot rest here without ignoring the stated image. However, if we can see this reason as explaining both the explicitly stated elements and the inferred frozen condition, we crystallize an eidetic image (an idea) and preserve the symbolism of the sonnet.

First, let us recur to the puzzling qualification that the swan is "without hope" (the third point). We are here oriented toward the past. The swan's being "without hope" thus has nothing to do with despair, the crumbling of the self in the face of unfulfilled and unfulfillable hopes. One can only despair relative to hope, i.e., within a futural orientation which, in addition, reveals nothing sustaining. Although the strictly visual image "fits," by itself it does not hold our interest: failure to migrate grounds only superficially the predicament, and would rightly occasion either desperate hope or despair. Rather, the orientation of the swan includes an acceptance of guilt: he recalls his own position (the first point). The guilt is directly revealed: he did not sing "the region where to live when the ennui of sterile winter came blazing." The eidetic image states what one *needs to do*. Within the complete image of the poem, the need is recalled too late to *do* what is needed, but not too late to *acknowledge* it. This acknowledgement constitutes part of *one* kind of deliverance or freedom (the fourth point).

So far, the eidetic image, barely extricable from the visual one, suggests that man (taking the swan ideationally, as locating the personage stuck in the human condition) needs to affirm articulately the impending region of his life precisely when the onslaught of circumstances exudes a distressing boredom (ennui), a non-productivity (sterility), and a lifelessness (winter). *This* need, and not hope, defines the proper, fulfilling orientation of man. The second quatrain acknowledges it as the reason for the common condition of being helplessly stuck. Only with difficulty do we accept the idea that man requires absolutely, for his fulfilment, articulate affirmation precisely in situations not "deserving" affirmation. Yet, as we shall see in the next section, our tradition includes many analogous ideas.

One further qualification relates to the predicament of the swan and to the stated reason: he has been all along "magnificent." This seems to be but a passing remark; after all, swans are generally impressive creatures. And he is hardly magnificent *because* he did not sing at the appropriate moment about the appropriate thing. Only the first verse of the final tercet clarifies the qualification, where the swan appears as condemned to the lake precisely because of his magnificence: "destined to this place by his pure radiance." Here the visual and the eidetic images run very close to one another. Visually, the swan dared not rouse himself to fly at the appropriate moment for fear of ruffling his feathers. Eidetically, a man can, just by being so strong in his own right, fail to give the needed attention (his song) to his abode: he may prefer, delude himself into, remaining self-incapsulatedly strong, thus fostering a contradiction of strength that leads to ultimate atrophy. In 1882 Nietzsche voiced a similar idea in his *Gay Science* (§277): "There is a certain high point of life; once we have reached it, we are with all our freedom... and yet in the greatest danger of spiritual unfreedom and have to endure our most difficult trial." The danger lies in the paradox: our own magnificence realizes itself and evolves as potency only in actively affirming if not forming a magnificence of the abode itself. Similar to crystal, our own magnificence, in refusing to reveal light other than its own, does not live up to its own nature.

The entire second quatrain both visually and eidetically (and receiving an immediate unity phonetically, in the sonority of the French) redirects the initial concern of the opening quatrain. A swan comes to his senses in and by an orientation toward his own failures of the past rather than in hope for the future. Acknowledging this failure he belatedly recognizes a very harsh destiny, unfulfillable now, to sing the pending region of life precisely when the situation annuls all affirmation. The concern proposed by the poem sends us to the region of our life at the moment when boredom, sterility, and winter blaze in on us— and, failing this, points us *back* to the failure and into a recognition of the entrapment due to our failure, and to nothing else. This concern directs itself to some one thing, the "region." It stands in contrast to other plausible concerns, notably the hope to escape the place of entrapment, and also the wish to preserve one's own magnificence.

While the previous quatrain specifies the personage, the first tercet speaks of the abode:

> His whole neck will shake off this white agony
> Inflicted by the space on the bird who denies it
> But not the horror of the ground where the plummage is caught.

The initial and final verses distinguish between what will and what will not be achieved in the course of the swan's effort. The imagery crosses the visual and the eidetic. Visually, we see the swan's efforts succeeding in shaking off his white . . . , but failing to loosen himself from . . . the ground. The success is ironic, then, since he only succeeds in losing his feathers. Eidetically, however, we see a reversed irony. The swan does shake off his agony, specifically the agony implicit in the experience of the preceding quatrains, the cause of which is stated in the middle verse of the tercet. This shaking off, expressed in the future tense, renders precise how the swan is freeing himself. But the deliverance from agony does not entail a deliverance from horror. What is the difference? Agony belongs to the personage, to the swan. The horror belongs to the ground, to the bit of earth (ice) "where the plummage is caught." Of course, the swan experiences this horror in the face of the ground. But while agony describes a psychic condition, horror here retains its reference to the abode and therefore reveals it (see the discussion in *Emergence*, page 70, of Mallarmé's statement: "The mirror reflecting Being toward me has most often been Horror"). The difference divides being stuck in one's condition ("for not having sung . . .") without "recalling" and "freeing" oneself (hoping all the while that circumstances will improve) *from* being stuck in one's condition while realizing that this condition is of one's own making. Agony marks the first moment. The swan frees himself from this agony. But in freeing himself he realizes that his own magnificence owes itself completely, preserves itself only, in the celebration of the "region where to live," and this precisely "when the ennui of sterile winter comes blazing." The reference to, and acknowledgement of, the region becomes evident in "horror of the ground where the plummage is caught."

The middle verse of the first tercet states that the "white agony" is "inflicted by the space on the bird who denies it" (it = space). Originally the swan was at fault "for not having sung the region where to live." The space where, visually speaking, the bird was to fly, punishes him for his transgression. The swan did not forget this space, he *denied* it. Visually speaking, he denied the claims of the climate and now pays for his error (as in the fable where the cricket pays for his lack of foresight, while the ant fares differently). However, we may also notice an accumulation of thought on the meaning of abode: one must sing the *region* of one's life, failure to do so leads to being stuck in the *ground*, whereupon the denied *space* takes revenge. To be oneself, even if magnificent, one must sing the region where one is to live; in one way (in the imperative "must"), the region lies always "ahead" of one, so that one's abode rightly includes movement (flying, migration), and one locates oneself indeed between the ground and the region. While one relates oneself to the region in song, one's relation to the ground in abstraction from the song and in denial of the space is one of entrapment: at first in agony, then possibly in horror.

The infliction of agony comes to an end. Evidently, the recollection and the liberation described in the second quatrain undoes the denial: the swan no longer denies the space, for otherwise further agony would be inflicted.

Yet the bird is about to die. In the final tercet the swan, now become the Swan, appears as a ghost:

> Phantom destined to this place by his pure radiance,
> He immobilizes himself in the cold dream of scorn
> Worn amidst useless exile by the Swan.

These three lines summarize the condition unfolded gradually in the previous eleven verses. Apart from the suggestion of death, the first verse underscores what the second quatrain leaves ambiguous: the swan's magnificence, his pure radiance, did indeed "cause" his troubles and now also his pending demise. The eidetic image provides, then, a complicated network of reasons: first appears the "fault" (not having sung), then the "source" (the space wronged by the denial), and now a further "cause" (the magnificence or radiance distracting from the requisite reference).

The significance of the last two verses escapes us at first. He (it, the phantom, the Swan) immobilizes himself (there will be no "beat of elated wing" after all) in a cold dream of scorn which he (now definitely and yet symbolically the Swan) shows in a useless exile.

Why the "cold dream of scorn"? The swan does not scorn the space, since he succeeds in shedding the agony that follows from denying space. Nor does he scorn the region where to live, since he acknowledges his earlier failure in this regard. And his relation to the ground which emprisons his plummage is one of horror: one can hardly scorn what incites horror. In fact, the "action" is not directly one of scorn at all. The Swan "immobilizes himself," loses all power of flying, is about to die. A "cold dream" characterizes the moment of death. The word *songe* (not *rêve*) means "drifting thought" which, though drifting, claims nonetheless to "touch upon" the real. This thought being cold, it delineates the moment of death, of being frozen in the "place." It is *of* scorn (*mépris*), *of* setting little or no value ("price") on things, *of* not taking them seriously, *of* not concerning oneself about them in a decisive way. Grammatically, the "of" may mean either (1) the swan immobilizes himself while scorning, the scorn taking the form of a drifting thought, or (2) the swan immobilizes himself while thinking about his failure to take things seriously. Different as these meanings are—the first implying that the swan continues in death the same illusion as when living, the second implying that the swan overcomes the illusion—, the two do, in one sense, merge. In truly acknowledging a failure (not just a correctible mistake) we necessarily "relive" it. While thinking about it we sadly resurrect it, seeing things *beyond* it while still being *in* it. These meanings necessarily merge as the sonnet retains its poetic integrity of relating a recollection including both deliverance and death.

Furthermore, the "cold dream of scorn" is *worn*, i.e., shown, by the Swan "amidst useless exile." The visual image suggests that the Swan belongs in the region to which he must, by his nature, migrate and where he would live with others of his kind. Relative to this region he is now in exile, at the moment of his self-incurred immobility dominated by resuscitative thoughts about undervaluing things. More accurately, the Swan is "*amidst* pointless exile." The choice of "amidst" (*parmi*) instead of the usual "in" (*en*) underscores the place (*milieu*), that the Swan is identified with it. And the qualification "useless" implies that there may be other, more "useful" kinds of exile. These turns of phrase evoke sketchily further elements within the eidetic image: for instance, that any "swan" can be in exile by the very nature of swan-hood, and that this particular exile differs from the more "useful" kinds incurred in poetry, philosophy, or any necessarily individual activity. *His* exile leads naturally to death. It was incurred by his "not having sung the region where to live when the ennui of sterile winter came blazing," by his consigning to death all else that did not reflect back to him his own magnificence. Condemnation of all else leads to self-destruction.

The idea has now been "extracted." Justice to one's condition

78

requires a certain kind of concern and activity. The sonnet reveals this justice through an experience of its opposite, through an acknowledgement of injustice, and at the special moment of death following naturally from the failure. The idea hovering over the poem takes the shape of an eidetic image superimposed upon or intermingled with the visual image of a swan on a lake. We have seen how this superimposition works in the sonnet under review. In the first quatrain the visual image breaks into an eidetic one at the moment when the lake is haunted by a "glacier of flights that flew not." The second quatrain marks the break by the "qualification" of the swan as one who *is* recalling and freeing himself, yet as one who is "of time ago" as well, while the ennui of winter "came blazing." Then the simple visual image of the first tercet (shaking off the white agony) fuses with the idea distinguishing between agony and horror and stating the cause of the infliction. And finally ideation inundates again the last tercet, since it only adumbrates the visual death of the Swan, while the reason for his predicament and the thought in or about it predominate.

This superimposition or intermingling, far from being a mere trick to convey or to obscure the idea, is the essential technique of symbolism conveying the experience of the idea insofar as the idea remains of (relates to, refers to) the thing which it expresses. The thought then funnels back into the real of which it, the idea, claims to state the reality. Thus it funnels *us* back to the real: to *our* lake which, as the ground of our condition, also has a space for us to fly and a region where to live. The predicament, the problematic of failure can therefore become ours. Reading the sonnet just as it stands, but after we have *thought* about it, thus *re*-reading it, leads us into an experience. On the other hand, a theoretical treatise on the subject of human being only prepares us for such an experience; in this preparation we can easily forget the experience to which our efforts are related and for which they are relevant.

3. MODES OF TRANSCENDENCE

Mallarmé's sonnet structures a development of finite concern. Although the work itself "funnels" both the idea and us back into an experience, it assumes from the outset that the idea can be "material" for an experience. Our participation in the work will be strengthened if we recall and appreciate the problematic arising already, as material, at the threshold of the poetic articulation. To be sure, understanding the idea in a reflective manner does not ensure an entrance into the experience provided by the poem. Perhaps we can even enter without any prior understanding at all, since the idea "comes upon us" by virtue of the sonnet anyway. But if we *refuse* the idea we also decline to enter, and to the extent that we resist it we attenuate the participation. In other words, it serves *some* purpose to ponder the problematic at a distance from the poetic work.

The structure of concern evident in the sonnet may be sketched as follows. We begin in everyday concern: hopeful prospects viewed from the outside ("dative of interest") and yet quietly laden with failures of the past. The recognition of individuality first breaks this everyday concern: it is he (*a* swan, who becomes *the* Swan—ourselves). This individuality contrasts with everyday egoism (magnificence and radiance reverting to oneself). Genuine selfhood is correlative to the fulness of thinghood. The exigency of individuality directs us (and the Swan) to the abode. This abode receives further structure from a ground where one is, a space where one should fly, a region to sing, and an assigned place.

Our earlier question asked: How is such concern possible? If the sonnet does "answer" this question (better: address itself, and bring us up to it), then the answer is: through recollection of the exigencies of pending death, such recollection including a belated compensation for failure and therefore a momentary fulfilment of the exigent selfhood and thinghood. The next section will further consider this answer.

Development accounting for one's situation (rather than simply expanding or securing it) is transcendence. Finite concern, it will be noticed, turns us in any case toward our assigned place. As we shall subsequently see, some such "turning" arises in nonfinite transcendence as well. The swan's transcendence is finite because the power requisite for this turn also confines itself within the swan's own situation. First of all, "the region where to live" bids the swan to sing. Second, the space of his possible flying inflicts the agony experienced by him. Third, the swan's own "pure radiance," earlier recognized by the swan as his "magnificence," distracts him from his task by supplying a specious substitute for the needed re-creation, through song, of "the region where to live when the ennui of sterile winter came blazing."

The challenge of finite transcendence, and so also the meaning of the development of finite concern, come out more clearly when contrasted with other modes of transcendence. We may refer to three: the story of Jonah in the Old Testament, one account of Socrates given by Plato, and a Chinese version stated by Lao-tzu.

Jonah, too, is debilitated, but in his case for not having sung *at* the region where God had assigned him. Like the Swan, who prefers not to ruffle his feathers "when the ennui of sterile winter came blazing," Jonah loathed the prospect of his own task, to preach truth. He has been assigned to a place, Ninevah, where truth is notably lacking and where the inhabitants receive poorly the truth-sayer. In Ninevah Jonah would certainly live in a painful but useful exile, amidst wickedness. But he "flys away" to Tarshish, thus landing in a useless exile which (he hopes) will be devoid of pain. However, his escape brings for him no better reception from his fellowmen (sailors and captain), nor from nature (first the storm and then the whale), nor ultimately from God whose presence he is fleeing. Only in the depths of despair and in the full acknowledgement of his failure (through a song-like prayer) is he spewed back upon the ground where he willingly affirms "the region where to live." Then again, however, when God forgives the inhabitants of Ninevah, who had taken no heed of Jonah's prediction of destruction, Jonah despairs: "this forgotten hard lake" called Ninevah "thawed" against his approval. Jonah must learn yet another lesson (the Bible does not say whether he does), namely that his own song will precisely lead to events which are not of his own making.

Transcendence always requires that we overcome the claims inherent in the unfolding of our everyday concerns. It also demands, at least in the modes here of interest, that we return to the *place* where we belong, namely that place and its "contents" forgotten, neglected, or ill-treated in the mere expansion and protection of our own concerns. Finally, this return, in the cases both of the Swan and of Jonah, expressly asks that we heed the opposite: magnificence should heed the ennui of sterile winter, the truth-sayer should heed those who deny truth. Both cases embody a similar paradox: one *is* in fulfilling one's task, and one's being (magnificence or truth) maintains itself not in a concern to preserve it but in a care for the things or people whose very existence denies, perhaps even destroys one's own

81

being. Swans and truth-sayers live in this paradoxical condition explicitly.

Yet Jonah's assignment comes from God, and in the end he can realize his task only in "useful exile," in preaching to the wicked men and women of Ninevah, and this (as the final episode tells) by leaving the fulfilment of his prophesy to God as He wills. Furthermore, God punishes him. Finally, he must proclaim the message of God. The tensions of Jonah's mission take definite shape primarily with his fellow human beings "through time" rather than in places and their changing countenances (at dawn, at the descent of winter). Jonah's song is either directed to God (from the belly of the whale) or mediated from God to his fellows (the message). The rest—the captain and his sailors, the tempest and the whale—appear only as God's instruments in the course of Jonah's development and ultimate return.

In the story of Jonah the transcendence roots itself beyond the finite situation of human life and labor. Jonah is not "invited" into this beyond, he is rather sent back into the place where his own being realizes itself as manifestly a task. However, the source of the assignment, the agony of his refusal, and then the horror of having to allow the task to be fulfilled as against his own intention, —these are all grounded outside the assigned place. Ultimately, the message, the agony, and the horror can only be endured by standing with God: in singing at Ninevah not because of the place or its people, but because of the truth which transcends them. This mode of transcendence may therefore be called *infinite*, in contrast to the Swan's.

Socrates' re-interpretation of the swan-song in Plato's *Phaedo* (84E) bears some obvious resemblance to Mallarmé's sonnet. The earlier Greek interpretation stated that swans sing best when mourning their pending death. Disagreeing with the reason stated, Socrates supplies his own: "although they sing at other times also, they sing more and better in their joy that they are departing for the presence of the god (= Apollo) in whose service they are." Socrates' special service is to speak coherently, challengingly, and convincingly with the Athenians, in Athens, about local affairs and the truth, or the need for truth, that hovers over and around these affairs. However, the broader argument establishes willingness to die as a mark of the philosopher, since in all his concern for local affairs he does not stake himself out within their boundaries, but rather bases himself on truth transcending these affairs with all the successes and failures, promotions and obstructions of ordinary interests in the course of their unfolding. Socrates claims he does not know the truth on which he grounds his songs. Rather his position allows him to know that concern for Athenian affairs receives appropriate orientation only when it rests on truths founding and defining these affairs and therefore not found in or defined by them. The arguments in the *Phaedo* justify a willingness to die, i.e., to depart, once one is based beyond one's circumstances anyway. But these arguments do not contradict those in the *Crito* which justify remaining in Athens, in prison and under the death penalty, because one owes allegiance to a place precisely to the extent that one has taken issue with its inhabitants. Already in the *Phaedo* a brief argument undoes the supposition that willingness to depart entails a desire to depart: on the contrary, the willingness indicates that one grounds oneself over and above the situation in order to concern oneself for it on this basis.

The development requisite for the fulfilment of human being receives from Socrates, too, an interpretation specifying an infinite transcendence. In order to take things seriously in one's finite situation one must, according to the Socratic teaching, base oneself above the situation. Although spatial, this metaphor of "above" takes on even more significance here than in the Jonah story, or in the Old Testament generally. For this late Greek metaphoric interpretation also suggests a certain "deathlessness" of the developed individual. Thus based, a man puts himself in a position where he need no longer take his mortality seriously: he lives like a god. Socrates never wavers, unlike Jonah—and unlike Jesus in the Garden of Gethsemane ("let this cup pass me by") or later on the cross ("for what purpose have you let me down?"). For Socrates, taking things seriously excludes any concern for mortality, even the direct sense of urgency of caring for things while one can.

Jonah receives a command from "above," but the Bible does not suggest that he himself has any ground to stand on beyond Ninevah: development of concern means hearing and heeding the command, and death continues to inspire fear or to occasion despair if he fails to heed or understand the command. Socrates, on the other hand, clearly states in the *Apology* that the only command he either hears or heeds (his *daimon*) directs him *away* from possibilities: he himself must—and he recommends this to others—figure things out entirely on his own, without any further commands from above. His transcendence is not only infinite, it is absolute.

Although Mallarmé's sonnet speaks for itself apart from the traditions, it resumes a problematic interpreted previously by writers and readers alike. Considering the traditional interpretations provides us with a perspective from which to distinguish between the "bare" problematic on the one hand and its interpretations on the other. All three interpretations develop an individuality of concern which singles out both the agent of this concern and the place where it develops: whether Jonah, Socrates, or the Swan, it is *he* who must come to terms with, do justice to *this* place, be it Ninevah, Athens, or a lake. Furthermore, this emergence of selfhood and thinghood out of oblivion must somehow bring the everyday concerns (wickedness, stupidity, ennui) into the event. For they configure the situation initially, and they "need" the convergence at a moment. —Yet, apart from this common denominator of concern, the interpretations differ radically among themselves.

The transcendence articulated in Mallarmé's sonnet is distinctively finite. The power of the poem therefore depends upon the extent to which such finitude has significance for us in our contemporary situation. The modes of transcendence exemplified in the Old Testament parable of Jonah and in Plato's account of Socrates' interpretation of the swan's last song, are powerful in themselves. They *did* provide potent models for our tradition. To the question, Why *finite* transcendence *today*? we answer: the contemporary world no longer tolerates infinite transcendence; our world, as configured politically by democratic government, shaped sensuously by capitalistic architecture, and explained theoretically by positive science, provides channels *only* for the unfolding of ordinary concerns (production, consumption, distraction). All contemporary roads lead back into ordinary preoccupations. If we fully absorb ourselves into the transcendence exemplified by Jonah or Socrates, we abandon the place where we live—in outright contradiction to one essential direction of movement in those ancient models. This paradox eventually surfaces in all efforts to resuscitate ancient modes of transcendence.

Furthermore, the ancient modes of transcendence have been absorbed and trivialized into our contemporary situation already. Not yet entirely abandoned, they cling to us even if we would rather reject them as mere "myths." Both models, although in differing ways, ask us to base ourselves *beyond* the place "where to live." This "beyond" was originally a "push off" point for returning to the place. The Jewish God and the Greek Apollo had the significance of "back-up men" for the requisite transcendence (the development of taking things seriously). Thus we abandon these traditions only partially: forsaking only the return, we retain the "beyond," namely in the primacy of "the future." For modern man, any given moment of activity receives its justification in terms of *what is to come*. Suspicious captains and sailors, violent storms and voracious whales cannot turn us from Tarshish; and even the arguments against suicide in Plato's *Phaedo* (based on the idea of service to be rendered in the name of the god Apollo) seem weak and contrived. Our tradition trains us to accept our situation only when we are "within hearing" of a "beyond." Today we proceed to the beyond itself, henceforth conceived horizontally, as an extension of the present.

Ultimately we experience the significance of finitude in our contemporary situation rather than in historical comparisons. Assuming, then, that we *do* agree to return to our present-day Ninevah or Athens, what do we find? Chapter One, the consideration of poems by Rimbaud, explored this question. The "answer" was worked out with a view to the titles of poems: we live in "cities," in a "metropolitan" conflux, not as points in space but as manners of responding to things ("Here's a people for whom these Alleghenies and Lebanons of dream rose themselves!"). The peculiarity of this manner was exposited in terms of the discontinuity experienced in the exigency to affirm where we live. Unable to affirm moments (things and people here and now), on the basis of the structural features of our own context (urban life), we find the context truly affirmable only if we "start" already with a moment and proceed "backwards" to the context. Modern organization of life refuses, in principle, to direct or aid us in coming to terms with moments as distinct from, because the convergence of, contexts. While no context can complete this affirmation for man, earlier organizations at least structured the need (church-based government, elitist education, property requirements, and so on). Today, and as individuals, we insist on self-reliance, and we conceive of society (the race, mankind) as gradually achieving dominion over nature (creation), not as receiving sustenance from it. These determinants (lack of contextual aid, insistance on self-reliance, drive for mastery) spell out for us a radical finitude in the face of any given moment, however "infinite" the power acquired in strictly organizational affairs.

The radical finitude of man in the modern epoch, simply evident in Rimbaud's poems, becomes the *issue* in Mallarmé's works. In the sonnet, the self emerges in the face of a place where the emergence of things has been and *is* the issue. In ways carefully developed in the poem, this issue has been skirted until "today," until the moment when it is, in a sense, "too late." Now the protagonist meets the issue (accordingly, it is after all *not* too late) in a fittingly finite transcendence: the self acknowledges the task (to sing the region where to live), the infliction (the agony, as distinct from the horror), and his failure (his earlier "wrong headed" concern to preserve his own "self-image")—*all* in terms of the situation itself. Such acknowledgement creates a moment that includes (by converging) the context without relying on any "outside" guidance at all.

However, Mallarmé's Swan does not sing, not before when he could and should have sung, and not today when he "immobilizes himself in the cold dream of scorn." According to the pre-Socratic tradition, a dying swan sings in mourning for his own death. For Socrates, the swan sings in joy for his departure, for his return to the basis (to Apollo, in whose service he is). In either case, the swan does sing. Can we discover a reason for the Swan's silence in the finitude of the transcendence itself? If so, light would be cast on the modern problematic of finite concern and its development.

Reviewing the sonnet with this question in mind, we note the following: (1) the Swan was to sing the region where to live, (2) a mood of a "cold dream of scorn," i.e., neither mourning nor gladness enshrouds the bird, and (3) the sonnet itself is a song about life *and* death; about life, because it evokes the chief exigency of life, and also the plight of the life which fails to respond properly to this exigency; about death, because the Swan in fact must die. If we allow our ideational propensities free rein, each of these points may be "generalized" beyond the immediate claims of the poem. Still, we may learn something by letting the propensity run its full course, if only we remember to rein it in again.

(1) Placing the duty of the Swan (to sing life) side by side with his silence in the face of death, we may provisionally conclude that the only kind of song possible for the Swan (and

so for us) is one celebrating life (even, or precisely when, "the ennui of sterile winter" comes blazing). Thus we would be warned that all postponements of our song are foolish and disastrous. The silence of the Swan at death would then indicate that the *only* occasions for song are those provided directly by our own situations, such as they are. Speech would then, indeed, be bound up with finitude.

(2)   Noting that the one explicitly stated attitude of the Swan (his "cold dream of scorn") stands in implicit contrast to both mourning and joy, we may provisionally surmise that a song celebrating life can *neither* embody a clinging to life *nor* an overall perspective upon life as it approaches its final threshold. At the actual moment of death only the strange "cold dream of scorn" remains. Generalizing again: if we forsake reality and hold ourselves aloof from life, the reality will return to us "in the end" and manifest the coldness, the dreaminess, and the attendant scorn in our very person. Even or precisely our acknowledgement of failure would not enable us to rise above it. Once again, if the human condition allows only a finite transcendence, then death will throw us back into our situation (*frozen* into it) and condemn us to silence. In any case, freeing ourselves by acknowledging our failure, shaking off the agony of the resultant condition, would not here place us in a position to speak well. In this regard, we may contrast Mallarmé's sonnet with Augustine's *Confessions*, where the need and the right to speak, and the elegance of the song, derive from admission of sin in the presence of God.

(3)   Finally, the sonnet, being itself a song, qualifies the hasty conclusion that only life occasions song and that the rest is silence. Generalizing this third point, we may provisionally formulate a theory of language: the fullest, the most genuine, originary and originating speech gathers together both life and death, celebrates "the region where to live" *and* recalls the ultimate immobilization. The sonnet as a whole exemplifies precisely this speech. *This* song turns us toward life by recalling the inevitability of death. Only *this* speech does justice to the finitude of the human condition by placing us in the "middle" between birth (original task) and termination of life where we look *forward* to life (*back* into the place where we belong: into *our* Ninevah or *our* Athens) and *recall* (neither mourning nor celebrating) death as the ultimate event *ahead*. Death then makes us take life seriously, not as "our life" or "life in

general," but the life anchored in and structured by the region, space, ground, and place where we happen to belong, move, freeze, and be. To this power and significance of death we shall return in subsequent sections.

Can we rightly "read" these ideas about the occasions of speech and silence into the sonnet? We can certainly read them *into*, but not at all *out of* the poem. The poem says what it says, and the ideas are *our* ideas. However, through the symbolism these ideas can receive a reference if we allow them to become transparent to the poem. In other words, the symbolism is essentially ambiguous, drawing our thoughts into it but hardly justifying our opinions and prejudices.

Yet, even if we "rein in" from the generality of the ideas (from the "alls" of "all songs sing life," "all failures lead to silence," and "all genuine language articulates both life and death") the proposal still remains that the decision to consider the human condition as finite *somewhat* connects with our subsequent understanding of a language which can do justice to this condition. Mallarmé's own theoretical views on language we have recorded and discussed elsewhere (see *Emergence*, pages 67-73). Suffice it to recall that generally transcendence has in Western literature been considered as supplying the mandate for significant speech. And in this regard the stories of Jonah, Socrates, and the Swan all agree: Jonah learns "the hard way" to return to Ninevah to *speak* the truth in the face of wickedness; Socrates all along understands his task as requiring and allowing him to *speak* to his fellow Athenians, and the Swan sees too late that swan-hood realizes itself in singing the region where to live. The difference in Mallarmé comes out against the background of an agreement: the Swan is reduced to silence, although not the singer or listener of the sonnet, and speech receives its mandate in a transcendence.

This background, shared by the three modes of transcendence discussed, comes itself into relief when we recall a tradition diametrically opposed to our own: the ancient Chinese tradition of Lao-tzu.

The *Tao Te Ching*, The Book of the Way and the Power, also contains a statement of transcendence, although the sayings composing the statement are enigmatic in form. We may consider five which appear to be interrelated in meaning.

1) Not self-seen (self-seeing), therefore illumined (illuminating). Chapter 22.

2) Whoever is self-seen (self-seeing) is not illumined (illuminating). Chapter 24.
3) Knowing its (his, their) clearness requires abiding with its (his, their) darkness. Chapter 28.
4) The Way which is illumined (illuminating) is like darkness. Chapter 41.
5) The ten thousand beings are clear in countenance when their backs are to the dark. Chapter 42.

These sayings are here rendered literally. The original Chinese is elliptical, aphoristic, and (from the Western standpoint) grammatically vague. In general, the Chinese language eludes the familiar but abstract subject-predicate structure, and tends to juxtapose concrete meanings which arrange themselves kaleidoscopically, crystallizing their momentary significance according to how they are "turned." Some essential ambiguities are indicated by the alternate translations placed in parentheses.

The context of the first saying tells us that the subject being described is "the sage": the man who, while not looking at himself (and perhaps not looked at much, either) is enlightened for this very reason and casts light onto the things around him. The second saying, the logical obverse of the first, describes the non-sage.

The possessive pronoun of the third saying is ambiguous: "Knowing the clearness of... requires accepting the darkness of... ." Clearness can mean glory, then darkness would mean ignominy, and the blanks would likely be filled by "oneself." Or we can complete the blanks with "things," and then the clearness would mean emergence, and darkness something like oblivion. In any case, the third saying adds the reference to *abiding* or "accepting": what is appropriate (be it a spotlight on ourselves or light cast on things) arises only through a willingness to take onto oneself the very opposite (be it the ignominy of oneself or the darkness of things). This willingness institutes a conversion on our part (enlightenment), but not one directing us to face the light, let alone to place ourselves at the source of it.

The fourth saying underlines a further feature of wisdom: the Way on which we experience light manifests itself as, without being in essence, darkness. This Way, where the possibility of light arises, appears to us as dark when we look at *it*, i.e., when we are not looking at the things under our care and jurisdiction (the book as a whole ostensibly speaks about the exigencies of ruling over a kingdom). Thus we not only have "no business"

89

looking at ourselves, or even looking at the light upon things as though this were their chief being, we also have "no business" looking at the Way, the apparent "subject" of the book. Our only task is to look to (take care of) things.

The fifth saying speaks metaphorically: one side of things receives the light of the sun and one side is in the shade. But in its context the saying almost appears "metaphysical": the Way gave birth to the one, this generated the multiplicity of things; *these* are "clear in countenance when their backs are to the dark," and the mixture of clear and dark allows them to continue to be (rather than disintegrating, falling completely into ignominy or oblivion). This "metaphysic" fades immediately in the book, whose purpose is chiefly "ethical," i.e., "way-pointing." *We* must preserve things in our care. The crux of this responsibility lies in abiding with the dark side of things—in a way that allows them to come into the light.

The transcendence of the Chinese "sage" is emphatically finite. For he concerns himself only with the "ten thousand things." Nothing nameable beyond these things (like Jonah's god) "empowers" this concern. And it is not guided by a vision of the way things really are or should be (as Socrates, at least in Plato's version, demands of himself and others that the "idea" of every matter of concern be worked out "ahead" of the matter itself). The darkness of things must here be taken seriously, and we are required to put ourselves in the shadow for the sake of the light which will come of itself upon things.

The Swan's task was to sing *when* "the ennui of sterile winter came blazing." The transcendence here, as also in Lao-tzu's account, is finite. However, Lao-tzu's work does not suggest that language issues from this transcendence. Quite the contrary, it contains at least one clear statement that the man who tends to his proper business speaks very little or not at all: "those who know do not speak, those who speak do not know" (Chapter 56). In fact the book never intimates that singing (writing, speaking) is essential to the human condition. Mallarmé's Swan, then, assumes an additional significance: agreeing with the traditions of Jonah and Socrates, rather than with the tradition of Lao-tzu, the sonnet articulates transcendence in the mode of a struggle requiring speech. All throughout Western literature, and now again in Mallarmé's work, the question of transcendence is both asked and answered within tension. The poles of this tension are (1) what is needed and (2) what immediately offers itself, and the vectors structuring it are words. The Western tradition sees the human condition as a battle, even if only the "strong" take up arms. And the "arms" are, since Plato, those of *logos*, language.

That the Swan does not sing, while the sonnet about the Swan does sing, underscores the finitude of man. As living, we must sing the region where to live while recalling death as the reminder that this singing is *all* we have. The singing itself is transcendence, here understood as finite.

4. THE EXIGENCY OF DEATH:
"PETIT AIR II"

The Swan dies, he *is* dying. His death is pending for him, and it never quite becomes an accomplished fact for us. Death as impending marks the moment when the possibility and necessity of "taking some one thing seriously" announces itself forcefully. At least the sonnet focuses on this moment. Is this choice of focus arbitrary?

When, within the horizon of our own concerns and labors, we see others dying, we perceive death as an occurrence, a termination of a linear unfolding of interests, the end point of a vector line, where things simply come to a halt. If we continue to concern ourselves beyond this halt, we proceed to move down *our* line, making the appropriate adjustments in the domain of the living: we redistribute the belongings of the deceased, go into mourning, realign our daily routines, and so on. We may of course foresee our own death and plan some of these adjustments for others. In making such plans, however, our *will* becomes a mere wish, since we shall not, by the hypothesis of the case, be present to enforce it. We foresee a helplessness in contemplating the occurrence of our own death: the "things" of our life after the terminal point fall under the will of others, not under our own will. The prospect of our own death considered as an occurrence, with its attendant impotence, may cause us much anguish. It casts upon us a displeasure similar to the one we experience in despotic organizations where the arrangements of things and our own attendant routines are determined solely by others. For this reason despots fear death more than anyone else.

Death as impending, as opposed to death as an occurrence, is

91

a modification of life itself, viewed from the inside as a being (*our* being) caught up short. In a figure, viewing death from the inside means willingly standing in the center of the region of life where one belongs as this region closes in on one, as the lines of one's daily labors gather themselves into one as spokes into the hub of a wheel, the far ends forming a circumference which contracts itself and compacts the entire contents—to the vanishing point. This figure contrasts with the familiar image of a linear unfolding which mysteriously comes to an end. However, the "standing in the center" of a circle that "closes in" requires further thought.

Thoughtful, and not primarily calculative, thought dissolves visual images for the sake of the event in which we ourselves have a crucial part. And in death we play an especially demanding part. In this case non-participative thought can never be *of* one's own death, or *of* any death at all, but is consigned to calculations and observations of life. The "death" non-participatively "thought" represents a strange gap to be filled. Assuming that participative thought of death is both possible and important, how can it *begin* without taking the outside view, without representing death as an occurrence of termination always "elsewhere"?

We can commence by noting that "death as an occurrence" merely emanates from "death as impending." Death is for us something like what philosophers have called an "a priori": only because we must, as human beings, stand in the center of a self-closing circle do we respond so remarkably to instances of death, and ultimately to our own. Unlike most if not all animals, we are "taken aback" by the death of our fellows, and often even by the death of animals. Unlike animals, we may fear death even when there exists no "reason" to fear it, no imminent danger; and, more soberly, we prepare ourselves and others for the event. What, then, in this "standing in the center" bespeaks mortality already and sensitizes us to death even "before" its occurrence?

Initially, the thought of death "brings home" an individual finitude. The interests defining my labors, interests normally represented as stretching out indefinitely in a linear series of "moves," are brought up short: I myself shall no longer "move" along the prescribed course. But this negative thought reveals, if we abide with it, the character of the human condition "all along." One's position in life is both one of no special rights and one of total responsibility. No special rights, because everything that appears as mine, as being there for me, may be "taken away" at any time. Total responsibility, because whatever I *am* belongs to the situation of my responses rather than to myself. These two go together. So long as I believe I have special rights, I also assume I shall not die, and also that I have a limited responsibility to my situation.And so long as I believe my responsibility is limited, I assume I have special rights and, again, that I shall not die. These beliefs in special rights and limited responsibility postulate an infinitude in the course of the unfolding of ordinary interests. This postulation constitutes the very illusion (oblivion) that is recurrently shattered, namely whenever the reality of the moment breaks in upon us.

The self is singled out correlative to things singling themselves out. Death does not so much take things away from us, we are taken away from things. Thus the thought of death brings the recollection that the complex of my labor's interests is only provisionally or temporarily "superimposed" on my environment, and shall eventually be "lifted." Initially, this recollection seems to leave things in my environment without special recommendation: Nothing (no person, no house, no flower) justifies my dealing with it seriously, each thing is "in itself" indifferent. But, once again, this negative thought can reveal something about our condition "all along": the ennui of sterile winter comes upon us at every moment, just "under" the superimposition of our interests. It is *our* responsibility, each alone as individual, to "differentiate" things (persons, houses, flowers) to accord them presence. This "task" does not belong to any specific job as distinct from others. Yet the detail assignments of our jobs make no sense, once the thought of death moves in upon us, except as they order themselves under the one strange task of creating and preserving a presence. This task of thinghood has been ours "all along."

These modifications develop in our daily work. Thus one who does not work, who never has had a job, cannot die: he either resists dying (good-for-nothings are generally cowards) or he does not really foresee death as impending (this is generally the case with children). With the common place of work in mind, we can restate how the various experiences of impending death interweave and qualify one another. Having no special rights means that we stand for the things of our region, not for ourselves. Being totally responsible means being ineluctably individual, not subordinated to any other locus of responsibility. Being taken away from things means seeing them as they are, not abandoning them as mere nothings. And, finally, the indifference of things "in themselves" bespeaks their inherent possibility, relative to our responsibility, of coming into a differentiated plenitude, providing that we sing, i.e., articulate and recreate "the region where to live."

In sum, the experience of death as impending is an originary experience of guilt and presence. Here, guilt is total: we owe every response to our "region"; once "in" the region, we may incur specific debts, feel bad about specifiable events. But guilt itself, allowing for specific instances of guilt, is correlative to presence. *This* presence, occurring within a responsibility fully assumed, sharply distinguishes itself from the kind of "here and now present" of mere distraction, as when we rush to see the results of an automobile accident. Genuine presence congeals a moment, but into this moment flows the entirety of our past, our accumulated deeds and skills, and we stand in the face of things as possibilities: as overwhelmed by the sterile winter and yet tentatively emergent in their being through our stand, our song. Without this genuine plenitude as a hope, we would never run after mere heres and nows distracting us from the rest. The present correlative to guilt has no "rest," since it includes already everything relevant to our responsibility.

Mallarmé's sonnet of the Swan poetically articulates the experience of death as impending. We can tune into the sonnet because death in this mode means something to us. The poem expresses this meaning in a definite way, yet without finishing the thought and so precluding further reflection. Rather, encouraging us to think into the symbolism and thereby into the experience itself, the sonnet invites thought.

The original question, How can we nowadays take some one thing seriously? was modified to read: How is finite concern possible? We answered: in the experience of death as impending, as revealing how we have been situated "all along." The abiding difficulty, adumbrated in the answer, lies in the distinction between the outside and the inside view of death. This difficulty is essential to the experience itself, since the experience of death requires above all a conversion of the ordinary patterns of human response, a conversion both modifying and retaining the realm of our concerns. Thus poetic articulations of death generally depict the development of the inside view, leaving the depiction of the "actual occurrence" to thrillers and the like.

Mallarmé's "*Petit Air II*" (*M*, 66; see following facing pages) also articulates mortality, but with direct emphasis on the exigency of the inside view, on the "transition" into it. The unattractiveness of the literal translation indicates the service performed by the phonetic dimension of the poem, deserving an analysis in its own right: the mixed high pitches of the first and third quatrains, the chiefly dark sounds of the second quatrain and the almost uniformly high pitches of the final couplet, create a tension of urgency for an imagery whose coherence is more directly ideational than visual.

The eight verses of the first two quatrains form one image with both visual and ideational purport. This image is separated from a second, presented in the remaining six verses, by the only period in the poem. The two images together bring death into evidence.

The order of the verses is essential. (1) "indomitably had to" evokes a power that cannot be overcome. The power is already established (the past tense), and its formation is (was) necessary (a matter of "duty," *devoir*). We are told *that* the power is present long before we hear what it does (the verb) or even what it is (the subject). This priority is, as we shall see, essential. (2) "As my hope rushes to it" introduces a narrator who, in a present action, responds in a futural mode (a hope) to what has been stated as necessarily established. This rushing locates a precipitous human response, full of hope for what is not yet understood (verb and subject are still untold). (3) "Burst forth up there lost" finally supplies the action: human response directs itself to a bursting forth overhead that not only already happened, but is now "lost." A *sound* elicits response in the mode of hope. (4) The bursting forth, indomitably necessary in the past and now evoking a hopeful response, occurs "With fury and silence": with fury *and yet* with silence. This qualification might appear self-contradictory, unless we recall the temporality of the entire quatrain. Fury marks the indomitable exigency of the as yet unspecified sound which did in fact burst forth. Silence marks this same exigency, now experienced by one who, in hope, rushes toward it: a sound that was, and that evokes hope, is, for all its fury, experienced as a silence.

The first quatrain brings together the essential dimensions of an experience into a whole vibrating with tension. The French,

PETIT AIR II

Indomptablement a dû
Comme mon espoir s'y lance
Eclater là-haut perdu
Avec furie et silence,

Voix étrangère au bosquet
Ou par nul écho suivie,
L'oiseau qu'on n'ouït jamais
Une autre fois en la vie.

Le hagard musicien,
Cela dans le doute expire
Si de mon sein pas du sien
A jailli le sanglot pire

Déchiré va-t-il entier
Rester sur quelque sentier!

LITTLE TUNE II

Indomitably had to
As my hope rushes to it
Burst forth up there lost
With fury and silence,

Voice foreign to the thicket
Or followed by no echo,
The bird that one never hears
Another time in one's life.

The haggard musician,
In doubt it expires
Whether from my breast, not from his
Welled forth the worse sob

Lacerated shall he, whole,
Remain on some path!

or course, displays a phonetic unity as well as visual and eidetic unities. The literal translation can retain only these latter unities and inevitably foresakes the first:

> Indomitably had to
> As my hope rushes to it
> Burst forth up there lost
> With fury and silence

As an intellectual question, and as an imperative internal to the experience, the vibration may be formulated as: Will presence be recovered?—It must! The temporality of the quatrain "locates" this exigency in the face of the "totality" of life: not as touching upon some one instance among others, but as recalling at a given moment what has been and what must be. The recollection, futurally if precipitously oriented, adumbrates a presence of mind and a presence of situation. However, as any genuine presence, it "hangs in the balance": it bespeaks mortality without naming it.

The second quatrain specifies a "subject" for the verbal event: a voice or, even more specifically but then also symbolically, a bird had, indomitably, burst forth up there, lost, with fury and silence. (5) "Voice foreign to the thicket" *places* the presence at, in, or near a thicket, a "little wood." But the voice itself cannot be explained by the place: its sounding is foreign to it. Perhaps, however, the thicket receives its "explanation" from the voice; i.e., by having burst forth, the voice, initially in the mood of hope, now brings the place into focus, making for a presence, however unstable. (6) "Or followed by no echo" states the significance of the voice's being foreign: "at least" no sound gives an answer, so that in *any* case the *self* must follow it up—nothing else will.

The remainder of the quatrain states more exactly and symbolically the carrier of the voice:

> The bird that one never hears
> Another time in one's life.

The voice of the bird is heard once and only once. Normally we would not ascribe to the hearing of a bird a one-time event indomitably necessary and evoking hope, sounding in fury and in silence, lost, and foreign to the woods. This first image needs an eidetic image to retain the force. Abstractly translated, the idea seems to be: each of us will experience one thing having power (not an evident meaning) for us, and from then on each of us, individually, must respond in a way preserving a presence in its terms. However, this "one thing" will not return to help us, nor will the situation before us echo it: nothing in the thicket of life will ever justify it; it itself is fury, but its significance for us lies in its silence: *we* have to break the silence.

These last two verses, terminating the first image, state clearly, and yet not distinctly, the idea. Clearly, because the statement brings one thing to mind: only "one time" will offer the guiding evocation for our subsequent vocation. Not distinctly, because the statement does not single out and present that "one time" to and for us. The lines adequately formulate but do not apply the proposed ideation: strikingly presented, it still floats over times and places. Yet it sets the stage by requiring already a convergence. The past sound and the future orientation, the extreme exigency (fury) correlative to a gap to be filled by us (silence),—these coalesce to demand a presence, an application, a distinct experience.

The third quatrain introduces immediately a player on the stage: (9) "The haggard musician." A musician's task is to be "a-mused" and to "a-muse" others, i.e., to respond to his Muse. This one, the poem calls haggard, i.e., wild, gaunt, and (as becomes evident in the final couplet) nearly if not completely destroyed.

According to the ancient origins of our intellectual tradition, the term "musician" includes or covers anyone who develops, in any manner, a way of responding to "life" as such. We can catch sight of this broad meaning in a passage from Plato's *Phaedo* (60D-61C), where Socrates explains why, in waiting for his day of execution, he has been composing poems. He states that a dream has often said to him: "make music, and work at it." Previously he had always assumed that the dream was encouraging him to proceed as he had been (as a runner proceeds when cheered on), since "philosophy is the greatest music." Now, however, and just in case the dream meant that he should make "popular" music (literally: suitable for country folk, i.e., those with whom he had never discoursed seriously), he has been composing poems. Socrates goes on to differentiate *mythos* from *logos* (probably the point of the interlude), and then he and Simmias agree that the poet (who has been wondering about Socrates' poetic exploits) is also a philosopher. —Plato's dialogue assumes, and does not prove, that philosophers and poets are also "musicians."

How are we to interpret the remaining three verses of the quatrain, interrupting the "story" and re-evoking the narrator? They read:

> In doubt it expires
> Whether from my breast, not from his
> Welled forth the worse sob

In effect, a question has been raised, one that first remains undecided (in doubt) and then finally withdraws itself (dies down as a question needing an answer). The question (whether...) speaks of both the narrator and the musician as having "cried tears," as having in some sense failed. The failure bewailed is not directly specified, but in the context it can only be a failure to respond to the voice, to "the bird that one never hears another time in one's life." Still, the poem states neither the how nor the why of this failure.

These three verses are strange because they institute a tenuous distinction between the "haggard musician" and the narrator evident earlier in "my hope" and now again in "my breast." The two appear at first as different from one another. Yet the question basing the distinction between them "expires" without being decided. Furthermore, the unresolved question only makes sense if the narrator somehow "identifies" with the wild, though perhaps now exhausted musician. We shall return later to this puzzling interlude.

The final couplet takes the form, as did the bulk of the first quatrain of the Swan-sonnet, of an emphatic pronouncement of what will (must?) happen:

> Lacerated shall he, whole,
> Remain on some path!

The couplet first of all completes the visual image. The musician is on a path, in or near the woods. He shall *remain* on this path. An earlier version (see *M*, 1484) reads: fall (*tomber*). This rejected version would change the entire meaning of the poem; "he" could then very easily recall the bird of the second quatrain, and we would then identify the voice and the bird with the musician, leaving the narrator as the sole listener, the one whose task it is to respond to the voice = the bird =the musician. In this version the source would then be destroyed (torn up, lacerated), leaving the narrator "free." In the corrected version, the musician remains on the path and the bird is "up there" even if "lost": the *man* is lacerated, not the source (a one-time thing anyway), and the narrator continues to be still strangely identified with *or* differentiated from this man.

The couplet also completes the structuring of an eidetic image. The previous quatrain had shown a haggard musician, a self returned to its wild nature, withdrawn from the human conventions upholding ordinary concern. The last lines evoke a lacerated self, yet one not disintegrated and scattered into parts. The self is, although in some sense defeated, still *whole*. As whole, he remains on some path. The alternative would be to leave the "beaten track," the particular path (one among many human paths intersecting to form a society of life) one happens to be on. However, *this* self shall not leave, *must* not leave. He will remain within hearing of the silence. Thus the circle closes.

The visual ambiguity (whether the musician is dying or finally dead, a miserable failure or only withdrawn into a pristine condition) completes the eidetic image. For the experience of death is first of all the experience of the ultimate task. This experience "brings home," on whatever path one may be (and *nowhere* else) the finality of issue in one's mode of response. Once *in* the self-closing circle of the human condition, once *remaining* there rather than trying to leave, we experience dying and failure as reminders of our position (technically: of our own negation) in the face of the "thicket," "the region where to live." Only from the outside standpoint does it become essential, as it sometimes does for a physician, to determine the moment of death as an occurrence.

The central idea articulated in *"Petit Air II"* appears to be identical with the idea in the sonnet of the Swan. No doubt the two do point toward the development of finite concern in the mode of finite transcendence. Yet the image of *"Petit Air II"* includes one striking element only weakly present in the sonnet *"Le vierge, le vivace et le bel aujourd'hui."* In the portrayal of the Swan a "dative of interest" was introduced to suggest the outside view which proves itself to be illusory. In this second poem, however, the strange relationship of the outside narrator to the inside musician recurs to structure the whole image. In the first quatrain the narrator, in the mode of hope, already rushes to the indomitable exigency of the bursting forth of the voice. This occurs in apparent independence of the musician whose chief

101

task is to respond to the voice. Then, again, three verses of the third quatrain distinguish and relate the self of the narrator to the musician in a question which expires without being resolved. This tension of personage constitutes in large measure the tension of the imagery, the sense of urgency and ambiguity already structured by the visual image (fury and silence, lacerated and whole, etc.).

The tension gathers the force of the poem to converge the articulation at the threshold. It allows for both an outside view and an inside view, and then "demands" (*exige*, the French can say) that we cross the threshold from the outside to the inside. The narrator looks on: first in the manner of a mere hope marking a distance to be covered, then in the plight he shares with the musician. But the basis of the distinction between the self on the outside and the musician on the inside is a question, one which remains unresolved and also ceases to be a question. In a sense, then, the narrator *is* the musician: as each of us *is* the one who stands in the center of a self-closing circle— haggard (pristine, whole, ultimately lacerated)—even though we recurrently deny this and even presume that it is someone *else* who dies.

The verses beginning "In doubt it expires," as well as the urgent imperative and strange prediction of the final couplet, structure the exigency of death, the demand that we move from the outside to the inside. Of course, the poem does not explicitly state the move or claim the identity: it allows for it. In this way we can *experience* the move and the identity. Any further statement or claim would reduce the experience to mere opinion and so "block" the idea.

5. INTERPRETATIONS OF DEATH

As an impendence of life, death marks the moment of transcendence—of taking things seriously. Transcendence having been variously interpreted, death has necessarily received differing interpretations in the course of history. And since these established interpretations crowd in upon our consideration of the event itself, deterring fresh attention to the matter, it helps to recall them insofar as is relevant to keep them from obscuring the vista directly opened by Mallarmé's poems.

In the West there are chiefly four interrelated traditions interpreting death. The Socratic interpretation is, as we have seen, closely associated with a view of death replacing an earlier one. And the interpretation of transcendence in the story of Jonah also, although not so obviously, included a view of death which was then challenged by the Christian reassessment of the Old Testament. The differences distinguishing these four views are obscured because the *later* interpretations—the Socratic, Platonic, and Aristotelian on the one side, and the Christian on the other side—joined together in the popular mind to form a single view.

A few lines at the end of Pindar's 8th *Pythian Ode* (written about 446 B.C.) capture and condense the spirit of the earlier Greek tradition abandoned already less than a century afterwards in Aristotle's *Nicomachean Ethics*. In literal translation, the lines from the *Ode* read:

> ... Suddenly does
> What is delightful to mortals shoot up! But then just as
> suddenly is it laid low,
> Brought crashing down by a telling mark.
> Creatures of a day! What is any one? What is any one not? A
> vision of darkness
> Is man. But whenever a god-given sunbeam does come
> A limpid splendor is upon men, and gentle times.

The entire Ode was composed to be sung at a victory celebration for a wrestler who had carried off a prize from the Games at Delphi. Earlier, the poet asks the gods not to be resentful of the victor and advises the victor himself to remember that the gods, not he himself, are the givers and to recall that his own victory spells also defeat, if only for the others. On the surface, then, these six verses warn against overweaning pride and recommend a humility on the occasion of victory. But they say much more. Five comments may suffice to elucidate the principle "behind" the warning.

(1) What is delightful comes and goes. The course of human affairs suddenly (in a flash) pleases us. Yet, for no particular reason, things suddenly "turn around" to displease us. Such is the nature of "delightful things." However, these are to be distinguished from "gentle times," the last words of the selected verses. Victories are delightful. Something else is at stake in gentle times.

(2) A "telling mark" (a *gnoma*) puts an end to the delightfulness of a thing. The *gnoma*, a mark or sign lets us know (or at least suspect) what a thing really is. Since the delightfulness of

things expresses our own satisfaction in the realm of human interests, it is by itself alienated from the actual offerings of the situation. For instance, the desire for victory precedes the actual events, and the glee lingers on afterwards. Satisfaction of human interests can, through anticipation and memory, seduce us into losing sight of present circumstances. A *gnoma*, anything demanding and directing attention but not fitting the occasion as we insist on construing it, re-establishes the reference to the present, undoes the dreaminess of anticipation and memory, and ends the delight. Any achievement distinctively ours is abstract: it abstracts us from the present.

(3) Thus human achievements are by nature transient. The single word translated as "creatures of a day," *epameroi*, asserts emphatically this transience. A generation before Pindar, Empedocles also calls us "creatures of a day," literally "ephemerals" (Diels, fragment 3). Only after the description of the ephemerality is "man" said to "fit" the description. To be ephemeral means to be for the day only, i.e., unable to "count on" either yesterday or tomorrow. Thus, when we look at man, at ourselves, we can ask, "What is any one?" The answer suggests: nothing; you may be a victorious wrestler, but this has no duration, for yesterday you were nothing and tomorrow you may again be brought down. Yet the poet goes on to ask: "What is any one *not*?" Thus, ephemerality not only closes, it also opens. Although we are closed off from being anything *in* and *by* ourselves, the closing is nonetheless correlative to being opened out onto anything whatsoever—to *everything*. The full meaning of ephemerality implies that each and every moment harbors a possible presence which actualizes itself as a full moment if and when we acknowledge it.

(4) It follows that man becomes visible precisely where he is transparent to the things of the moment. Transparency means understanding our achievements, anticipations and memories as but transient garments of what presents itself here and now. In short, man becomes himself, and therefore visible, where he is invisible. Pindar defines man as a dream, a vision, a special kind of seeing. Yet far from being a vision of things controlled and understood, this seeing is a vision *through* these modes of victory *toward* what can only be given as a gift (of chance), never captured as a booty. This vision (often translated as "dream") is *of* darkness (often translated as "shadow"). The "definition" of man as a vision of darkness follows from a commentary on

104

the victor's enjoyment of "delightful things," on the way these things come crashing down.

(5) The light which momentarily dispells the darkness is *given*, it does not originate with man. We merely "achieve," therefore anticipate and remember. On the other hand, the gift of transparency allows us to *be* anything and everything, if only ephemerally. When this gift comes, not only does it institute a reference, a plenitude, "gentle times" for man's undertakings, it comes upon *men*. The plural deepens the meaning here: victory may be mine, in a sense; yet if the fulfilling meaning of this triumph lies only in a *given* transparency, then the substance of the event, the light momentarily dispelling darkness, comes *upon* the situation, upon all the people involved in it. As a gift, enlightenment is never a private affair.

These five remarks suggest an interpretation of death. The verses already address us as mortals, a designation very common in Greece until precisely the moment when Socratic thinking came to power. Superficially, man appears as mortal in these verses *because* he is powerless to effect a constancy, *because* his victories are transient. At bottom, however, Pindar calls man the "mortal one" because of his ability and his task: he must become transparent and must allow his victories to be transparent to any and every thing of the *present*. To fulfil this task we must be willing to "let go" of victory. Most certainly we are not to "give up" in the wrestling match, but we are to realize that victories ahead or behind are not, as human accomplishments, sustaining and therefore are not to be taken seriously. Even at any moment *in* the match, victory does not occupy the attention of the good wrestler, rather the present hold or move. We must take the present seriously—and humbly too, since it is given as a gift. Human beings distinguish themselves from other creatures through this task; it makes them distinctively mortal. Only those beings who have to learn to renounce, without giving up, and to accept the present as a gift, are beings who must die, i.e., beings for whom death means something.

For Pindar—and for other pre-Socratic writers—human being fulfils itself in renunciation for the sake of the present, and death signals the necessity of this renunciation. Although this thought may have been formulated in a way inviting subsequent modifications, only later did these evolve into a genuinely Western thought. Mallarmé's two poems suggest the difference. In them, human being is fulfilled by the acknowledgement of a *mission* to preserve a presence, and death (as an impendence of life, not as an occurrence in life) appears as absolutizing this mission. In both cases death bespeaks the possibility and necessity of presence, but in Pindar the presence is a gift to be appreciated by transcending (here = letting fall away) all drives for achievement. Mallarmé's verses do call for some kind of drive:

> The bird that one never hears
> Another time in one's life.

and

> For not having sung the region where to live
> When the ennui of sterile winter came blazing.

We are more familiar with Plato's interpretation of death than with Pindar's. Plato interprets life precisely as a mission and death as recalling the character of this mission. The *Phaedo* exemplifies the war waged against the earlier interpretation. Here the swan's last song indicates an infinite rather than a finite transcendence. Aristototle's *Nicomachean Ethics* (Book X, Chapter 7) presents a more direct, less mythical version of this transcendence. The subject under general consideration here is *nous*, "intellectual intuition" or direct insight into things. Elsewhere this intuition is described as "the origin of knowledge" (end of *Posterior Analytics*) and as a kind of "at-oneness" with beings (*Metaphysics*, Book XII, Chapter 9). In *nous* lies the possibility of presence and so of human fulfilment. The passage in the *Ethics* reads:

Yet the life of *nous* is greater than the life of man. For not by being man does he live it, but by something divine emergent in him.... If, then, *nous* is divine in comparison to man, the life of *nous* is divine in comparison to human life. So we must not follow those who advise us to think of things human, since we are humans, or to think of things mortal, being mortals. Rather, we should aspire to immortality insofar as is possible, and do our utmost to live according to what is greatest in ourselves. For though it be tiny, it surpasses everything else in power and value.

The conclusion is clear: some way of life delivers us from our mortality. Not that we are, as humans, immortal. We shall surely die, each in his or her turn. But some part of our nature can be developed into a style of life within which death recedes—a path on which things appear as divine and immortal rather than as human and mortal. This conclusion stands explicitly in contrast to Pindar's and to the pre-Socratic view generally: "we are not to believe those who... ."

What are the *reasons* for the advice Aristotle proffers? The *Ethics* in its entirety answers this question. The opening paragraphs of the book remind the reader that all human involvements have goals and then ask around which *one* goal (*the* good or the *best* thing) all our other goal-oriented activities gravitate. For man, this central goal is evidently his own happiness. However, Aristotle immediately qualifies this term: happiness resides in a certain sense of completeness (we have everything necessary) and self-sufficiency (we can proceed on our own). Whatever our involvements in life, we intuitively recognize two extreme possibilities: on the one hand, we can grudgingly perform our "duties" in order to achieve a reward or avoid a pain; on the other hand, we can become involved in our tasks (whether cleaning the house or designing a bridge) with a sense that *we* are doing it, enjoying both the flexing of our minds and bodies and the influx of things into the field of our attention. In the first case we are not ourselves, and the things we work on are also alien: *absence* characterizes this pseudo-performance, and we ardently await its termination. In the second case we are ourselves, and things in our environment are momentarily ours: *presence* of mind and of circumstance characterizes this happy performance, and time flies.

In fathoming this intuitive sense of happiness, Aristotle asks, "What is human performance, then?" Literally: What is man's functioning (*ergon*)? In answering, Aristotle departs from common conceptions: man functions as himself only in "activity of soul according to *logos*." Both Aristotle and Plato define man as "the living being conditioned by *logos*." The Greek word may be aptly translated as "articulation," i.e., "joining things together." Man stands inevitably within an articulation, and the only question is whether he is joining things together *well*. Thus the definition of human happiness is restated to read: "activity of soul according to excellence." Aristotle here refers to the harp player, who in any case articulates, but whose happiness will lie in articulating well, in playing excellently according to the standards essential to music. This introduction of excellence leads to a division of topics, the discussion of which occupies the larger part of the *Ethics*.

Toward the end of the *Ethics* (shortly before the passage quoted) Aristotle restates the activity of man as an activity of *nous*, of seeing things in an immediate presence. Aristotle calls this *complete* happiness, most properly the "activity of the gods." It is the second kind of performance never beleaguered by the first kind. To the extent that we enact it, we do exactly what we want to do, we are our own masters, we contemplate each thing as it comes along, never doing or noting one thing for the sake of something *else*, something absent.

Yet the first kind of performance does in fact beleaguer us. We find it necessary to deal with many situations simply to "get done" with them. During such dealings we are not ourselves and things are not truly present to us. As Aristotle makes clear, our task is to pull ourselves as much as possible out of this morass. In so extricating ourselves we do not abandon the *beings* of our situation, on the contrary we see them for the first time in their full being. Much of Aristotle's technical discussion in his *Metaphysics* directs itself to the question of *what* we see or contemplate once we have extricated ourselves from the distractions of incomplete and unself-sufficient performance. As central to this discussion the point emerges that all beings (*ta onta*), not just human beings, find or manifest their being (*ousia*) in their respective and distinctive modes of activity (*energeia*).

According to the late Greek view, we fulfil our nature to the extent that we extract ourselves from extrinsically purposeful activity and plunge into intrinsically purposeful (complete and self-sufficient) activity. Our concrete position is, at best, *in* this transition. In fact, only in this stance (only as "philosophers") can we recognize the two possibilities. Owing to our everyday involvements with the social and natural things of our environment, we *can* concern ourselves chiefly or even exclusively for what is, was, and will be happening to us. This attitude, the worst, literally the pathetic one, renders us essentially passive, dependent, wafted. However, owing to the nature of man and the nature of things, we also have to *respond* to things which happen to us: calculate or steer them. Thus we can concern ourselves for *how* we are responding, for *what* we are doing, concentrating first of all on the activity rather than on the passivity. We are then *aloof* from things in the usual sense: ordinary concerns, apparently "dictated" by society and nature, are not accepted as self-evident in meaning and final authority. But, while not frenzied or "worried to death" about things, we are essentially *attentive* to them—not to how they will "turn out" (a matter of guesswork anyway) but to how we shall act toward them at each moment. In sum:

1. Concern for what happens to me shrouds every moment of

108

my life with mortality since what I undergo is never up to me and will in the end destroy me in disease or old age. Death here necessarily becomes construed as an occurrence, a termination in the sequence of what "comes over" me.

2. Concern for how I am responding to things unfolds in *logos*, in the articulation of things. This concern is *active* and *mine* individually. Yet the activity is essentially "at one" with the being of beings. Thus my aloofness places me in a realm of activity in which I am both independent of *and* referred to the natural and social things of my environment. Such independence of mind that also retains an essential contact with things belongs to the gods. And since these are immortal, I too am immortal—insofar as I can maintain the requisite mode of concern, i.e., extricate myself daily from ordinary concerns.

Aristotle's conclusion obviously disagrees with Pindar's. Yet both thinkers agree that *presence* is the ultimate issue of human nature, the fulfilment of man. And both agree that such presence requires us to overcome ordinary distractions and temporal dispersion. Wherein, then, lies the essential difference?

According to Pindar's formulation of the human condition, we not only have to strive for achievement ("silence of obscurity descends on those who will not endeavor"—4th *Isthmian Ode*), but must also renounce these human pretensions for the sake of simple presence. The difference is one between successful oblivion and god-given moments, the first giving way to the second.

Aristotle accepts this difference, but not as fundamental. He scrutinizes the presence, analyzing it into two sorts: active (noetic and energetic) and passive (aesthetic and pathetic) presence. This distinction marks the birth of Western philosophy. By according to man even a "tiny" share in noetic presence, in pure aloofness contemplating the moment, Greek philosophy inaugurated the thought that "gentle times" are not necessarily god-given, that man himself can achieve them, i.e., become a god. Aristotle states this thought in the strongest possible terms: "nous *is* man more than anything else."

Mallarmé's Swan suffers death precisely *because* he assumed an aloof position. And death undoes this aloofness insofar as a belated acknowledgement can rectify a long-standing error. Yet Aristotle's and Mallarmé's accounts agree on the centrality of *mission* in the fulfilment of human being. The basic human commitment is to sing. Furthermore, singing "the region where to

109

live" *does* place us at a distance from the region, extricates us from the web of suffocating concerns for daily survival. About writing, Mallarmé himself says (*M*, 481): "whoever accomplishes it completely cuts himself off" (the adverb seems to qualify both verbs). How do Aristotle and Mallarmé differ, then?

In Aristotle's view, recollection of death occurs only insofar as we "bother" with mortal things: with changeable circumstances affecting us in here and now situations, with what is here today and gone tomorrow. According to Aristotle, "mortal things" lie essentially under the veil of oblivion. Concern about death therefore bespeaks concern for "what does not matter." In this same tradition Spinoza could write two milleniums later that "the wise man thinks of nothing less than of death." For Aristotle and this tradition, oblivion, and so death, are to be forgotten. Here the difference becomes clear: Mallarmé's two poems articulate the breaking or dissolution of oblivion. We are therefore not incited to forget forgetfulness, but rather to recall it for the sake of a transparency to a presence of place. In this regard, the poems agree more with Pindar's *Ode* than with Aristotle's *Ethics*.

Parallel to the development of Greek philosophical thinking runs a strikingly similar change in Jewish religious thought, a change which gave birth to Christianity.

In the story of Jonah death becomes an issue on two occasions. Jonah is first fearful at the prospects of death contrived by God, and then later he wishes death upon himself when God had mercy on the people whose destruction Jonah had predicted under instruction from God. In both cases typically human illusions engender Jonah's thoughts on death. *Genesis* recounts how death *originally* came into the human condition, as a reality rather than as an illusion:

...Out of the ground the Lord God made grow every tree that is pleasant to sight and good for food; the tree of life also in the midst of the garden, and the tree of knowledge of good and evil.... The Lord God commanded the man, saying "Of every tree of the garden you may freely eat, but of the tree of knowledge of good and evil you shall not eat: for in the day that you eat thereof you shall surely die." ... And the serpent said to the woman, "You (two) shall surely not die, for God knows that in the day you eat of it your eyes shall be opened, and you shall be as gods, knowing good and evil." And when the woman saw that the tree was good for food, and that it was pleasant to the eyes, and a tree to be desired to make one wise, she took the fruit

110

thereof and ate it, and she gave some to her husband with her; and he ate it. And the eyes of them both were opened. . . .

For this "eye opener" both Eve and Adam pay a price: pain in child-bearing and obedience to her husband, and again pain in eating of the ground. This ground, "out of which the Lord God made grow every tree," is now cursed in regard to man. Henceforth, Adam knows he must "return to the ground" since, as God goes on to say, "out of it you were taken; for you are dust and to dust you shall return." After a short interlude, the story comes to a climax:

And the Lord God said, "Behold, the man has become one of us, to know good and evil. Now, lest he put forth his hand and take also of the tree of life, and eat, and live forever,—" the Lord God sent him forth from the garden of Eden, to till the ground whence he was taken. He drove out the man and he placed at the east end of the garden of Eden Cherubims, and a flaming sword which turned every way, to guard the way to the tree of life.

According to this account, death enters the human condition upon a decision that defies the transcendent source of creation. But how does this "explanation" of death affecting Adam and Eve help *us* understand our *own* condition as mortal? To answer this question we must fathom the "before" and "after" conditions recounted in the biblical story.

Before the decision, Adam and Eve live without taking fruit from either of the two trees singled out for special mention. Genesis does not indicate that they are immortal—only that they shall die "in the day" they take of the tree of knowledge of good and evil. They are not forbidden to take of the tree of life, and apparently they don't since God later says that they would live forever if they had. Before the decision, then, they were neither mortal nor immortal: they simply "lived along," i.e., survived with eyes closed.

After the decision, Adam and Eve live in pain. They are not pained by their defiance, but by their concrete existence, by child-bearing and field-tilling. In addition, they know they shall return to the ground from which they came. However, the serpent did not lie: they do not die; they go on living, Adam for 930 years. Later (Chapter 6) the Lord decides that his "spirit shall not for so long abide in man," and he limits human life to 120 years. Thus the serpent had told a partial truth: life for Adam and Eve *begins*, in the story, with the expulsion from the garden. With open eyes, man is simultaneously both living and mortal.

In the transition, death becomes an issue for man: not an immediate occurrence, but a pending possibility. The difference between "before" and "after" resides not in the contrast between living forever and living only for a limited time. The possibility of living forever is not realized before the decision, and only afterwards does it vanish as a possibility. In becoming an issue for man, death makes life itself into an issue. Although neither Adam nor Eve apparently "worry" about either one, subsequent accounts in the Bible express profound anxiety about life and death; e.g., Psalm 116:

The bonds of death compassed me, and the pangs of hell got hold of me....
Return to your rest my soul, for the Lord has dealt bountifully with you. For Thou hast delivered my soul from death, my eyes from tears, and my feet from falling. I will walk in the presence of the Lord in the land of the living.

From death as an issue we can be *delivered*. However, this does not mean that we become immortal. Delivered from death, we are free to face it, face the inevitable, and in such freedom we can walk in the land of the living—and, like Jonah, in the presence ("before the face") of the Lord.

The story, however, clearly states a *reason* why death becomes an issue: knowledge of good and evil. This knowledge leads to death. What *internal* connection is there between these two? What does knowledge of good and evil mean? Such knowledge "opens our eyes": we notice each thing not simply at the given time and place, we judge whether it "passes muster," whether it is good or evil. We raise ourselves *above* any given *ground* by refusing to take things straightaway as they appear, by looking above them. As the serpent predicted, we become "as gods"; even God confirms the serpent's words: "the man has become one of us." Insofar as we raise ourselves above creation—if only to judge it—we are gods. If this transcendence were to end here, we would concern ourselves henceforth strictly for what is *above* things, for what makes them good or evil. The things themselves would fall into oblivion. To thwart this eventuality, God introduces death as a reminder—that we shall *also* "return to the ground" out of which we and the trees were taken. We are

112

delivered from death in accepting this return, in willingly fore-going our godhood. We are "compassed by the bonds of death" when we refuse to return.

In the Old Testament we understand death as the counter-move to our god-like extraction from the immediacy of life. Willingness to face death is then the key condition for fulfilling life, for coming down to earth. In returning to dust we are not, however, returning to paradise: we never abandon our know-ledge of good and evil, we can at most concretize it, i.e., return with it to our concrete situation. Here we truly "walk ... in the land of the living."

Genesis agrees with Pindar in one crucial respect: death un-does the transcendence containing the germ of oblivion; it takes us back to things and is therefore central to presence of mind and of circumstance. Yet in contrast to Pindar, *Genesis* envisions a remarkable tension between man and presence, a love-hate relationship between the self and the ground from which it came. The ground is *cursed*, man's daily return to it is *painful*: "cursed is the ground for your sake: in pain you shall eat of it all the days of your life." Thus the presence man can henceforth achieve must be appreciated not so much as god-given as *of* God: we "walk in the presence *of the Lord* in the land of the living." Return is therefore possible only in reference to a transcendent source, and we realize this possibility in becoming "again" obedient, in undoing the initial disobedience of the Adam and Eve in each of us.

On the Christian interpretation, not deliverance from, but only *abolition* of death suffices for the human condition. In the *Gospel* according to John (5:24) Jesus says:

Whoever hears my account (*logos*) and has faith in him who sent me, has life everlasting and is not coming into judgment (*krisis*) but has passed over out of death into life.

Hearing a *logos*, we stand *in* it, we follow and obey it; a *logos* is not an utterance, but an articulation, a way of putting things to-gether. And to have (*echein*) everlasting life does not mean to possess it privately: it means being characterized or conditioned by it. Thus, once we have "put things together" the crisis vanishes, we need not worry about any future decision; the "chief thing" in and for life has already been decided. (The Greek *krisis* means a "parting," a place where things are decided one way or the other. When we ourselves move through

113

a *krisis* we translate it as "decision"; when we are moved by another we translate it as "judgment".) Finally, when we partake of the Christian *logos* we put death behind us for the sake of life: only life remains. This claim is underscored as John continues (verse 29):

the hour is coming in which all those in the tombs will hear the voice (of the Son of God) and come out, those who have done good things into the resurrection of life, those who have practiced vile things into the resurrection of judgment (*krisis*).

In this instance of hearing the *logos*, the alternatives reappear: life on the one side and crisis on the other—death in this case remaining definitively behind.

Although the New Testament terminates in a victory over death, it *commences* in a more fundamental thought about *krisis*. According to the account of *Genesis*, the decision has already been made and we today must live it out. In the accounts of the *Gospels* the decision is always being made—here and now. Consequently, a mood of urgency dominates the *Gospels*. An interesting example occurs uniquely in Matthew (12:36-37):

every idle utterance (*rhema*) men and women speak they will render an account (*logos*) of it in the day of judgment. For by your accounts (*logoi*) you will be justified and by your accounts (*logoi*) you will be condemned.

Much of what we say in life serves no purpose and detracts from the truth of our condition. Jesus tells us that every one of these utterances will "come back" to us "someday." At this time we must answer for worthless utterances. And according to *how* we account for them we shall find ourselves either cleansed of them or explicitly sullied by them. In short, we must carefully consider every utterance we venture. Being human, though, we are bound to utter worthless words. The question is whether we can *re*articulate them: the *rhema* sows the seed and the *logos* of it determines whether the fruit should be retained or discarded. A doubly harsh destiny for each and every moment of life.

In the *Gospel* according to Matthew the impendence of decision still appears in the Old Testament context, and Jesus can still say (5:17):

Do not think I came to destroy the law (*nomos*) or the prophets, I came not to destroy but to fulfil.

However, in the fulfilment of the law (*nomos*) the decision between the life of oblivion and an enlightened life shifts into the pending present: it is no longer a fate anchored in a distant past, nor a promise for the distant future. Significantly, neither death nor everlasting life are thematic in this Gospel.

In the *Epistles* of Paul the Christian thought of judgment grows definitely into a theology of death and everlasting life. The first *Epistle* to the Corinthians (15:26) states that "the ultimate enemy, death is to be rendered ineffective (*katargeitai*)." For the Jews, death returns us to the ground, and so undoes our pretentions to wisdom, our aspirations to rise above things and to be as gods. In Paul's account, grace (*charis*) accomplishes the "rendering ineffective of death" and, being a gift of God, also undoes inhuman pretention: but we are *not* returned to the ground. Death here has a different meaning entirely. What is this meaning and how does it grow out of the "relocation" of judgment?

According to *Genesis*, man has already decided to take into himself knowledge of good and evil. For this decision he must die. In the interim, however, we live in and by law (*nomos*), a condition which follows from our knowledge of good and evil and from the sense of fate. Paul draws the logical conclusions: First, if sin spells death, and if the circumstances of death dictate law, then sin, not enlightenment, becomes the meaning of law. Furthermore, if the significance of law lies in sin, and if Jesus' message undoes sin, then it also undoes law: in a way, the law and the prophets have been destroyed after all. Finally, if sin has been undone, then its consequence, notably death, must also be abolished. The following references establish this line of argument:

Just as in Adam all are dying, so also in Christ all will be made alive. I Corinthians, 15:22.
While the sting of death is sin (*hamartia*), the power of sin is the law (*nomos*). Ibid., 15:56.
Sin will not lord over you, for you are not under law (*nomos*), but under grace (*charis*). Romans, 6:14.
For while the wages of sin are death, the gift (*charisma*) of God is life everlasting. Ibid., 6:23.

Besides shifting judgment into the present of our life, the New Testament also stipulates that the issue of death be raised and decided in the middle of life—rather than in the beginning (with Adam) or at the end (in the distant future). First sin and death

115

are upon us, afterwards comes grace and life that is "for all ages" (*ainios*) or "everlasting."

Living in sin we lead a dying life. In pre-Christian technical usage, *hamartia* is a kind of error. In it we do *not* miss the universal principles governing things (e.g., failure to recognize the social nature of man); rather, fully knowledgeable about universals, we fail to recognize an instance requiring application of such principles (e.g., we fail to treat the human being in front of us according to his nature). For example, Aristotle explains tragedy partly in terms of *hamartia*, and in the context the word is generally translated as "tragic flaw." In any case, *hamartia* is functional oblivion, a forgetfulness allowing us to "work" well in the sequences of ordinary concerns. In the specifically Christian context, sin characterizes the human condition *per se* (a point not insisted upon by Aristotle), and it can only be expiated in mediation through Jesus. And since we are *per se* sinful, expiation is death itself, the end of our first self. Thus the same word (to "render ineffective") describes what happens both to death *and* to the body of sin. Paul writes (Romans, 6:6):

The man (*anthropos*) of old in us was impaled with (Jesus) in order that the body of sin might be rendered ineffective, that we should no longer be slaves to sin.

Two general points emerge from these four sketches of our traditions interpreting death.

First, the two later views—the Aristotelian and the Pauline—did in fact merge in subsequent theology, despite their evident differences (e.g., the *hubris* of the one and the *charis* of the other). For both traditions advise us to adopt a way of life in which "the mortal is clothed in the immortal" (I Corinthians, 15:53). The conversion to this manner of living must occur *now*, and when we live in the right way death ceases henceforth to be an issue for us—at least from the perspective of *this* now.

Imbued with Christianity and with the late Greek philosophy incorporated into its theology, we today find no element in our socio-historical environment which could encourage us to take death seriously. For these traditions instruct us to surmount death already during our life and then to forget it. The popular view, always but the residue of traditions, encourages us to forget death, to live as though we were never going to die.

Second, Mallarmé's poems not only counteract the popular view, they also penetrate *through* the traditional interpretations *to* the basic elements of the experience. Thus they stand closer in meaning to the earlier than to the later two views. Yet even here they pierce the interpretations for the sake of the experience.

The relationship of Mallarmé's work with the Judaic and the Christian interpretations is especially noteworthy. The relationship is negative, since the poems do not in any way articulate presence as bringing us face to face with God. In this regard they present a much harsher destiny than does Baudelaire's *"Recueillement,"* a poem which rivals, in its peaceful mood of transcending presence, the Psalms of the Old Testament and the poetic works of the Christian mystics.

Yet unlike the two pagan interpretations, Mallarmé's poems articulate the materials of the human condition as both brutal to encounter and difficult to sing:

> His whole neck will shake off this white agony
> Inflicted by the space on the bird who denies it
> But not the horror of the ground where the plummage is
>   caught.

and

> Lacerated shall he, whole,
> Remain on some path!

The religious interpretations construe the elements of the human condition as so harsh that they can never be properly faced in their own right. We can encounter things properly only by facing their *source.* In both accounts, the ground is *cursed.* As Paul says (Romans, 8:21), we can at most *hope* that "creation (*ktisis*: established circumstances) may be freed from slavery and corruption." Until then, man finds not only the ground cursed, but also himself cursed *from* the earth by the voice of Abel's blood crying up from the ground (*Genesis*, 4:10-11). Both the Old and the New Testaments rule out a *direct* presence of things, as recommended by Pindar and Aristotle.

While Mallarmé's poems depict circumstances as brutal and difficult, they also suggest that the presence possible and relevant for human kind is mediated solely by "song." It is mediated then, but not by a transcendent source. Presence becomes a mission for man. Our mortality hovers over every moment as the possibility that we may fail to re-present our circumstances in song.

117

6. UN COUP DE DÉS

Convergence of the human condition, the making of a moment out of the flowing configurations of human experience, has traditionally been associated with a human attitude toward the destruction of configuration. Earlier traditions recommend a stance accepting mortality, later ones enjoin a hope for an immortality. All agree that "naturally" (ordinarily, initially) the human condition is one of oblivion. The question of mortality or immortality arises in the effort to interpret the dissolution of the oblivion.

Mallarmé's *"Le vierge, le vivace et le bel aujour'hui"* and *"Petit Air II"* articulate conditions in which death is impending. In these poems we experience finite transcendence. Death enters into this experience as sealing the development dissolving the oblivion.

We may turn to Mallarmé's *Un Coup de dés jamais n'abolira le hasard* for a direct articulation of the encounter with death, with the convergence of configuration (see following pages). This is a longer poem, very innovative in form and complicated in structure; obviously, we must restrict the analysis to those features of it relevant to the one theme of death.

The poem tells of a shipwreck. Evoked are a situation at sea, a shipmaster, the varying attitudes of the master toward the event, and what happens and does *not* happen as the ship founders. The story unfolds penetratingly, not linearly: in the sequence the single event becomes progressively unlayered and unveiled.

In its printed form, the poem occupies eleven double pages. The words on the first two double pages fall onto the right space only, while the remaining pages vary in directionality from a sloping downward to a shuttling back and forth; for instance, on the fifth double page the words build up on the left and then finally explode toward the right. Even more striking is the variation in type faces (eight in all); this device allows each dimension of the sequence to be interrupted, integrated with other dimensions, and then abruptly resumed. As a result of these two techniques of typography the poem reads (visually) as a choral chant enacting (audially) the tempest which, though not itself verbally described, sets the scene of the shipwreck. Thus is unified the manifold of happenings which implode simultaneously, true to the experience of destruction.

The bold centrality of the idea evidences one conspicuous

"novelty" of the poem: the complete title actually reads as a proposition, a *claim*. Traditional epics and dramas portray characters at the center of things, and lyrical works evoke a narrator anchoring the sentiments. These works provide ideas epiphenomenally: an idea congeals gradually out of the encounter of the personages with the circumstances. Mallarmé's poem reverses this usual order: the idea, as stated enigmatically in the title and ramified by further "verses" in bold typeface, dominates the entire work. Our attention moves from the idea toward the personage and the circumstances. The "story" itself unfolds only episodically, in the small cursive type of the printed text.

UN COUP DE DÉS

JAMAIS

QUAND BIEN MÊME LANCÉ DANS DES CIRCONSTANCES

ÉTERNELLES

DU FOND D'UN NAUFRAGE

SOIT
　　que

　　　　l'Abîme

　　blanchi
　　　　étale
　　　　　furieux
　　　　　　sous une inclinaison
　　　　　　　plane désespérément

　　　　　　　　　　d'aile

　　　　　　　　　la sienne
　　　　　　　　　　　par

avance retombée d'un mal à dresser le vol
et couvrant les jaillissements
coupant au ras les bonds

très à l'intérieur résume

l'ombre enfouie dans la profondeur par cette voile alternative

jusqu'adapter
à l'envergure

sa béante profondeur en tant que la coque

d'un bâtiment

penché de l'un ou l'autre bord

125

LE MAÎTRE

surgi
 inférant

    de cette conflagration

       que se

     comme on menace
   l'unique Nombre qui ne peut pas

         hésite
      cadavre par le bras
plutôt
  que de jouer
   en maniaque chenu
     la partie
    au nom des flots
        un

    naufrage cela

hors d'anciens calculs
où la manoeuvre avec l'âge oubliée

        jadis il empoignait la barre

à ses pieds
      de l'horizon unanime

prépare
  s'agite et mêle
    au poing qui l'étreindrait
un destin et les vents

être un autre

      Esprit
         pour le jeter
            dans la tempête
          en reployer la division et passer fier

écarté du secret qu'il détient

envahit le chef
coule en barbe soumise

direct de l'homme

    sans nef
      n'importe
        où vaine

ancestralement à n'ouvrir pas la main
                              crispée
                    par delà l'inutile tête

         legs en la disparition

                         à quelqu'un
                                   ambigu

              l'ultérieur démon immémorial

ayant
         de contrées nulles
                   induit
le vieillard vers cette conjonction suprême avec la probabilité

                              celui
                                   son ombre puérile
caressée et polie et rendue et lavée
                         assouplie par la vague et soustraite
              aux durs os perdus entre les ais

                              né
                                   d'un ébat
la mer par l'aïeul tentant ou l'aïeul contre la mer
                   une chance oiseuse

                                                       Fiançailles
dont
         le voile d'illusion rejailli leur hantise
         ainsi que le fantôme d'un geste

                    chancellera
                    s'affalera

                         folie

N'ABOLIRA

COMME SI

Une insinuation

au silence

dans quelque proche

voltige

simple

enroulée avec ironie
                    ou
                        le mystère
                                    précipité
                                            hurlé

tourbillon d'hilarité et d'horreur

autour du gouffre
                    sans le joncher
                                    ni fuir

                    et en berce le vierge indice

COMME SI

plume solitaire éperdue

sauf

132

que la rencontre ou l'effleure une toque de minuit
et immobilise
au velours chiffonné par un esclaffement sombre

cette blancheur rigide

dérisoire
                en opposition au ciel
    trop
         pour ne pas marquer
                   exigûment
                        quiconque

prince amer de l'écueil

s'en coiffe comme de l'héroïque
irrésistible mais contenu
par sa petite raison virile
                            en foudre

soucieux
        expiatoire et pubère

                muet

La lucide et seigneuriale aigrette
au front invisible
scintille
puis ombrage
une stature mignonne ténébreuse
en sa torsion de sirène

par d'impatientes squames ultimes

134

rire

     que

SI

de vertige

debout

   le temps
      de souffleter
bifurquées

    un roc

   faux manoir
       tout de suite
          évaporé en brumes

       qui imposa
          une borne à l'infini

C'ÉTAIT
issu stellaire

CE SERAIT
    pire
        non
            davantage ni moins

                    indifféremment mais autant

136

LE NOMBRE

EXISTÂT-IL
autrement qu'hallucination éparse d'agonie

COMMENÇÂT-IL ET CESSÂT-IL
sourdant que nié et clos quand apparu
enfin
par quelque profusion répandue en rareté
SE CHIFFRÂT-IL

évidence de la somme pour peu qu'une
ILLUMINÂT-IL

LE HASARD

Choit
  la plume
    rythmique suspens du sinistre

          s'ensevelir
        aux écumes originelles
    naguères d'où sursauta son délire jusqu' à une cime
          flétrie
      par la neutralité identique du gouffre

RIEN

          de la mémorable crise
               ou se fût
                  l'événement

accompli en vue de tout résultat nul

humain

N'AURA EU LIEU
une élévation ordinaire verse l'absence

QUE LE LIEU
inférieur clapotis quelconque comme pour disperser l'acte vide
abruptement qui sinon
par son mensonge
eût fondé
la perdition

dans ces parages
du vague
en quoi toute réalité se dissout

EXCEPTÉ

    à l'altitude

          PEUT-ÊTRE

                aussi loin qu'un endroit

fusionne avec au delà

           hors l'intérêt
          quant à lui signalé
                 en général
selon telle obliquité par telle déclivité
                   de feux

    vers
       ce doit être
          le Septentrion aussi Nord

                 UNE CONSTELLATION

       froide d'oubli et de désuétude
                pas tant
             qu'elle n'énumère
        sur quelque surface vacante et supérieure
          le heurt successif
                  sidéralement
       d'un compte total en formation

veillant
      doutant
         roulant
           brillant et méditant

                avant de s'arrêter
         à quelque point dernier qui le sacre

          Toute Pensée émet un Coup de Dés

Without attempting to reproduce in English the exact typography, much less the multiple phonetic and semantic interrelations nourished by the typography, we may translate each double page with a view to the overall relationship between the visual and eidetic images (see following pages).

"A throw of dice—never will it abolish chance." The claim spreads through the poem on four separate double pages (I, II, V, and IX), where it receives immediately a strengthening qualification (II): the chanciness, the unpredictableness and the danger, will not be overcome by a throw of dice "even when cast in circumstances eternal from the depth of a shipwreck." Besides introducing the "story," the qualification suggests that being in the "depth of a shipwreck" is an eternal condition. In any case, the force of the idea appears initially as negative. The last two double pages (X and XI) both reaffirm and mitigate this negativity: "Nothing will have taken place but the place, except perhaps a constellation." A shipmaster's typical concern, namely to extricate his ship from the circumstances, will not be fulfilled. But something else happens: the *place*. Through the master's efforts the place itself, as distinct from himself and from the construction for which he takes responsibility, will be preserved. But something further might *also* happen: a constellation, an arrangement in some sense new, *over* the place. The final comment returns to the original act: "Every thought emits a throw of dice."

One logical paraphrase of the idea reads: In those rare moments when we actually think, we initially wish that our thoughts will undo the uncertainty of things. Yet this wish remains ultimately unfulfilled. While we would like to believe that our thoughts can institute something *in* our situation, something which will save *us* from the disasters inevitably occurring therein, we discover that our rare moments of thought only preserve the situation as a whole, nothing *in* it, least of all ourselves. At most our thoughts may, in addition, lead to a "new" configuration *for* the place.

Structurally, the poem is a "well-formed formula." But what do all the "variables" mean?—a throw of dice, abolishing chance, taking place, constellation, thought emitting a throw of dice. The episodes of the idea, the story of the poem, answer in part this question. The visual image of a situation of shipwreck provides a reference for the eidetic image of the human condition in which death—and so life—is impending.

I

A THROW OF DICE

II

NEVER
EVEN WHEN CAST IN CIRCUMSTANCES
ETERNAL
FROM THE DEPTH OF A SHIPWRECK

III

GIVEN

That the Abyss
whitened... extensive... furious
beneath an inclination
glides desperately
with wing... its own
in

       advance fallen back, straining to trim the flight
       and covering over the gushes
       cutting into the swells

       gathers up, far in the interior
       the shadow buried in the depth by this alternative sail
       enough to fit the (wing-) span
       its yawning depth as the hull
       of a construction
       listed to one or the other side

143

IV

THE MASTER
                    beyond calculations of old
                    where maneuver (is) with age forgotten
(has) risen
(is) inferring
                    formerly he took the tiller in the hand
from this conflagration
                    at his feet
                    from the unanimous horizon
that there is
                    readying itself
                    working itself up and mingling
                    in the fist that would grasp it
as one threatens
                    a destiny and the winds
the sole Number which cannot
                    be another

                    Spirit
                    to hurl it into the tempest
                    to flatten the division and pass proudly on
hesitates
a corpse, by the arm
                    separated from the secret it holds
rather than playing
as a hoary madman
the part
in the name of the waves
one
                    invades the head
                    flows into the submissive beard
shipwreck, this

                    direct of the man
                    without a ship: no matter where vain

144

V

ancestrally not to open the hand
clenched above the useless head
bequest in vanishment, to someone ... ambiguous
    the subsequent immemorial demon
    having, from null lands, induced
    the old man toward this supreme conjunction with probability
he—his puerile shadow
    caressed and polished and rendered and washed
    softened by the wave and withdrawn from the hard bones lost between the planks
born of a frolic
the sea by the forefather trying, or the forefather against the sea
a futile chance

(The Rituals of a) Betrothal whose veil of illusion (has) rebounded, their haunting
like the phantom of a gesture
will stagger ... will collapse
madness

WILL ABOLISH

VI

AS IF
An insinuation
           simple
in the silence
           enwrapped with irony
           or
           the mystery ... flung down, roared out
in some nearby
           vortex of hilarity and horror
hovers
           around the gulf
           —without strewing it, without fleeing—
           and cradles the virginal sign of it

AS IF

VII

quill solitary (and) bewildered
except
                       that a cap of midnight meets it or grazes it
                       and immobilizes
                       in velvet crumpled by a somber guffaw
                       this rigid whiteness
                       preposterous, in opposition to the heavens
                       too much, not to brand ever so slightly whoever
                       bitter prince of the reef
                       dons it as something heroic
                       irresistible but contained
                       by his small virile reason
                       in lightening

VIII

concerned
conciliatory and puberal
mute
               laugh that
                   IF
The lucid and lordly aigrette
            of vertigo
on the invisible brow
sparkles... then darkens
a dainty, shadowy stature
               upright
in its twist of a siren
                 the time to flout
with terminal impatient scales
             forked
             a rock
             false manor immediately evaporated in mists
             which imposed a limit to the infinite

IX

(IF) IT WAS
progeny of stars
       THE NUMBER
       Were it to *exist*
       otherwise than hallucination scattered by agony
           Were it to *begin* and to *end*
           emergent as denied, sealed when apparent
           (and) finally spread thin by profusion
           Were it to *add up*
       evidence of a sum-total, however small
       Were it to *illumine*
IT WOULD BE
worse
no more, no less
indifferently but as so much
       CHANCE

       Falls the quill
       rhythmic suspension of calamity
       to bury itself in the original foams
       whence but recently delirium sprang to a summit
       withered by the identical neutrality of the gulf

NOTHING
of the memorable crisis
—or the event might have
       consummated itself, with no human result in view—
       WILL HAVE TAKEN PLACE
       an ordinary height dispenses absence
       BUT THE PLACE
       below indifferent lapping as though for dispersing the empty act
       abruptly
       which otherwise
       by its lie
       might have founded perdition
       in these latitudes of the vague into which every reality
         dissolves itself.

EXCEPT
in altitude
PERHAPS
so far as one region

      fuses with a beyond
         apart from any interest
         this being signalled in general
      according to such an obliquity, by such a declivity
        of fire

      towards what must be
      the Seven Stars, also North
      A CONSTELLATION
      cold from oblivion and disuse
      not so (cold) that it does not enumerate
      on some surface, vacant and high
      the successive shock, starwise,
      of a total account in formation

      watching
      doubting
      rolling
      shining and meditating
      before stopping
      at some final point which consecrates it

    Every Thought emits a Throw of Dice

First, the master, the locus of responsibility. He enters at stage IV, after the scene has been set, and must respond to the Abyss earlier described: visually, to the lack of support for his ship. The "construction" is primarily in danger, only derivatively the master. This ranking of the endangered sets the tone of the entire poem. For the moment of death penetratingly unlayered brings into focus first of all the givens of the situation. The focus is there *for* us, but it does not primarily fall *on* us (except insofar as we verge toward frenetic fear). Not simply about the shipmaster, the story evokes the "coming into focus"—the convergence bespoken by death.

The master has risen. Whence? Out of the "calculations of old where maneuver is with age forgotten." Ordinarily, we meet given moments with established methods of calculation and then maneuver our constructions through circumstances: we figure things out at the moment with a view to continuing the operation (the voyage), and this becomes a matter of routine. However, in the face of *the* Abyss, the means and procedures established in the configuration of our vocation (sailing) are not adequate to the moment. Not that the master attempts to employ them. As we see him, he has already risen beyond them. Again, this level of experience determines the articulation as a whole; if we presume the initial level we hear the poem in the wrong key. Having risen beyond configurative calculation and maneuver he will at first try something else: a throw of dice.

The master is inferring. Whereas previously he "took the tiller in the hand" to *steer* the construction on its voyage, he now *thinks*. The final "verse" of the poem reveals one enigmatic result of such thinking: a throw of dice. At the present stage, however, the *structure* of thinking appears.

First, the thought assesses "this conflagration," the utter destruction of the ship, of the place where one stands (XI resumes the image of fire). This kind of assessment acknowledges that the horizon of one's endeavor is of *one* mind ("unanimous"). Visually, the image suggests that the storm, sheer blackness and rage, closes in upon one. Eidetically, a "unanimous horizon" evokes an unequivocal coming-into-focus.

Second, the master infers from the destruction and closure "a destiny and the winds." The two terms qualify one another. The destiny is not vaguely futural but specifically correlative to the winds: *these* locate the thought of destiny. This destiny is also "readying itself, working itself up and mingling" in the very fist

149

(*poing*) which had formerly grasped (*empoignait*) the tiller but now holds the dice soon to be thrown. Thus the destiny here inferred remains associated with the elements raging against him; it also depends on—calls upon—the master himself. In so rising and thus inferring, the master has a menacing aspect, his fist raised "as one threatens." Defiance initially indicates the power both embedded in what one confronts and lodged in one's own response. A simpler instance of such defiance may be discerned in the rage of the man who is summoned from a deep sleep by the pleading voice of a servant come to deliver an urgent message.

The *third* moment in this structure of thoughts is the direct object of the inference: "the sole Number which cannot be another . . . ." The shipmaster thinks not only *from* the "conflagration" *toward* "a destiny and the winds," but also directly the one *solution* which allows him to meet these. In the visual image, only one combination will suffice. Yet the title lines of the poem state that *no* throw of dice will ever abolish chance (the danger). Thus, in the full eidetic image the one solution the master "has in mind" is either a figment of his delusion or a thought not at all intended to extricate him from his concrete plight. Double page IX resumes this dilemma; for now we may simply note that, however the question will be resolved, the master appears as one who *thinks* in a fully structured manner: he does not simply meander, much less tremble, since he has risen "beyond the calculations of old."

The remaining half of page IV introduces, in the vocative, a mood of exigency: "Spirit to hurl it into the tempest, to flatten the division, and to pass proudly on." The master's wish or need for this Spirit expresses itself in a syntactical ambiguity. The entire semantic unit ("Spirit... proudly on") stands in free bondage with either or both the images preceding and succeeding. That is, the Spirit to hurl, flatten, and pass may *be* the unique Number. In this case, the master thinks the Number (solution) which cannot be other than the Spirit itself. However, the two may be distinct, and a continuous reading (as would be appropriate for a chant) leaves the clause semantically oscillating: at one moment the Number (solution) *is* Spirit (a manner of solution), at the next moment the Number is a correct solution and the Spirit a manner of response in view of the solution.

The semantic oscillation of this key clause expresses precisely the master's actual manner at the moment when, suspended

150

over the Abyss, he has risen beyond the calculations of old and thinks the situation fully: he *hesitates*. Hesitation becomes the dominant mood of the entire description, manifesting itself in an elementary way already in the shuttling of the typography left and right. Eidetically, the master hesitates between *hoping* for a solution and *identifying* a stance of his own with the solution. Visually, the hesitation expresses itself as a doubt whether he should cast the dice—an act which, we are already told by the title of the poem, can never result in the abolition of the danger.

In Sophocles' account, Oedipus searches boldly for a solution only to discover that the answer points back to himself; here hesitation occurs in straight passage from an assumption *about* Number to the assumption *of* Spirit. In the Biblical account (*Matthew*, 8:23; repeated with variations in two other Gospels), Jesus simply flattens the division and allows the boat to pass on; here the man embodies directly the Spirit and chastises his disciples for hesitating to believe in Number on the basis of Spirit. These ancient interpretations of human responsibility over the Abyss lurk contrastingly in the background as the modern shipmaster hesitates in the face of death. The "story" of the poem unfolds at the level where hesitation essentially marks both the man and the moment.

As hesitant, the master appears virtually dead: "A corpse, separated by the arm from the secret it holds." Visually, he stands on his ship (say, on the bridge) facing the gale, and with outstretched arm he clasps the dice for a throw, the resultant Number of which remains unknown. Eidetically, the man is separated from the requisite Spirit to face the tempest itself, and this separation spells death. On the visual level: to hesitate at the moment of crisis causes one to lose out, to die. In this case the line predicts what does indeed come to pass. But the "it" in the phrase "the secret it holds" can stand for Spirit as well. Then the master is a corpse because separated from the secret which Spirit holds. Visually as well as eidetically, death results from the hesitation.

Why does the master hesitate at this juncture of Number-as-solution and solution-as-Spirit? The next lines seem to answer this question: "rather than playing, as a hoary madman, the part in the name of the waves." The master hesitates to "play the part," to give himself over to the elements in the manner which would make of him not only a *wild* man, but also an admittedly *old* man. The Northern pagan blood in our veins sus-

151

pects that Spirit over the Abyss can mean joyous willingness to engage in mortal combat and to go down fighting. If we die "with sword in hand" we give ourselves over to the elements. However, this pagan Spirit merges with the essentially mythic conviction that growing old, inevitable in any event, brings us closer to the gods and returns us to nature. Today such heroism lacks the appropriate mythic support. Thus the master hesitates between the futility of an extraneous solution and the incredibility of the immediate alternative. Since he cannot rightly *choose* Spirit, the question is whether Spirit will "choose" him.

The last image on the page stands in free relationship with several possible subjects. Something, either Spirit or shipwreck or Number, "invades the head, flows into the submissive beard." In any case, the head and the beard are overwhelmed. *By what*? The "head" (*le chef*) connotes thought, "beard" connotes the elements. Spirit belongs to the one; the swamping of the ship fits the other. Concretely, however, the event, the master's foundering, is single. We experience one shipwreck, with both a manner of response and a savage sea. This event is direct, and it is *of* the man (or simply "of man") who appears "without a ship." A shipwreck without a ship! At the moment of death, one loses the construction (as double-page III calls the ship). At this moment man is without construction, nude. But, the last lines emphasize, this lack makes no difference. Here and now the problem is not to procure or preserve a ship. With or without one, the problematic remains the same.

The description of the master recalls the configuration of voyage in the mode of convergence. The ordinary exigencies are transcended, the moment assessed (danger, destiny, a solution), the fundamental possibilities acknowledged (Number and Spirit), and the ultimate responsibility stated. These lines can stand alone, in the way certain passages from Proust or Homer can. However, they also fit into the larger context of the poem and gain in significance in the sequel.

While the last three (IX, X, XI) resume the visual and eidetic imagery of the ultimate moment, the intervening four double pages present the temporal modification of appearances experienced by the master as he has just risen. The conversion of the master's stance entails a modification of past, future, and present.

(V) The past normally appears as the achievements of one's vocational life-time. Constructing a ship, learning calculations, and succeeding in maneuvers form one's contextual past. The necessary condition of our present place, this "past" determines where and what we are—without, however, sufficing to consolidate any given moment of our being.

Visually, the new past wrought at the moment of transcendence recalls the master's long-standing refusal to open his clenched hand and an unclarified legacy which now disappears. It evokes the fact that some demon (both infinitely antecedent and subsequent) "caused" the master to enter into the situation, the fact that his shadow had been ensconced in the bones lost in the planks, and the fact that he was born of a frolic. Finally, this past includes a marriage whose veil of illusion is now lifted and whose haunting is about to end and perhaps to abolish something as yet unstated (assuming that "WILL ABOLISH" ties in with the episode).

Drawn back toward the moment described, an eidetic image of the past looms concurrently with the visual one. The master has *all along* refused to put Spirit into the voyage, i.e., to take his stand in the manner of his response rather than in the outcome of his manipulations. Thus the one thing of importance, both for himself and for mankind, is bottled up and in danger of extinction. This refusal to put ourselves into the situation in which we supposedly find ourselves, marks the distinctively human past emerging at the moment in inexorably impending death. We can always blame something as having brought us into straits. In the *Iliad* a *daimon* or some god "makes" things happen the way they do, e.g., leads a lion to the wounded stag, thus frightening all else away (Book Eleven, line 480). Interestingly, Socrates suffered the charge of blasphemy at a later date for claiming that *his* "demon" never led the way but only restrained him along his own way (*Apology*, 31C). But the master's true self, until now "in hiding" because identified with the easy self of an officer and simply integrated into the construction of the ship, withdraws from its hiding place, from its specious even if necessary past, and is "caressed and polished and rendered and washed, softened by the wave." It is made manifest and real, flexible and responsive to the circumstances appearing at the moment of death. The true self is born in conflict: either brought forth by the elements with the help of one's forebears or issuing from the forebears' defiance in the face of the elements. One is never the *first* shipmaster, but rather the "last" in a long line of established efforts and conflicts. Thus when we

153

venture out on our own for marriage with the elements an illusion sets in. We assume that voyages take care of themselves, requiring only calculation and maneuver on our part. Now, however, the ultimacy of the moment dispels the illusion and reveals a new sense of the past: the Rituals of the Betrothal (*Fiançailles*) re-emerge in their original significance, as a haunting and like a phantom which, owing to the evanescence of the moment, commands special attention. The true self clothed in the new past only *emerges*: it cannot and will not dally as something merely emerged.

(VI) A simple insinuation hovers around the gulf without either undoing it or fleeing in the face of it, but rather preserving its virginal "index." The semantic force stresses that *one* "something" winds its way into the situation of shipwreck. It enters into the silence. Irony enwraps it: this "something" is not explicitly named.

The future ordinarily appears in the plans we have and make. The next destination on our voyage, the pending tasks, and the projected solution to the irksome dilemmas currently experienced, form the contextual appearance of "future time." It is a necessary dimension of one's vocational life-time, the mapping of one's job. Such "future," however, hardly leads to the making of a moment. On the contrary, orientation within it (the merchant's orientation) essentially distracts one from each and every moment. The distraction is evident in the way we view the alternative possibilities: things will either work or fail to work out as planned; in the first case, we pass directly by the event and plan for the next, while in the second case we become vexed by the event and disown it in the name of its missing brother.

Beyond "calculations of old" inferring "a destiny and the winds," the master faces the truly futural dimension of his situation: an undetermined outcome as this bespeaks the savage situation. Facing the shipwreck as he does, even in hesitation, the master acknowledges the claims made upon him and admits that he himself does not know its "contents," i.e., cannot reduce them to his own schemes. The waves, the winds, and later the stars, simply *are*; they introduce themselves, wind themselves (as do the words printed on the page) into the situation as they are in themselves. Thus they enter in silence, enwrapped only in a statement of this silence. No courtly page announces things in advance, forewarning the master and allowing him to say. "Oh, yes, I know who you are already."

154

In confronting the unknown we can either meet it as unnamed (and undetermined) or, calling it such, toss it into a pile labeled "miscellaneous/unclassified." For the genuine future demands that we be true to its sense, and this demand raises the possibility of our being false to it. The poem states the alternative: "or the mystery is thrown down, roared out, into some nearby vortex"—not into the Abyss but into something like it, off to one side. Visually this vortex appears as one "of hilarity and of horror"—and fittingly so, since "insinuation," once classified as mysterious, seems ridiculous while nonetheless horrible, as does the insinuation of death when interpreted as a voyage to heaven or hell.

An "as if" embraces the entire experience of insinuation. This mood of uncertainty carries over onto the next double page.

(VII) Ultimately, the sense of the future "strikes home" only as we rise to meet it, i.e., step forward to face the unsettledness, the indeterminateness. Of course, the question remains whether we can and will do it. In *this* "whether" the *full* impact of our futural being discloses itself—rather than in the uncertainties pertaining to things.

Visually, this seventh double page introduces a quill, a feather, all alone and lost; then also a *toque*, a cap formerly worn by men and often including a feather in its composition. However, the images strain against one another. The cap is *of* midnight, it meets or at least grazes the feather, it immobilizes "this rigid whiteness," and its velvet is "crumpled by a somber guffaw." The whole appears "preposterous" and anyone who "dons it" (presumably the cap) becomes branded "ever so slightly" as "bitter prince of the reef." Penultimately, something (presumably the reef) is "irresistable but contained by his small virile reason." Finally, everything flashes "in lightning," with possibly a special reference to the master's "reason."

The inner conflict of the visual image forces the reader also onto an eidetic level. In the nineteenth century a quill served as a writing instrument. A *toque*, also a "hair-do," covers a man's head. At midnight a man writes, namely when the racket of daily configuration has died down. Writing catches a moment, makes the configuration stand still for the sake of an emergence. Concern for the moment collides head-on with the ordinary mode of response, and a man becomes disheveled in it—sadly but also comically. In part, the unrelenting terror of the elements (the rigid whiteness of the waves) is caught (immobilized).

155

Devoted to the making of a moment, the effort appears indeed preposterous, for it moves in opposition to the overall givens of the situation. Yet in responding thusly, one becomes indeed marked (ever so slightly) as a prince, in some evanescent sense as heroic. This bitter experience, the response essentially for the moment, the poem in turn defines precisely by the reference: by the reef. The master is prince, but prince of what destroys him. He himself, no matter how virile, does not locate the essence. And the response enlightens the moment only, whereupon darkness resumes.

An idea, however, makes concrete sense only when transparent to an immediate situation. The visual image supplies the immediacy and, as reference, continues to dominate the experience.

(VIII) The present is apparently the time of direct perception, the arrangments directly perceived and therefore shortly to be by-passed in the course of the voyage. However, in the genuine present we respond, we consummate the arrangements perceived. Perhaps the distinction between the apparent and the genuine present becomes intelligible only when the arrangements themselves absolutely preclude any by-pass.

The first lines of this page describe the poise of the master: concerned, concilliatory, puberal, mute. *Now* one must strike as best one can. It is "the time to flout a rock," that which appears to be the firm ground of salvation but which actually bespeaks destruction. The poem calls the "rock" *false* either because it offers no place to stand or because it is simply the crest of a new wave crashing against the construction.

Experienced seafarers already know, apart from the tale of Odysseus and the sirens, that during a storm sailors sometimes plead with the shipmaster to steer the ship in close to the shore, in the false but plausible belief that there lies safety. A rock is a false manor which, once dissipated, appears retrospectively as having "imposed a limit to the infinite."

In any difficult situation there looms always some "firm ground" which, as we generally learn too late, brings immediate destruction: the mighty solitary tree for the man caught in a lightning storm, the reckless deed for the cowardly man. These "easy ways out" are false because with them we attempt to shut out the "hard fact" that we confront something which, although absolutely demanding, does not fall into any class prescribing the response. They are false because they impose a limit upon

156

what allows of no limitation. The response adequate to the moment can never be pre-scribed. If we face the moment truly, we face it nakedly.

(IX, I, XI) From within the master's situation wells the reflection terminating the poem. Such reflection issues from the solidity of the moment comprising a new past, a new future, and therefore a new present in a genuine temporality.

One element on the previous page reads: "laugh that IF." The purport of this laughter, which itself may be "concerned, concilliatory, puberal, and mute," is now stated: "IF IT WAS THE NUMBER IT WOULD BE *CHANCE*." If the solution envisioned turned out to be the correct one, it would be merely a coincidence, not a true product of calculation and maneuver, nor an adequate answer to the exigencies of impending death. Now, however, one laughs at the vanity of this interpretation of NUMBER. The short block of dramatic "asides" articulates the detail of this illusion.

First, Number considered as a projected solution is simply "hallucination," and this in turn does not persevere: agony scatters it, the agony experienced in flight from the givens of the situation.

Second, if such a Number were to arise (begin) we would immediately disclaim (deny) it, while if it were to come to completion (end) we would experience it as over and done with. Construed as a solution, Number is inadequate to the moment. The situation itself, in all its multiplicity, would dissipate the solution. Any solution one *has* is a mode of response based on a projection into the future, i.e., away from the present. In experiencing our mortality we acknowledge the irrelevance of this mode of response.

The remaining two dramatic "asides"—"Were it to *add up*" and "Were it to *illumine*"—suggest the transition from Number-as-solution to solution-as-Spirit. A solution *may* allow us to get out of a scrape. But it can *also* allow us to "make sense" out of our predicament, to add it up—if not into a sum total, at least to the extent that such "total sense" appears possible. However, the solution then illumines the situation and what *it* contains. Thus the tables are turned, and were the Number to exist it would be Chance itself, the solution would be to *face* the danger. The key term of the poem, *Le Hasard*, means one thing to the unconverted (coincidence, the predictable and controllable) and another to the converted (danger, the plenitude which must be faced).

In every situation, one stands before the same "parting of the ways." A student entering a professor's office to confer about an assignment can either search for a Number which will allow him to put the problematic behind *or* place Spirit in face of the problematic. A professor entering a faculty meeting "prechooses" similarly one way or the other. American television abounds in heroes carefully fabricated to have *both* the Number solving every problem and the Spirit to face the danger "and pass proudly on"; thus they survive unscathed and, like the early Puritans, they continue to believe that God himself had assigned man to open and master the New World.

At the parting of the ways one experiences—perhaps not without humor—death. Whether as ignominious flight from, or as frontal encounter with the givens of the situation, one's response henceforth precludes forever any pretended self-sufficiency or invulnerability. Once we have arrived at the parting, the law of excluded middle is in effect. Here, failing to face the situation entails frantic flight and so loss of self (a loss prefiguring death). Alternatively, not fleeing entails a giving of oneself to the situation, a loss of the easy self and a recovery of the self which *is* the response to the givens of the moment. Such a gift not only rehearses death in a figurative sense (giving up not the spirit but the pretense), it ultimately foreshadows it in the fullest sense. For, willing to give up pretense, one is also willing to die. Thus when "hazard" is upon us our views of ourselves are put to the test.

Although the poem exudes a rather definite mood, the lines here do not explicitly describe the *master* in the throes of death. Rather, the quill, which was first introduced on double page VII, *falls*. Visually, the image becomes increasingly unstable. Earlier the feather is described as "solitary and bewildered, except that a cap of midnight meets it or grazes it and immobilizes (in velvet crumpled by a somber guffaw) this rigid whiteness." Now it falls "to bury itself in the original foams." But even earlier the eidetic image suggested itself. As a writing instrument, the quill marks the possibility of a decided response. Now it evidently functions to suspend, in rhythm, the calamity. Language manifests and preserves human response, and the craft of writing especially preserves the delicate balances of response when human construction hovers over the Abyss—when

158

configuration is about to converge. Eidetically, the master's power of preservation falls. This power being finite, it must fall back into the raging elements of the Abyss itself. To this origin human response must return. From the standpoint of such an origin Spirit is delirious (off the track: the French reads "*son délire*"—his *or* its delirium). While the word normally connotes a failure to respond, here it denotes the character of the ultimate response: having reached his peak of full-bodied response, a man essentially runs "off track" and will inevitably be withered by the gulf below. The gulf, itself neutral (neither devil nor god, neither evil nor good) recurrently makes the same claim upon Spirit.

If we think the drama has ended, we are surprised to see that the poem continues: "NOTHING of the memorable crisis... WILL HAVE TAKEN PLACE BUT THE PLACE." The future pluperfect tense makes us abide with the present moment. Nothing will have taken place as a result of the response. Neither the voyage nor the construction are preserved. And the master does not "make a point." Nothing whatsoever is *accomplished*. Yet now, in the realization of death, one foresees what has hitherto been overlooked: the place. *This* "will have had place" (*aura eu lieu*). One views the place *futurally* as having *been*. What does this mean?

As a crisis, the event is memorable. We usually remember a "time" because we learned something, stored something away from it. However, nothing has been accomplished. If the crisis is memorable, the event might still have accomplished itself with precisely the nullification of every human result. The *human* side comes to nothing. But in the nothingness of death the place asserts itself. Now comes to the fore precisely the *other* side essential to the nothingness of death.

A contrast juts into view: "an ordinary height dispenses absence." The moment of mortality bespoken in the poem dispenses a *place*. Ordinary human experience and its indifferent death dispenses the opposite, *absence*. The master stands at the parting of the ways where one can either hope for a solution delivering one from the plight (Number as solution) or be delivered from the *sheer* nothingness of death (absence) by acknowledging the situation as demanding absolute self-giving (solution as Spirit). Being at no ordinary height, the master is willing to stand at the parting, to hold a cast of dice in outstretched fist. Consequently, the nothingness of death reveals its correlate: the pending plenitude of the place as it has been.

One telling perception marks the moment of this insight. Looking down, one sees "indifferent lapping" of water. The elements may have tamed themselves, but the water at least remains strictly for itself, indifferent to human results. The poem immediately raises this single perception to an ideational plane: "as though for dispersing the empty act." So the act, presumably the master's response, was empty after all! Empty because solution-as-Spirit is ultimately void of any presumed Number-as-solution.

At the parting of the ways the alternatives always remain. Thus the act which rises to the occasion carries within itself, as a mist to be recurrently dispersed, the Lie: the essential possibility of resuming the attitude of calculation and maneuver. Rising to the occasion *can* inaugurate illusion rather than insight. Thus the popular television heroes rise to contrived occasions *only* to secure some realm of calculation and maneuver, so unlike the Achaian heroes of Homer's *Iliad* who rise *to* the god-determined occasions and so *above* their ever-present interest in homecoming, and who die. The act of rising must be dispersed because it acknowledges its own emptiness for the sake of the fullness of the place. Undispersed it becomes a lie unto itself and, if allowed to stand, "might have founded perdition"—precisely as television heroes regularly debilitate millions of children in North America.

Still, we may ask, what and where *is* this "place" which will have had (or taken) place? The shipwreck? But, as a disaster for every "human result," this is precisely the "absence" dispensed by "an ordinary height." Or, the "indifferent lapping" below? Again, how can this be a place? Or, the "total account in formation" *above*? But constellations take place *over* the place; no matter how essential to the place, they are not identical with it.

Place manifests itself in the poem as a *happening*. While no accomplishment within it will occur, the place asserts itself *as* place. The self finds itself situated in this event, as do also the elements. Place in this verbal sense means place*ment*. Essentially evanescent, such placement is a moment made by a convergence, it is *not* an achievement registered within the configuration.

Two literary examples may cast light on the thought of place as placement.

Conrad's *Lord Jim* tells of a man who has led an indifferent life, one marked chiefly by flight (often the Number of prudence). Seeking refuge on a remote island, he achieves a happiness of sorts, and an honored position among the natives. Yet, by another error of judgement on his part, his best friend, son of the local chieftain, is killed by rogish men of his own race. Instead of fleeing (and he has every abstract reason and concrete ability to do so) he chooses to face Doramin, the father of his now dead friend. At the very end of the work, the narrator describes the event as Jim walks into the camp of the natives:

'He came! He came!' was running from lip to lip, making a murmur to which he moved. 'He hath taken it upon his own head,' a voice said aloud. He heard this and turned to the crowd. 'Yes. Upon my head.' A few people recoiled. Jim waited awhile before Doramin, and then said gently, 'I am come in sorrow.' He waited again. 'I am come ready and unarmed,' he repeated.

After describing Doramin slowly rising to shoot Jim point-blank in the chest, the narrator continues

... They say the white man sent right and left at all those faces a proud and unflinching glance. Then with his hand over his lips he fell forward, dead.

These lines suggest that in the end nothing much matters but the place, in Jim's case the placement of self, his own ability to face circumstances whatever they are.

Melville's *Moby Dick* tells of a man, Captain Ahab, who at all costs rises to master the elements which have harassed him, most centrally the white whale which had foiled him and robbed him of one leg. His defiant response proves to take not only his own life but all the crews', too, save one (aptly described by the last word of the novel as an orphan, one who has lost the context of his life). Apart from the brief epilogue, the book ends with a one-paragraph description of the final result of the desperate hunt, the fierce battle with the whale, and the sinking of the ship:

Now small fowls flew screaming over the yet-yawning gulf; a sullen white surf beat against its steep sides; then all collapsed, and the great shroud of the sea rolled on as it rolled five thousand years ago.

The sea now takes place as having always been there, since the beginning. From the standpoint of human aspiration, it is as

161

though we were addressed from the whirlwind, "Where were *you* when I laid the foundations of the earth?" (*Job*, 38:4). In any case, the sea has been there all along—when Ahab was ranting at the crew and when these were cutting up the blubber. Now, however, this placement is revealed. The tale has told essentially of this event. We may experience such an event when, after stooping with troubles in an artificially lit parlor and breathing its stale warmed-over air, we step out for a stroll alone and stand upright, discovering the simplicity of the earth's crust, the clarity of the sky, the refreshment of the cool evening breeze, all these as a background not of our own making, against which man-made and man-suffered troubles appear as naught and are renounced.

The last qualification on double-page X locates the *where* of the event: "in these latitudes of the vague into which every reality dissolves itself." Placement occurs where the realness of things vanishes! What can this mean?

Placement has long been understood in Western intellectual history as requiring of man both hope and patience. Thus the futural orientation so deeply ingrained in our civilization. Conrad's *Lord Jim* unfolds in anticipation of Jim finding his place. Melville's *Moby Dick* anticipates the sea and its leviathan. In contrast, Mallarmé's *Un Coup de dés* articulates placement from the strictly finite standpoint, and the futural orientation remains only as a vestige. If the master can assume his *own* place, if the sea can assert *its* place, and if this finding and this asserting are essentially momentary, then the master appears as one who can also *lose* his place, and the sea itself appears as about to dissolve back into the vague whence it arose. In the experience of placement human responsibility consists in accepting its correlate, *dis*placement.

With the statement of that "into which every reality dissolves itself" the drama climaxes. Visually, the image has been completed. But the poem continues. Double-page XI adds a whole new thought and extends the visual image to the heavens above.

We realize that "nothing will have taken place but the place." With one possible exception: "A CONSTELLATION" *might* take place. The episodic details of this last double page describe the conditions on which this exception might occur.

We look to a constellation to guide us on our voyages. However, we seldom *see* "face to face" the relevant constellation. When we *do* see it, it "takes place" for us. Is the constellation, then, a *new* one? It is certainly renewing, and in that sense a "newness" for us. Yet the poem states that the event has a pre-set direction: "towards what must be the Seven Stars," i.e., the constellation of the Little Bear. The "new" constellation, then, takes its bearings according to something very old, the *guiding* North Star, the one heavenly body relatively stable in location. Newly envisioned and newly functional, the constellation is also very old.

The first condition of this special event is that "one region fuses with a beyond," that the region of the shipwreck can have a relationship with what remains afterwards. Whereas the first ten double pages gather temporal dimensions into the making of a place, this last double page has a temporal mood in the more usual sense: it speaks of what might happen further along the line of time.

The second condition is that the fusion itself occurs "apart from any interest." If, in responding to the ultimate moment, the master should leave a new guide for posterity, he will do so because he faces his own moment and so abandons his interest in further moments. If, on the other hand, a shipmaster turns his attention toward the future, he fails to face his own moment and so leaves no guiding star for others.

The exigencies of human response are paradoxical. To be worthy of retention (fusion with a beyond), man must look away from the beyond. Most of all, *we* (who are "beyond" the master) need assurance that response to the moment—*our* moment—is indeed possible. A "guide" who ignores his own moment for the sake of ours sets a poor example. In fact, such "interest" on the part of a would-be master embodies the bane of human existence, the indifferent generality of non-convergent configuration, even though it receives the general spotlight: it is "signaled in general."

The fusion of one region with a beyond depends on the placement of self and things in that one region. In this event of selfhood/thinghood we must distinguish between distractive "interest" and the human response which directly, as Spirit, faces the moment. Yet the distinction is peculiar. For every guiding star, every great thought or deed, enters into the fund of "general interest," becomes a part of "culture," of that swarm of signals which are generally looked at rather than allowed to send us toward what they signal. We see the comedy of "culture" most easily in the mock-hero who declares "I shall ignore all the prudent advice of men and gods—just as Achilles did" or "I shall conceive of deeds never before realized by men—just as Napoleon did" or "I shall write unprecedented poetry—just as Mallarmé did."

That "general interest" and the "fusion" possibly resulting from placement mingle confusedly with one another in "culture"—this accounts for the double-duty of the line "according to such an obliquity, by such a declivity, of fire." These words connote the way seamen determine the latitude and longitude of a ship, the fire then being the sun. But "obliquity" carries the more colloquial sense of "deviation," being "out of the way," and "declivity" means literally the "slope" along which things fall. The fusion of the region with a beyond takes place (possibly) according to a deviation and by a place of falling. Similarly, the general interest, which must be overcome for the fusion to take place, is signalled according to this very same thing: both "fusion" and its antipode, the "general interest," refer to "fire" for their bearings. Thus placement occurs (and may possibly endure) only when we acknowledge the burning issue, yet the drifting (non-convergent) configuration likewise remains in the throes of the issue, since it takes its shape from the "left overs" of great thoughts. Elsewhere, Mallarmé calls this "the resurrection of infinite blindness in vertical plaster casts, with no sheltered fountain nor emergent greenery, but only the buts of bottles and awkward fragments" (*M*, 384; see *Emergence*, page 28).

Placement always "deviates" from the norm and inevitably "slides" down into a specious location. If the master of thought cannot accept both the deviation and the fall, if he cannot take the moment just as it is, then the place can "have" place but no "fusion with a beyond."

As already remarked, new as the looming CONSTELLA-TION may be, the fusion directs itself toward the ancient guide of sailors, the North Star of the Little Bear. In one sense, then, there is not, never has been, and never will be but *one* guiding star for the human condition: placement of self and things. A given region will most surely *not* fuse with a beyond if the human response claims that its significance lies in presenting a new guiding star. Death recalls the *one* that is, was and will be—without at all distracting from the here-and-now exigencies of the voyage for which each man is irreplaceably the one ship-master who himself must guide the ship.

164

The block of verses describing A CONSTELLATION under-scores the paradox. Although appearing in the mode of a pos-sibility governed by conditions rarely fulfilled, the constellation is already "cold from oblivion and disuse." In fact, it has been overhead for so long that one first of all realizes the oblivion in which it has fallen and the human failure to use it. Visually, the heavenly fire giving direction both to "fusion" and to "general interest" does not become cold simply because we ignore it. Eidetically, however, the burning issue of placement does in-deed become cold. The ultimate realization of death can stoke the fire, whereupon placement occurs in any event, and some-thing of this event may remain for future moments.

Again, however, ordinary unconverted and unconverging configurations do not escape unscathed the CONSTELLA-TION which has become "cold from oblivion and disuse." This stellar formation never becomes *so* cold that it does not continue to "enumerate on some surface, vacant and high, the successive shock, starwise, of a total account in formation." *In any case* the guiding issue repeatedly delivers a shock, *the* shock to our oblivion. What unsettles, if only distantly from the stars, is a "total account in formation": the incessant suggestion that things *do* in fact add up, even if we are not yet "with it." Myriad angels and devils whisper this shocking news in our ears. An "addition" is not yet a convergence, but perhaps we first awaken to the possibility of a convergence when reminded of the possibility that hitherto unknown configurations loom over-head—as when professors tantalize their students with fanciful cosmologies and shock them with dialectical arguments.

The final string of verbal forms—"watching, doubting, rolling, shining and meditating before stopping at some final point which consecrates it"—is ambiguous as to subject. "Watching" can be either a human act or an attitude of the stars overhead; "doubting" is strictly a human act; "rolling" de-scribes either the ship or the dice; "shining" recalls the stars overhead; "meditating" suggests a human possibility; and "stopping at some final point" must refer either to the dice or to the ship. In any case, these descriptions, and also the typo-graphy, create a mood of final precipitation resolving a tremen-dous tension. As in the story of *Lord Jim*, one breathes easy as the calamity at last takes place.

The "final point" at which all things come to a halt conse-crates, makes sacred. What? Grammatically, the "it" can refer back to the *shock* of a total account in formation, or simply to the *account*; conceivably, it may refer forward to the *throw* of dice. Or "it" may stand for the whole experience of the master above the Abyss.

In any case, there *is* a watching, a doubting, a rolling, a shining and a meditating, and there *is* a stopping at "some final point," namely death. Mortality marks the parting of the ways, and death not only tests our solution-as-Spirit but terminates our effort to discover a Number-as-solution by destroying our constructions. This marking, testing, terminating, and destroying can still lead to a fulfilment. Not to "better times," since the promise of such "times" secretly insinuates postponement and procrastination, and so Number-as-solution. The sacred allows of no postponement, no procrastination. Fulfilment first of all revises such specious "times" in a realization of the true past and the true future consummating a plenitude of presence: placement. But fulfilment also opens us to the guiding-star of life, the constellation over the head of every human being.

If "every thought emits a throw of dice," thought is rare. Genuine thinking occurs *only* over the Abyss, *only* when we are already "beyond calculations of old where maneuver is with age forgotten." *Then* thought means primordially a giving of oneself to the situation—we do not "give up" but accept the convergence of the configuration in its full temporal plenitude. Thought qualifies as such only in the overcoming of specious modes of experience, specifically the specious past, the specious future, and the dimensionless "present" caught between the two.

But if the throw of dice never abolishes chance, then thought which casts itself into the situation cannot, by that act, undo the danger. The act precisely accepts the moment for what it is, namely as gathering past and future back upon the fullness of the moment over the Abyss. The momentousness of this moment cannot but elicit awesome hesitation on the part of any genuine master. It therefore unfolds as a drama. The dramatic act-which-receives rehearses death— and fulfills life.

7. A CONCLUDING THOUGHT

In differing ways, Mallarmé's three poems tell about human mortality. They "interpret" death as marking the human condition with the exigency of finite transcendence. Thus we can turn to these works for a poetic or an eidetic presentation of death.

But if we could simply read these poems in order to discover the idea of human mortality, they would be mere couriers of opinion—and rather poor ones at that. Moreover, reading the poems as simply "about" death, we would assume that poetic language is a directly accessible medium through which a "subject" can present itself. No interpretation of the language of literature could be farther from the truth. Non-poetic speaking and writing may indeed "come easy" to most of us, but precisely because here our language has become an indifferent medium relating arbitrarily to "subjects" already familiar to, and therefore not *thought* by us. In short, ordinary language re-presents and re-assures. In contrast, reading and hearing truly original (origin-bespeaking) language deprives us of our own comforting opinions and bids us to view matters as they themselves dictate. Poetic literature opens a world to us, but only if we enter the opening and so depart from our usual locale. This experience has its painful moments.

But, furthermore, can we genuinely partake of great literature without realizing our own mortality? Must not our mortal nature be unveiled *prior* to entry? How could we ever participate in the articulation of Mallarmé's poems unless we admit that we are mortal? Does not a refusal to acknowledge mortality bar us right at the entry? If so, then the "subject" "inside" the poems cannot first present us with mortality. Rather, our own mortality may possibly present the work to us.

Mallarmé's poems articulate the human condition with a view to the one development conditioning not only the fulfilment of human life but also the full appreciation of, and this means genuine participation in, literary work. In short, his work is reflective as well as poetic.

Unwilling to die we will not allow the configuration (in which we move, live, and have our initial being) to converge. For convergence undoes the direction of movement, the human pretentions, and the self-interpretations formative of the configuration—it undoes them in order to funnel them into the

167

moment. Furthermore, to read a literary work we must affirm the convergence. For the power of the work lies in the readiness for convergence, whether consummated (as in Mallarmé's poems) or retained as readiness (as in Rimbaud's poems). Thus an unwillingness to die entails an inability to read and, conversely, the ability to read indicates a willingness to die.

A quatraine of Mallarmé's, dating from 1894 and designed as an inscription for a library in a private home (*M*, 162), states the human position in the face of literary works:

> Ci-gît le noble vol humain
> Cendre ployée avec les livres
> Pour que toute tu la délivres
> Il faut en prendre un dans ta main

> Here lies the noble human flight
> Ash folded with these books
> In order that you deliver it all
> You must take one (book) in your hand.

From the noble human flight only the ash remains in the multiple books composing a library. As these are lined along the shelves, the flight, which makes them what they are, lies dead. —These first two verses read clearly as an epitaph on a gravestone. Yet the ash can be "delivered" if only I take a book in my hand. It sounds so simple. Yet these last two verses obviously state only the necessary, not the sufficient condition of the "deliverance." The first two verses, while singing the flight of Spirit as it has become ash, elucidate our *task* once we take a book in the hand: one must deliver not the dead, but the ash of the dead, and not different ashes for different books, but the same ash for any genuine book: the ash of the noble human flight. In contrast, the dead worry about the dead, and they do so not in order to deliver, but rather to bury.

CHAPTER THREE

BUTOR AND THE AMERICAN HERITAGE

1. THE QUESTION

A heritage encompasses the whole in which we live and think. Thus it is not genuinely available for inspection. Rather, it invites participation. Let us therefore contemplate the function of a heritage which is now encapsulated, in some sense completed, and thus set off at a distance for an "inspection" of sorts.

We may imagine an Athenian of the 5th century, B.C., listening to a rhapsode singing the *Odyssey*. He hears the honored and aged Nestor, king of Pylos, telling Odysseus' son Telemachos about the return of the Argives after the sack of Troy. Nestor recounts several details surrounding the homeward journey, and then remarks (Book III, verses 276-9):

> Now we sailed on our way from Troy together,
> Atreus' son (Menelaus) and I, friends with one another.
> But when we came to holy Sounion, the cape of Athens,
> There Phoibos Apollo (attacked) the helmsman of Menelaus.

Today, "holy Sounion," "Phoibos Apollo," and "Menelaus, son of Atreus" all enter into our field of vision as products of our imagination, and preoccupation with them distracts us from our own world. But our Athenian knows Sounion as a place, like Argos, Pylos, and Troy. For him, Apollo was in fact the cause of the turn of events delaying the homecoming, while Menelaus and Nestor represent himself, the listener, inasmuch as they respond effectively to the god-given turns of events but without claiming themselves to be the causes of the occurrences.

Athens, Argos, Pylos, and even Troy are *places* for our Athenian. Thus the rhapsode voices where the listener himself lives: in a network of close and distant, disparate, yet variously related city-states. If imagination aids his understanding of this network, he still perceives these places as preceding his own images. Ultimately, the rhapsode's song and his own train of thought bear upon the very world in which he lives.

Yet the rhapsode evokes *times* which are distinctively not those of the present. For our Athenian, the tale tells of an era when some men were of greater stature and nobler mind than those of his own time: men strong enough to face whatever the

169

gods dealt out to them (*moira*) and to assume responsibility for a position they themselves did not make. For us, the temporal distance between the era told and the era of the telling most likely calls into question the accuracy of the tale. However, to the Athenian the gap of three to six hundred years does not diminish the credibility of the account; rather, it guarantees the worth of the place where he lives and the legitimacy of the recommended manner of human response to the course of affairs.

Recitations from the *Iliad* and the *Odyssey* tell of events in time. In fact, our Athenian understands them as history. Yet their most important function we most likely miss. These songs distill *place* out of *time*: they teach geography in the name of chronology.

The event of heritage consists of telling of the way things *were* which imbues a people with a sense of where they *are*. The "telling" here alternates between its two most prominent meanings. Most obviously, stories speak of events. Yet from this telling we should be able to determine where we are. Reading the *Iliad* and the *Odyssey* today, we often proceed as anthropologists, philologists, or entertainment seekers, and we do not participate in the event.

Turning now to the contemporary American heritage, we may note some functional analogs to the Greek epics.

Viewing detective serials on television, we experience places such as New York, San Francisco, and Honolulu: these cities then become part of our world. Yet generally these serials do not carry much sense of history, except insofar as they incarnate the singular idea of "good conquering evil" (on a human, yet wholesale plane), a distinctively Western if not American view. Similarly, the situation comedies generally locate us in a place without much of a temporal dimension. Unlike those of Aristophanes, most modern television comedies situate the drama mainly in the human psyche, and the polis of the given psyche is intentionally irrelevant—so that anybody, anywhere in the world, can "understand" them.

The "westerns" do in fact suggest the historical dimension of contemporary life. In telling how the American frontier was opened, these films have contributed remarkably to the formation of whatever heritage we have. Yet they fail to complete the formation. They represent and recommend a manner of human response which alienates us from *where* we are, from our actual location. And the alienation functions at various levels. Most obviously, we no longer live in genuinely rural communities or ride horseback to town. Unlike the Greek of the 5th century listening to tales already hundreds of years old, we can hardly identify with the life-style even of our grandfathers, let alone of our distant forebears. Secondly, the portrayals of the West are naive; and more recent filmmakers have created anti-westerns eliminating any doubts we may have entertained in this regard. Finally, and at the deepest level, we can see in the distinctly American version of "good conquering evil" a force working directly against the formation of heritage. This last, the interpretation of evil, provides the key, if not the solution, to the problem.

The Greek absorbed in the *Iliad* and the *Odyssey* calls "evil" anything violating the present course of affairs. Thus the concept makes sense only from the inside of a given endeavor. For a warrior here and now on the battlefield before Troy, the man opposite could be honorable, yet he is called evil, for he obstructs the sack of Troy. Thus one calls even an "impersonal" force, e.g., a wind, evil if it blows one's ship off course. Contrariwise, anything which aids one, helps one to face the violence of circumstance, is named good.

Our tradition, however, namely the heritage immediately in evidence for us, stipulates that we judge only that evil which violates a principle. The man committing a deed, vile in our eyes, essentially fails to fit in with an impersonal ideal, and only incidentally violates our own interests. The television detective films have distilled this moralism into its pure essence, for their problematic inevitably gravitates around the question whether the evil man is responsible or not for his deviation from the ideal. Here and in the psychological comedies, we see the true heirs of "frontier life."

The difference between the ancient and the modern meanings of "evil" is common philology, and its application to the founding of America has become a cliché. Many first settlers and subsequent Founding Fathers were convinced that God had sent them to this wild country not only to establish a new order in obedience to Christian principles, but also to stamp out the heathen who had infested this otherwise virgin corner of divine creation. Despite its many variations during its brief existence, the American mind has never lost its unique spirit of negativity. To be eradicated, or at least subdued, were first the Indians, then the bears, then the timber, then the newly released Blacks in the South, then the Yellows in the West, then the wayward segment of the Whites, and finally the land itself. Although some historians like to see within these modes of opposition the spirit of adventure, an acceptance of a challenge (even if sometimes perversely construed), and so in the Westward Ho! a new Odyssey, one peculiarity does appear: the foe in each case violates not the man directly (be he adventurer, pioneer, or social reformer), but a principle, and the modern "hero" emerges as the earthly and transient defender of a heavenly and eternal ideal.

Recalling that a heritage functions to make a *place*, a home where we can dwell and respond in stipulated ways to the things arising new each day,—recalling this we can begin to understand why the American heritage functions only half-heartedly. For it states that what lies directly before us violates a principle which we must defend first of all by negating the actual for the sake of the ideal. Unfortunately no place, no abode, no home can crystallize out of such negation.

For a glimpse of the affirmative powers of heritage, let us return to the Greek epics. The themes of homecoming (*nostos*), earth (*gaia*), and death (*thanatos*) saturate the atmosphere and the events of the *Iliad* and the *Odyssey*. Together, they intertwine to interpret evil in a way allowing heritage to function. And, so far at least, they are all three unwelcome in the American heritage.

The *Odyssey* actually tells, diachronically, of a homecoming. In doing so it illuminates the background motivation for human action described in the *Iliad*. In this latter, homecoming dominates synchronically: nobody goes home because the poet unlayers only one event, ever so gradually. Achilles' decision not to fight pinpoints the single many-layered event. Unraveling the causes and consequences of this decision, the *Iliad* takes us into the encounters on the battlefield before Troy. Here the whole Trojan war unmasks itself as an engagement devised for very abstract purposes and depriving all concerned of what they really desire. At the beginning of the account, nearly all the Achaians, heroes and henchmen alike, fervently wish to cease fighting after ten years of fruitless siege. Only the goddess Athene can bewitch them back into the battle (*polemos*) and away from going home (*neesthai*). Two lines (Book II, 453-4) describe the completion of this trick:

172

> And now battle became sweeter to them than returning home
> In their hollow ships to the beloved land of their fathers.

Doing battle is a *means* of being, while each man *is* in reference to the homecoming. Thus the touching phrase recorded upon the retrieval of dead Patroklos (XVIII, 238). What *is* he now? Answer: "one who never again came home to be welcomed." And thus also the sense of sacrifice, the religious renunciation developing in Achilles when he notes the possibilities (IX, 411-15):

> If I remain here and wage war before the city of Troy,
> Then my homecoming is lost, but my glory will be
> imperishable;
> If I head homeward to the beloved land of my fathers,
> Gone is my glory, but long my lifetime.

It is the death of Patroklos which, much later, makes him prefer the first course, while he in general chooses the second and recommends others to do the same.

Heritage distills geography out of chronology. Yet it functions genuinely only when the geography itself becomes transparent to the place where we live: our home. The Greek listening to a recitation of the epics hears not only of the details about the region of his life, but also of the desires of the personages to renounce their alienating activities and return to their homes, each to his own in the vast network of city-states. How do the recitations familiar in the *American* heritage bid us to return home? Before answering this question we must think further into the nature of homecoming.

The heroes and henchmen of the *Iliad* hearken to an origin named "the land of our fathers." This land (*gaia*) is, more properly translated, the *earth*. While a human construction called a house or a home (*oikos*) might locate, spatially, the goal of homecoming, the *meaning* of this location lies in the role of the earth in human life. For the Greeks of the Homeric age the earth is still the source of life: of food, of birth, of a place to stand and to endure. Earlier yet, in Minoan times, it was Mother Earth, and human response adequated itself to this origin in total submission, as a child to its mother. In Homer, on the other hand, human response takes on the meaning of construction. In this era life is construed as requiring one to do battle, and the virtues of a warrior (*heron*) define the adequation of human response to circumstances. Yet from this battle one still

173

turns in order to go homewards (*oikade* or *oikonde*). And the earth, not the house, names the origin.

Furthermore, only that point of origin can be one's own which was "of one's fathers." Ultimately, the origin becomes one's own not by ruthless force or by arbitrary agreement, but by genealogy. Thus "the land of our fathers" is the earth for our forebears and, as such, the source of our being.

Perhaps we can come close to understanding how heritage can relate us to the earth if we consider the full implications of "raising children." We train them to stand up and so to enter into the world of human construction. However, raised *into* our world, they are also raised *out of* the earth. The earth, besides continuing as the place where we stand and the materials of our constructions, also remains the source of our vitality: as our very first mother to whom we inevitably return. And if we remember that we ourselves were raised out of the earth by our immediate parents, and they in turn by theirs, then the phrase "the land (earth) of our fathers" begins to take on one concrete meaning of heritage. For the phrase unites the superhuman and the human origin to which Odysseus and the warriors on the battlefield of Troy long to return.

Yet our Athenian listening to his rhapsode hears that the return to the earth, far from being merely a desirable event, is the inexorable destiny of each and every man, whether he accepts it or not. For each man is mortal: *a* mortal. And Homer, i.e., the Greek heritage sung by the rhapsode, emphasizes clearly what this mortality means. Just as each is supported by the "life-giving (*physizoon*) earth" (cf. *Iliad*, III, 243: *Odyssey*, XI, 301), so giving up one's life means precisely returning to the earth. The earth "pushed" us out (*faire pousser*, in French) and therefore when we no longer "grow" we collapse back into this origin. The two men Diomedes slays (*Iliad*, VI, 19) "enter into the earth." Hektor says of his brother Paris (VI, 282), "would that the earth opened beneath him." Menelaos reproaches his peers for their cowardice (VII,99): "may you become water and earth." Apollo complains (XXIV, 54) that Achilles, in abusing dead Hektor, "dishonors the dumb earth (= corpse) in his fury." Perhaps the double, reciprocal meaning of the origin speaks especially loud in the story of Althaia who pounds on the earth, calling to Hades and Persephone, the guardians of the unseen and also of the powers of growth within the earth, to give death to her own son: here earth is given the epithet *polyphorbos*,

174

"who gives nourishment to many"—but takes all in death (see IX, 568).

Thus, besides instructing our Athenian in geography, the rhapsode tells him where he belongs and how he should understand the passage from where he in fact is to where he ultimately must go. The experience of listening, later of reading, rehearses the human sojourn inasmuch as this sojourn can and does become transparent to its own origin.

We today must ask: Can we "have" a heritage which simply forms our "way of life" but does not return us to our origins? Can heritage realize itself, can it function as a salutary power, without distilling a place and returning us to it?

The question may sound rhetorical. Yet we today busily contribute to making a non-heritage. For a "way of life" is in fact developing which emphatically *forms* us and yet fails to refer us to an origin while actually *denying* that we need any such reference. Failure is nothing new, but institutional denial of the need is indeed new. Soon this way of life without any origins may be our heritage.

For instance, when a series of advertisements displaying the readily available quick-foods, insurance policies, and automobiles interrupts a television "talk show," situation comedy, or detective story, we experience no real discontinuity. The two kinds of recitations differ in explicit purpose but agree in essential purport. In both cases the goals and norms of life are firmly and unquestionably established. Both recitations claim that man has no origin but only desires. All ages have had, and even exhibited for posterity, an abundance of "suckers," but only our age actually structures and encourages a formation of life with express lack of any in-built signal for or path toward origins. The governing institutions as a whole present this formation to the public. Each generation as a whole inherits it as a non-heritage.

Based on desires or imaginary needs, the consumer society of today can hardly refer us to origins. It must deny them, and thus it essentially and forcefully disrelates our involvement with the very earth on which we stand: How can we, the consumers, revere "goods" as gifts of the earth? These "goods" are incidental by-products of an economic system structured and encouraged by industrialists who chiefly seek profits and politicians who set their sights on full employment. Finally, rootlessness manifests itself perhaps most strikingly in the modern American insistence that death is but a disappearance, a simple vanishment, rather than a return. If we do not respond to things as gifts, how can we acknowledge the inevitability of their absolute withdrawal from our ken? We must pretend that death comes by mistake.

How, then, can our heritage, which tends to evolve into a non-heritage, be re-formed to set a standard or a "tone" *directing* us toward the earth and stamping our movement with *finality*?

Rimbaud's poems, particularly those we considered in Chapter One, articulate the historically evolved *place* where we live, i.e., the modern directionality in reference to the earth. Mallarmé's poems then articulate the *ultimacy* of the human condition in a mode appropriate to modern times. Although the works of these two poets speak *out* of the modern problematic of heritage, they do not address themselves *to* it.

The question is: How can the chronology of our traditions distill a geography? How can there arise from the account of the *way* things have been a sense of *where* we are? The consideration of Greek heritage not only suggests the strange fragility of our own place in regard to homecoming, earth, and death. It also leaves us with a clue for understanding the tone of the account we must give of our traditions. It indicates obliquely that whatever appears as an obstacle must reappear in the account as a possible ground on which we can stand. Yet the question itself can only receive an answer if we raise it in the face of an actual effort to articulate the American heritage. Without this reference, without a grounding in an example, the question becomes "academic" and the answer floats as an opinion. If the answer is to keep in touch with its subject and not stand as one more testimony to its absence, then we have no choice but to begin with an articulation of the very thing, the American heritage, which we hope to understand.

There have been many noteworthy efforts to articulate the American heritage in the fullest sense of homecoming, of earth, and of death. Faulkner's novels and Whitman's poems certainly count among the most powerful. There have also been interesting commentaries, e.g., Tocqueville's *Democracy in America*, Part II. Furthermore, instructive histories, e.g., John Anderson's *The Individual and the New World* or Dee Brown's *Bury My Heart at Wounded Knee*, have focussed on the subject. Last but most numerous are the inspired harangues which, although very often accurate and informative, alienate us from our heritage by their very nature.

Since the heritage with which we endeavor to keep in touch must be unified and whole, we choose only one work for critique. The critical effort would itself bear witness to the wisdom of the choice.

2. *MOBILE*: THE STYLE OF ADDRESS

Michel Butor's account of the American heritage presents its materials in the mode of fragility. In various interrelated ways, *Mobile* brings the elements of our heritage into articulation, yet their coherence and ultimate purport remain tentative. However, since fragility precisely characterizes whatever American heritage asserts itself, the book, by displaying the material in this mode, very aptly addresses itself to the question—a question haunting not only the American spirit but also the spirits of all nations drawn, willingly or unwillingly, into its orbit: Can the configuration converge? Are homecoming, earth, and death somehow possible within these historically evolved structures of life and way of thinking?

Mobile's sub-title reads: "Study for a representation of the United States." The book assembles and arranges alphabetically, under the names of each of the fifty States, a wide variety of materials, starting with Alabama and ending with Wyoming. We may consider as an example "North Carolina," the first State escorted into view with "Welcome to..." (*F*, 16-19; *E*, 16-19; see following pages and "Prefatory Note"). For now it is daylight, and our vision in unimpaired. Although the States appear in alphabetical order, each also comes into view at a different, unique hour within a two-day span. Those appearing at night are not heralded by the familiar sign posted in airports and on roadways.

To *what* are we welcomed in "North Carolina"? What passes here under review? A restaurant, the elements experienced at the sea shore, snippets about the Indians, and a man; —then suddenly we pass out of the State, first into bordering Georgia with *its* seas, *its* Indian history, a woman; —then into a neighboring State, Florida, with *its* sea, *its* Indians, and more people. Besides bordering on one another, these States share a common town name, Concord, a name which the American mind associates with Massachussets and the "shot that was heard around the

177

BIENVENUE EN CAROLINE DU NORD

il fait déjà jour depuis longtemps à
CONCORD, temps oriental, où vous pourrez demander, dans le restaurant
Howard Johnson, s'ils ont de la glace à l'abricot.

La mer,
          les vagues,
le sel,
          le sable,
l'écume,
          les algues

Les Indiens Cherokees invitèrent les missionnaires à venir s'installer parmi eux et à ouvir des écoles pour leur enseigner leurs secrets; mais ceux-ci, jugeant que la langue des Indiens ne pouvait pas s'écrire, et ne modifiant nullement les méthodes qu'ils avaient apportées d'Angleterre, n'obtenaient que peu de résultats...

Noir.

Le marais d'Angola, «Hello, Al!» — Passée la frontière du Sud-Ouest,

CONCORD, GEORGIE, côte atlantique (for whites only)
(dans les États du Sud, une partie des autocars
ou des tramways est interdite aux gens de couleur).

La mer,

178

                    la marée,

la houle,
                    la brise,

les îles,
                    les lagunes.

Houx noirs,
                    lauriers-roses,
                                    myrtes dahoon.

Les tumulus d'Ocmulgee révèlent les traces de six civilisations successives, la plus ancienne pouvant remonter jusqu'à 8000 avant Jésus-Christ, la plus récente mourant au XVIIIᵉ siècle...

Noire.

«Hello, Mrs. Greenwood!»—L'immense marais d'Okefenokee, —en continuant vers le sud,

           CONCORD, FLORIDE (... whites only),—la
                    réserve des Indiens Séminoles.

Tornades,
paquets d'eau,
toits arrachés.

          Geais de Floride,
     cailles colombes de Key West,
gobe-mouches à queue fourchue,
     coucous de Maynard,
          oiseaux royaux gris.

          La mer,
                    conques de combat,
          coquilles ailes de faucon,
                    arches pesantes,
          coquilles ailes de dindon,
                    conques à la reine.

               Bananiers,
       orangers de Valence,
orangers de Jaffa,
               feuilles de cuivre,
       plantes chenilles,
               agaves.

                    Les premiers explorateurs découvrirent au sud de
                    la Floride de nombreuses tribus indiennes. Les
                    Calusas par exemple, plus de trois mille en 1650,
                    chassaient, pêchaient, ramassaient des coquil-
                    lages. Excellents marins, ils voyageaient au moins
                    jusqu'à Cuba. En 1800, sous la domination espag-
                    nole revenue après un court entracte anglais, ils
                    n'étaient plus que quelques centaines. En 1835,
                    sous le joug des États-Unis, les derniers survivants
                    furent déportés dans l'Oklahoma, alors appelé
                    territoire indien, avec la majorité des Séminoles.
                    Quelques-uns s'enfuirent à Cuba.

                    Noirs.

               Le gigantesque marais des Everglades.
GREENVILLE, sur la rivière du Goudron, chef-lieu de Pike, CAROLINE
     DU NORD (... only),— ... des Indiens Cherokees.

La mer,
               coquilles à grelots,
tellines lever du jour,
               Vénus rayon de soleil,
chitons,
               coquilles Saint-Jacques calicot.
Noires.

Un Indien Cherokee nommé Sequoyah, se méfiant de l'enseignement des
missionnaires, s'abstint d'aller à leurs écoles, mais étudia leurs livres avec grand
soin et décida d'inventer un système d'écriture. Grande méfiance dans les
missions et chez les autres Cherokees. Nouvelle sorcellerie puissante qu'il vaut
mieux étouffer dans l'oeuf...

Sur la route, une Oldsmobile grise, très endommagée, qui dépasse largement les soixante miles autorisées, «il faudra prendre de l'essence au prochain Caltex»,—les marais des Houx et Sinistre.

GREENVILLE.

GREENVILLE.

CLINTON, chef-lieu de Sampson.

Des noirs.

La mer,
        coques atlantiques,
coques papillons,
        dents saignantes,
coquilles tulipes,
        homard épineux.

Les Indiens Cherokees encouragés par les missionnaires brûlèrent la maison de Sequoyah et les papiers qui s'y trouvaient...

Flying Service,—les marais Vert, du lac Waccamaw, de la forêt nationale de Croatan,—passées les montagnes Fumeuses,

        CLINTON, sur la rivière du Rivet, qui se jette dans le Ten-
                nessee, affluent du père des fleuves, TEN-
NESSEE, le Sud (... only). En continuant vers l'ouest,

                CLINTON, ARKANSAS (... only).—Vers
                l'ouest,

                        CLINTON, sur la rivière Wachita
                          qui se jette dans la
                        rivière Rouge, frontière du Texas,
                        affluent du père des fleuves,
                        OKLAHOMA, middle-west
                        (... only),— ... des Indiens
                        Osages.

WELCOME TO NORTH CAROLINA

it has already been daylight for a long time in
CONCORD, Eastern Time, where you can order apricot ice cream in
the Howard Johnson Restaurant.

The sea,
            the waves,
the salt,
            the sand,
the foam,
            the seaweed.

*The Cherokee Indians invited the missionaries to settle among them and to open
schools in order to teach them their secrets; but the missionaries, supposing that
the Indian language could not be written and refusing to modify the methods
they had brought from England, obtained negligible results...*

Negro man.

Angola Swamp, "Hello, Al!"—Across the southwest state line,
            CONCORD, GEORGIA, Atlantic Coast (for whites only)
                        (in the Southern states, a section of the street-
            cars and buses may not be occupied by colored people).

The sea,
            the tide,
the swell,

182

the breeze,
the islands,
the lagoons.
Inkberry,
rose laurel,
dahoon holly.

The Ocmulgee mounds reveal traces of six successive civili-
zations, the oldest dating back to about 8000 B.C., *the most recent*
dying out in the eighteenth century...

Negro woman.

"Hello, Mrs. Greenwood!"—The enormous Okefenokee
Swamp,—continuing south,

CONCORD, FLORIDA (... whites only),—
Reservation for Seminole Indians.

Tornadoes,
tidal waves,
roofs torn off.

Florida jays,
Key West quail doves,
fork-tailed flycatchers,
Maynard's cuckoos
gray kingbirds.

The sea,
fighting conchs,
hawk-wing conchs,
incongruous arks,
turkey wing shells,
queen conchs.
banana palms,
Valencia oranges,
Jaffa oranges,
bronze-leaves,
caterpillar plants,
aloes.

The first explorers discovered numerous Indian tribes in southern Florida. The Calusas, for instance, numbering over three thousand in 1650, hunted, fished, gathered shellfish. Excellent sailors, they traveled at least as far as Cuba. In 1800, under the Spanish domination restored after a brief English interlude, they numbered only several hundred. In 1835, under United States rule, the last survivors were deported to Oklahoma, then known as Indian Territory, with the majority of the Seminoles. Some fled to Cuba.

Negroes.

The gigantic Everglades.

GREENVILLE, on the Tar River, county seat of Pike County, NORTH CAROLINA (... only),—...for Cherokee Indians.

The sea,
        jingle shells,
sunrise tellins,
        sunbeam Venus clams,
chitons,
        calico scallops.
Black women.

A Cherokee Indian named Sequoyah, mistrusting the teachings of the missionaries, refused to attend their schools, but studied their books closely and decided to invent a system of writing. Great opposition in the missions and among the other Cherokees. A new, powerful witchcraft, which it was wiser to nip in the bud...

On the highway, a battered gray Oldsmobile going much faster than the 60-mile speed limit, "have to get gas at the next Caltex,"—Dismal Swamp and Holly Shelter Swamp.

GREENVILLE.

GREENVILLE.

184

CLINTON, county seat of Sampson County.

Negro men.

The sea,

        Atlantic clams,
butterfly clams,
        bleeding teeth,
tulip shells,
        spiny lobsters.

Encouraged by the missionaries, the Cherokee Indians burned Sequoyah's house
and the papers that were inside. ...

Flying Service,—Green Swamp, Lake Waccamaw, Croatan National Forest,
—across the Great Smoky Mountains,

        CLINTON, on the Clinch River that flows into the Tennessee,
                  a tributary of the Father of Waters, TEN-
        NESSEE, the South (... only). Continuing west,

             CLINTON, ARKANSAS (... only).—west,

                  CLINTON, on the Washita River
                        that flows into the
                  Red River, forming the Texas state
                  line, a tributary of the Father of
                  Waters, OKLAHOMA, the
                  Middle West (... only),—...
                  Osage Indians.

world." But then we return to North Carolina where we once again witness a parade of the sea, of women, of Indians, and this time a car. Finally, the town of Clinton occasions brief associations with the "Clintons" in Tennessee, Arkansas, and Oklahoma.

Who speaks to us in "North Carolina"? From whom do we hear the story? A distinct narrator, one rising above and therefore presuming heritage, is conspicuously missing in *Mobile*. However, we can detect at least three *voices*. The first informs us that one may hope for apricot ice cream at the Howard Johnson Restaurant. This voice of commerce-for-the-people pervades *Mobile*, assuming a wide variety of forms expressing all the multiplicity of consumable goods. The second voice, that of local history, issues from a past which *antedates* the "American Europeans," as we ourselves are called later in the book (e.g., *F*, 131; *E*, 125). The third is the voice of the present-day Americans themselves as we indeed hear them: "have to get gas at the next Caltex" (the choice stemming, we may surmise, from the credit card one happens to possess) and "Hello, Mrs. Greenwood!" Still other voices are already faintly audible: the recurrent "(for whites only)" and the customary commentary on this sign.

Without directly answering the questions—What passes under review? and Who speaks to us?—we may already note that the reality of the "what," thinghood, and the "who," selfhood, will eventually present itself through the attitude evoked and articulated in the account. Attitude, the "middle term," stands in convertible relationship with the things and the people of any historical epoch. The attitude of things, i.e., the way they lean toward us, depends on the human bearing toward them, the way we "take" them. Yet the attitude of the people, i.e., the way they incline toward their environment, also stems from how things make demands upon human response: we are *born* in "North Carolina," and we grow up in response to the givens and voices of the land. In Butor's work this "middle term," the dominant attitude itself, comes to the fore and receives a statement.

The attitude of the things and the people of an historical epoch structures without, however, realizing a heritage. It configures the appearance of things and the formation of our thoughts without guaranteeing a convergence. No matter what the attitude, thinghood and selfhood are still outstanding. *Mobile* articulates the configuration on the brink of convergence. Thus we must ask first *how* the work gathers the materials of a configuration to create this sense of imminent convergence. In the process we may implicitly assess whether the proposed attitude does indeed "represent" the United States—as the subtitle claims.

The general attitude looms already in *Mobile*'s unique style of address, where, as in any poetic work, "content" and "form" merge into an inalienable unity. Two direct comments in *Mobile* state how things and voices speak to us.

In "Connecticut," and in the first entry on the "Quilts of the Shelburne Museum" of Vermont (*F*, 29; *E*, 28; see also *F*, 181; *E*, 173; ff.), we read: "this 'Mobile' is composed somewhat like a 'quilt'." Indeed, Butor's work at first impresses the reader as a "crazy quilt" composed of scraps randomly placed across the 300-odd pages. Such is the United States itself, as any map will show which differentiates the States by color. Yet *Mobile* provides no "bird's-eye view," but rather lands us into the detail of the "quilt." We start with a Howard Johnson Restaurant in Concord, arrive at the sea, hear snippets of history about the Cherokee Indians and the missionaries—and then pass on to the "Concords" in a chain of bordering States, Georgia and Florida. The figure of the "home" State is sewn together with two others. But "North Carolina" is itself a figure, and only thereby connected with adjacent ones. *Mobile* is indeed somewhat (*un peu*) like a "quilt," but it is appliquéd with great care.

As an art work, an appliquéd quilt shows discretely significant figures which capture our attention briefly and then direct us on toward their neighbors. Quilts vary, of course, but the materials of their composition naturally create a whole in which each figure contributes a part. Furthermore, the purpose for which quilts are designed dictates prima facie that sovereignty belongs to the quilt as an entity in itself—for battling the cold and the drafts. Every art work institutes some sort of relation between part and whole, but in many the relation is the reverse of that typically found in a quilt. Thus Bruegel's two paintings *Hunters in the Snow* and *Triumph of Death* very strikingly suggest a whole of life. However, our attention gravitates to the plights and conditions of individuals (things and people) in these works; *from* the whole, each *is*. Compared with a Bruegel painting, *Mobile* does truly resemble a quilt.

When contemplating the New World, the European even today perceives first of all the "wide open spaces," the freedom

187

of movement from one place to another. Actually, though, his first thought posits release from the Old World, where places appear essentially cramped. And this outside thought of the New World's inner character determines in large measure the attitude *making* the land "wide open." This thought, neither new nor confined to those still outside America, was the founding principle of the nation, and is now embodied in the people's attitude toward the land.

According to the fundamental thought, any *one* place makes sense to us and remains viable for us only in terms of *other* places. Unless we deliberately counteract the initially prevalent American attitude for a moment, we face "the sea, the waves, the salt, the sand, the foam, the seaweed" in North Carolina simply in comparison with *another* place, e.g., the variations of the scenery in Georgia and Florida. This tendency to understand places only in interrelation surfaces most obviously in the tourist who lives always for the *next* place and compares the "present" place with "how it was" elsewhere, in a kind of idle and garrulous "sceneriology." Yet these obvious cases merely embody, perhaps in caricature, the basic attitude of the "European Americans" who supposedly abide in definite places.

Just as the first settlers came to North America in flight from inconvenient pressure, so successive generations struck out for westward settlements whenever the pressures of their "latest" mounted beyond convenience (see F. J. Turner's *The Frontier in American History*). The willingness to tear up one's roots, the faith that the hovering possibility of a change makes one's present place bearable, promising at least transient salvation, —this willingness and this faith have imbued American perception and now constitute an a priori form for the faculty of sight. *Mobile* presents the United States through this form; it *re*presents the attitude of the U.S.A. as we experience it "somewhat like a quilt."

Place as interrelation with other places embodies itself perhaps most remarkably in the economics of the modern world. Whether as consumer or laborer, merchant or industrialist, the man or woman living in North Carolina "lives off" distant places. Producing, selling, or consuming on a local scale makes no economic sense: just as industrialists and merchants have roots only incidentally in an actual town, so today's laborers, the new itinerent workers, are expected to migrate to places where they are needed. And the vacationer re-enacts the

188

basic drama in his endless "drives," like the occupants of the cars recurrently racing throughout *Mobile*.

Place as anciently experienced, as formed centripetally by economic and religious forces, has no positive exemplification in the distinctively American attitude of the land. Rather, all forces operate centrifugally, drawing attention forever away from wherever we are nominally located.

The *second* direct comment on the manner of address is the title itself: the work is a "mobile," a moving sculpture. Alexander Calder (b. 1898) seems to have originated and named this particular kind of art work. A closer consideration of a mobile's nature may suggest the aptness of the title of Butor's work and may further define the style of address.

The construction of a mobile varies in technique. Typically, though, such a work consists of rods, usually tipped by a figure (called a finial), suspended from one another in balance, and ultimately either from the ceiling or from a stand which belongs to the sculpture. Thus a mobile shapes space by means of movement. Often, a slight breeze or draft suffices to set the rods into multiple circular motions, on several planes at once, so that the finials sweep in and out of view, displaying ever-changing shapes as the perspectives vary. This creation does not proceed from an effort to dominate space; rather, it results from a delicate interfusion of daintily suspended, forever shifting forms.

The essence of a mobile's space-creating motion is free repetition. The same figures recurrently appear, but in a forever unique arrangement of appearances at any one time. For a viewer who "drops in" for a brief moment on a mobile at two or several different times, its charm lies in its appearing each time as a new configuration. Yet if we abide with the work we begin to realize that it forms a totality: it creates space not at all by any one or finite number of positions, but by infinite *accumulation*. It is an essentially open-ended *event*. Thus we experience the work primarily in *time*—time not as a sequence, but as accumulation, and accumulation not of new elements but of the same elements in their varying perspectival combinations. Hence a mobile creates space for us by virtue of a special temporal articulation. This shaping of space, and the concomitant sense of freedom in repetition, appeals to us: for it recalls the possibility of responding meaningfully to the context of our lives.

Through accumulation *Mobile* creates a space for each State and for the United States as a whole, "somewhat like a quilt." But the manner of the accumulation is essentially temporal, too. "North Carolina" sets the pattern which repeats itself throughout the work. The sea appears this way, that way, and then another way. The American Indians appear in a snitch here, a snitch there, and then still again. A Negro first appears as a man, then as a woman, and finally as a collectivity. Each theme rotates on an independent axis, and also in unison with the others. Furthermore, the work formally progresses *through* time: each State comes into view for "one hour," starting in "pitch dark" with Alabama, proceeding to an even darker Alaska, to Arizona still dark an hour later, then to "not so dark" in Arkansas, to "pitch dark" again in California, and finally to full daylight in our example of North Carolina.

The real, as distinct from the formal accumulation becomes most evident in the flow of information about the American Indians. Although the "finial" of the Indians comes and goes and remains integrated with the flux of other finials (the sea, the Negroes), it appears in varying perspectives which begin to "add up" if we abide with the movement. Later in the work analogous strains of history appear as finials and rotate integrally with still others. History, often but an hypnotic and meaningless narration, is thus partially dissolved back into its originary form of heritage: the formation of, and integration with, a place.

The American attitude would like to believe that the individual marches through time in a purely linear progression. However, instead of a straight narrative, *Mobile* presents fragments of this progression interspersed with other fragments, finials among finials. Moreover, in the presentation of these voices of history the conflict among them grows into a full-scale opposition. We may refer to a passage later in the text (*F*, 250; *E*, 239) where the testimonies of Benjamin Franklin and Andrew Carnegie on social mobility and cooperation stand in blatant contradiction with one another:

"... A little Money sav'd of the good Wages they receive there, while they work for others, enables them to buy the Land and begin their Plantation, in which they are assisted by the Good Will of their Neighbors, and some Credit..." *Benjamin Franklin*

"... All intercourse between them is at an end. Rigid castes are formed, and, as usual, mutual ignorance breeds mutual distrust ... Under the law of competition, the employer of thousands is forced into the strictest economies, among which the rates paid to labour figure prominently..." *Andrew Carnegie*

An inherited attitude inevitably contains conflicting voices. In preserving their conflict in its own articulation, *Mobile* turns the "march through time" back onto itself, ultimately to create a space.

A mobile also allows its finials to recede momentarily when others become prominent. In "North Carolina" this receding or muffling occurs ominously. We notice that the first mention of segregation in the United States, "(for whites only)," is partially explained in the customary manner. Thereafter the designation becomes increasingly abbreviated, from "(... whites only)" to "(... only)." The fact itself does not recede: it re-emerges with increasing force already in "South Carolina," while the designation diminishes to the minimum. After all, we consider it improper to talk about segregation, we try simply to live with the fact. Occasionally, we might insist, approvingly or disapprovingly, on the fact, but it is impolite to ask that one respond to the *voice* of this fact. Too many other voices interfere to demand a hearing.

The same recession of finial, muffling of voice, marks the appearance of the Indians, that other episode in American history which darkly speaks to us, and continues to form our attitude. Already in "Arizona," in reference to the Navajos, we hear of the Reservation for Indians (*F*, 9; *E*, 9):

(Most of the approximately five hundred thousand Indians of the United States live on reservations scattered throughout the country, to which they have gradually been confined during the occupation of the land by the white invader. It would not be kind (*gentil*) to compare them to concentration camps. It would even be rather *(un peu)* unfair: some of these reservations are tourist attractions.)

Although ironically stated, all this is "true," and as a *fact* we know it well. Yet our forefathers' dealings with the native inhabitants of the land stand in marked opposition to the views we ascribe to them: that the land was empty and that every man had a right to his fair share. Thus we tell our children *once* that Indians live on reservations, and after that we no longer say, "Over there is a reservation for Indians," but rather simply, "Over there are some Indians." Just as "(for whites only)" dwindles as time goes on, so do the designations for the original inhabitants of the land: from "Reservation for Seminole In-

191

dians" to "... for Cherokee Indians" and finally to "... Osage Indians".

With its accumulation of history—appearance, fading, reappearance with growing force—*Mobile* seems at first to address us according to our initial awareness of time as a linear sequence. But the integration essential to the accumulation transforms this illusory experience of temporality into a sensibility for repetition. Although "new" finials come into view as the work progresses, their newness immediately contributes to the formation of a whole. Spatially viewed, this transformation may be described as either a circle or a spiral of time. In any case, history *comes back hauntingly*. It haunts (bothers) ourselves and it haunts (abides in) nature: the sea and its varying elements, the swamps, the rivers, the birds. Thus is preserved the possibility that history can be converted into heritage, the making of a place.

In the following sections we shall return to each line of force defining the attitude of America: space as "somewhat like a quilt" with centrifugal rather than centripetal signification; time as accumulation with a repetitive rather than linear signification. The structure of this attitude cuts short, already in "North Carolina," the naive propensities of these lines of force. We raise the question: How can this attitude become transparent to the ultimate issues of heritage, to thinghood and selfhood?

3. THINGHOOD IN AMERICA: THE COMEDY OF *MOBILE*

From the standpoint of any given individual, America appears foremost as the land of wide-open, *unending* spaces, with a forever displaced horizon. Urban centers may sprawl into the countryside, but the automobile carries one swiftly to the edge of the latest suburban housing development, where things present themselves once again in their pristine dynamism. Perhaps the grain fields out there do belong to some man or to some corporation, but the fields lie now free, and the grain grows itself. The woodland, too, no doubt belongs to somebody or to some institution, but extends too far and wide to be guarded, and one suspects that the State owns much of it, calling it perhaps a National Forest. As one wanders across hill and dale—

more likely, drives *through* the hills and *over* the dales—the thought recurs: there is always more.

The American heritage incorporates a sense of abundance which stems from the land itself. The attitude of things, the way they lean toward us, announces variety, replaceability, quantity. And we ourselves are left ever again with choice, with the presumption that we may change our choice, with the task of gaging numerically the value of what we choose. Thus the critical mind nowadays asks: Is the overall attitude embedded in the American heritage adequate to, a "good match" for the realities of the land?

Mobile articulates a response to a question lying deeper than the critical one: How does the abundance actually re-appear in the American mind? For prior to any reform, this re-appearance must become transparent to the originary appearance of things. We have to appreciate the "happening" of heritage before we can rightly assess the illusion, the reality, the inevitable interplay between the two, and finally the better course.

Abundance re-appears first of all as a multiplicity of places. A "Concord" or a "Clinton" evokes immediately *other* "Concords" or *other* "Clintons." We consider the greatness of the United States as vouchsafed by the extent of the arena where one can freely move. This affirmation of mobility surfaces, for instance, in the lurking intolerance of dissidents; after all, if things don't suit you here, you are free to move on to the next place.

Besides enumerating places in a manner suggesting an infinitude of mobility, *Mobile* lists items in America which more directly represent the American response to movement: the recurrent, generally shabby automobiles, along with the gas stations feeding them: "On the highway, a very battered gray Oldsmobile, going much faster than the 60-mile speed limit, ... Flying Service..." In the book, these automobiles answer most visibly to the wide open spaces; certainly they embody very emphatically the most steadfast of American values. The book and its "subject" then co-operate to raise implicitly the critical question whether the undeniable attitude of the land receives adequate response in the way of life promoted by the American heritage: here, automated mobility.

Of course, within each place there re-appears another plenitude: an abundance of nature. In *Mobile* several kinds of things appear in an overwhelming variety: the sea and its elements, the land and its trees, but most conspicuously the birds of the air. Lists of these last recur throughout the work, but begin in "North Carolina" (*F*, 17; *E*, 17):

> Florida jays,
> Key West quail doves,
> fork-tailed flycatchers,
> Maynard's cuckoos
> gray kingbirds.

As we continue through the work we discover hundreds of varieties. The abundance of these feathered creatures has fascinated newcomers since the first sighting of the New World. Thus bird-watching has its home in America.

What channels of response to the abundance of nature does the American heritage cut for us? Regarding birds, the response most lauded by our heritage comes down to us in the work of John James Audubon, whose *Birds of America*, first published during 1826-1828, contains 435 life-sized colored engravings made from his original water colors. Most of the originals were diligently created in the wild environment of the winged creatures. As these portrayals became accepted ingredients of the American heritage, the approved human response to nature took the form of *sentiment*. For Audubon's birds idealize nature as excitingly colorful while at the same time safely contained. These birds neither address us, nor do they tell us anything about nature herself; for they already represent the American mind, they express *us*, how we would like to face nature. Showing themselves *to* us, they display themselves precisely *for* us. The first four Audubon descriptions in *Mobile* exemplify this exhibitionism:

Two yellow-billed cuckoos, on a branch of blemished leaves, the one on the left exposing its white belly, the one on the right grasping the body of a large butterfly. (*F*, 12; *E*, 12: note that these birds do not eat butterflies.)

The prothonotary warbler, clinging to a cave vine, head and breast bright yellow, black and white fan-shaped tail, . . .

The parula warbler, perched on a large salmon iris known as the Lousiana flag, . . .

Two pairs of mourning doves billing on a bush with large white flowers. (*F*, 13; *E*, 13.)

Already in "Arkansas," and then again in "Colorado," *Mobile* informs us of Audubon and suggests that these descriptions recall not things in nature but things in Audubon's representation of nature. These depictions then accumulate explicitly.

In contrast with the otherwise typically brutal American attitude toward nature (the rape of the woodland, the massacre of the natives), the delicacy of Audubon's portrayals seems to suggest and recommend the possibility of a blissful reconciliation with, and a peaceful contemplation of, the pristine and abundant American landscape. Yet in *Mobile* these portrayals, interspersed with the other elements of the American scene, reappear as efforts rather than as accomplishments. The art work reminds us that the idyllic contemplation of birds stems more from a need to compensate for the hostility of nature and our antagonistic response to her, than from a genuine encounter. There is irony, then, in the one mention of an Audubon drawing in "North Carolina": "The Carolina parakeet, a species extinct since 1904. . . ." Nothing remains to be said, since this bird *is* no longer: the greed of feather hunters brutally eradicated to the last member the entire, once overwhelmingly abundant species. These birds did not die out, they were killed.

If Americans respond inadequately to abundant nature, and if *Mobile* integrates this response in a way portending an adequation, we must ask, first, why the inadequacy (specifically in the case of Audubon's work) exists and, second, how *Mobile* transforms it into its opposite.

A paradox. Any effort to depict nature "just as she is in herself" produces a work of pure expression, a work which prevents nature from addressing us, since things appear already as we would like them to be. In Bruegel's *Hunters in the Snow*, on the other hand, the birds perched on the branches of leafless trees above the hunters, and the one swooping down over the skaters on the ice, connect heaven and earth in a matter-of-fact-way, for they address us at the specific time, season, and place of sober work and cramped play. Here the birds and the other wintry givens of nature retain their identity and integrity, and address us accordingly, but not at all because they are singled out away from us and placed on exhibition. For the painting supplies a context wherein we can recognize the human condition through which nature can speak to us as and for herself.

Mobile does not describe America as it "really is," i.e., either nature apart from the human context or society apart from its material environment. Nor does it prescribe how America should be, i.e., how its human constructs should be built out or improved. Rather, *Mobile* configures the American heritage on the brink of convergence, rendering our heritage transparent. Audubon's depictions are opaque, since they actually obstruct a clear vision of nature and thereby indirectly contribute to the rape—just as much psychoanalysis obliquely bolsters the supremacy of mercantilism and industrial interests: by providing compensation on the level of sentiment. But when *Mobile* integrates this very opacity with a flow of place names, automobiles, snitches of history, and above all birds *without* idyllic depictions, the internal forces of the representations are "caught up short" and no longer appear self-grounding. Thus an otherwise merely expressive mode of encountering nature becomes transparent to the things themselves. The otherwise incestuous signification becomes now genuinely sensuous: it is converted to allow nature to speak for herself, to address us. To allow is not yet to ensure, but the alchemy has begun.

While early Americans (first of all Englishmen and Frenchmen) received Audubon's depictions as responses to the abundance of God's creation, we today are more likely impressed by the abundance of *society*'s creation in consumer goods: nature remade in the image of man. In "Idaho" we are introduced to the first of the recurrent series of extracts from sales catalogues (*F*, 50-51; *E*, 48-49):

Agates, —Snow and Elk Peaks, —through Sears, Roebuck & Co., a huge mail-order store serving every part of the United States, you can obtain "three superb wall decorations in dramatic natural color ... idyllic American landscapes transform your wall into a window open onto the world. Marvels of space... Enliven the office, the den, the living room, bedroom or playroom. Covers more than twenty square feet. A special process permits the faithful reproduction of the most delicate color photographs. Paste your decoration directly onto the wall (see page to left for pasting instructions), or on beaverboard or cardboard, frame it and hang it as a picture. Easy to clean; a damp cloth is all you need. Choose from:

A) Jackson Lake and the Grand Teton Range. An awesome panorama! Notice the refined, delicate coloring of the mountains framed by majestic trees in the foreground. A refreshing scene.

B) Cape Sebastian. The rocky coast of Oregon. For those who like to feel the call of adventure...

196

C) Cypress Gardens. 'I remember that,' you'll often hear apropos of this gem taken in Florida's famous park. Its myriad colors makes it one of our most popular decorations."

Barely do agates and peaks appear, when we hear of the possibility of purchasing representations of nature. And just as so *much* of it exists, so too there is a *variety* of representations—something for everyone!—for those who like something refreshing, something vicariously adventurous, or something supposedly conforming to the tastes of others. We need not face nature directly, we can stay at home and simply transform a wall into "a window open onto the world."

This is comedy. Americans boast of the rich vastness of their land, and yet *Mobile* shows this pride expressing its appreciation in terms of representations of it purchased by mail order and installed at home. An adequate response to mountains would require at the very least that we journey into *them*. And no doubt we occasionally do this. But more typical is the disposition just restated comically: we take to ourselves our own image of mountains. It is as though there were simply *too much*. We North Americans are born into a land with so many mountain peaks and rivers, mineral deposits and forests, that we tend to settle for a pre-packaged summary, an imaginary *idea* of the land.

As more finials move into view, we note the availability, thanks to Sears and Montgomery Ward, of live Mexican burros ("Shipped express from Freeport, Ill., with health certificates"), three varieties of monkey ("Your choice of species, not sex"), autoharps ("... sounds like a banjo, harp, or guitar... No need for musical training"), douchbags ("to avoid being embarrassed, buy by mail order, discreetly!..."), and do-it-yourself Rembrandt water-colors ("no need to be an artist, from now on all you need to do is paint by numbers... "). What is happening here? According to Hegel and his followers, the history of Western Civilization traces the development whereby *things* become increasingly the expression of *man*. However, directly evident is the fact that things have become consumer goods—priced items on a shelf, purchased rather than made and so disposed of arbitrarily. Consumerism attains the heights of comedy when such items re-appear in a special context as *denying* "the obvious," as refusing their origins. Ultimately, one must go to the burros, give oneself to music, admit one's bodily condition, perceive with humility the inimitable works of great artists. Out-

197

rageous denial of this ultimacy turns comical when it appears as impotently self-deluded. For then we, as observors, recognize and acknowledge the origins beyond the smoke screen of delusion, and therefore need not even rail against the deception:

Or, through Sears, Roebuck & Co., an assortment of seven knitted nylon or rayon panties artistically embroidered with the days of the week:
"... Choose from
- white for Sunday,
    - The Last Supper, with The Sermon on the Mount,
- yellow for Monday,
    -Autumn Landscape, with The End of the Day,
- blue for Tuesday,
    -Sunset at Sea, with Homecoming,
- pink for Wednesday,
    - Thoroughbred, with The Foxhunt,
- white for Thursday,
    - Scenes from Swan Lake (Ballet),
- green for Friday,
    - Venus and Adonis."
- black for Saturday,
"please include hip measurements..." (*F*, 174-5; *E*, 167-8.)

To the abundance of nature, which suggests exhibition rather than contemplation, and to the multiplicity of consumer goods, which incites arbitrary choice without genuine discretion, *Mobile* adds the profusion of religious institutions bespeckling the American land- and mind-scape. The sheer variety of sects has been a source of unending amazement for and speculation by visitors, at least since the Englishwoman Frances Trollope (*Domestic Manners of the Americans*, 1832) and the Frenchman Alexis de Tocqueville (*Democracy in America*, Part II, 1840). On the one hand, the variety seems to correspond to the diversity of the landscape itself: since no one place or force dominates the land, providing a center of definition, no single interpretation of creation can predominate in defining man's unique role within the universe. However, Tocqueville already penetrates deeper when he notes that the variety of sects still retains a conformity to the base—and engenders not only a uniformity but also a complacence of opinion. In the opening pages of his work he writes:

In the United States, Christian sects are infinitely diversified and per-petually modified; but Christianity itself is a fact so irresistably estab-lished that no one undertakes either to attack or to defend it... Hence

198

the activity of individual analysis is restrained within narrow limits, and many of the most important of human opinions are removed from the influence of such analysis.

Indeed, the variety is somewhat strange. India also houses an overwhelming multiplicity of faiths, yet each exacts the whole being of its adherents. In America, the variety arouses a need for indifferent choice—ultimately as indifferent as the color of a catalogue item or the flavor of an ice cream. In all these cases, the assortment varies chiefly because of the lack of genuine difference, and because the drabness would otherwise lead to no choice at all. Addressing the British Academy on January 30, 1918, George Santayana describes his American colleagues and the tradition which begets the "younger professors of philosophy":

Religion was the backbone of that tradition, and towards religion, in so far as it is a private sentiment or presumption, they feel a tender respect; but in so far as religion is a political institution seeking to coerce the mind and the conscience, one would think they had never heard of it. They feel it is as much every one's right to choose and cherish a religion as to choose and cherish a wife, without having his choice rudely commented upon in public.

To these now traditional *critical* observations, *Mobile* incorporates *comical* vision. With a sequence on clock radios we read:

The Seventh-Day Adventist Church, —the Nodaway and Platte Rivers that flow into the Missouri, —Apple River, tributary of the Father of Waters, —or another, cheaper model, "Ward's high quality. Wakes you to the sounds of sweet music. Fast colors. Comes in white, gray, or turquoise." ... Mark Twain National Forest, —the Church of the Assemblies of God, —the Grand River that flows into the Missouri, —or "our cheapest model. Recommended for local reception only." (*F*, 67-68; *E*, 64-65.)

One may choose one's church the way one chooses ice-cream flavors at Howard Johnson's or clock radios from Ward's; in both cases, the variety corresponds to the diversity of natural phenomena. While the choice of religion supposedly takes one *beyond* such materiality, in America one's religion marks, purely and simply, one's general willingness to alienate spirituality from materiality; as Frances Trollope notes in her Chapter on "Religion," little does it matter *which* sect one joins, what counts primarily is *that* one chooses. Thus Spirit and Material

199

stand in a strange conspiracy. The intended objects of choice differ radically in the two spheres, in fact they are separated from one another as nowhere else in the world. Yet the mode of intending, the attitude in choosing either a religion or a clock radio, is the same. Thus the comedy of *Mobile* portends a reality, namely our inherited channels toward the real.

So a comical discrepancy arises between the meaning of what is intended (the faith of one's choice) and the meaning of one's intending (the attitude of selection). But how did the conflict between the two ever occur? Why the insistence that the choice of church *does* differ from one's choice of radio or ice cream? By "explaining the joke" we may indeed destroy the comic effect for a moment; however, we thereby penetrate into the dark recesses of the heritage out of which *Mobile* speaks.

The American tradition fosters an attitude toward things which is *alternately* spiritual and material. The student of the United States cannot but be amazed how religion was, and still is, the "backbone" of the land, while commerce and its consumerism, the active and the passive correlates of the material disposition, characterize the country as a whole. Efforts have been made to bridge these two antitheses, to show how the religiosity led to a secular counterpart (see, for instance, Max Weber's *Protestant Ethic and the Spirit of Capitalism*, 1904-05). But the heritage within which we presently live knows no bridge. Although historians and sociologists may construct a continuity, the devout man or woman divides the two absolutely.

The line between the two has been drawn variously, of course. Starting with spirituality in its purity, the Puritans viewed the actual things they worked with as sheer materiality. Thus Cotton Mather sees the Puritan effort located in places "which were once the Devil's territories" (see John M. Anderson's account in the opening pages of *The Individual and the New World*, 1955). Perhaps the Puritans were indeed firm "realists" owing to their conviction that, being essentially evil, everything material demanded all one's energy and attention. However, the overwhelming abundance of the land obviously encourages "idealists" as well in the opposite attitude, a faith that nature herself, in her own right, deserves attention and energy as the source of everything beneficial to man. The materiality of America overwhelms both the visitor and the resident and requires that it, too, receive its proper due. Whether or not this circumstance evokes an optimistic "idealism" decreeing the New World to be "virgin country" rather than "Devil's territories," a line has been drawn between Spirit and Material. After all, the American "idealist" enmeshed in the exigencies of divine nature also "takes time off" to acknowledge the spiritual dimension; in his case the materiality simply comes first.

The alienation of the spiritual and the material destroys both. When we endeavor without spirit to respond to things, the thinghood of things merges with commerce and consumerism, and things themselves appear simultaneously as all-important for our personal happiness, and as *mere* things, since the ore of the earth or the items in our household are but stages on life's way. Swinging subsequently to the other side, we try to recoup our true selves at specifically appointed moments, but at these times (so carefully prescribed by law for our forefathers) nothing focuses response. In fact, at the extreme, we define spirit as the nothingness of matter: concretely, we don our spiritual form, whether during the Friday night "sensitivity training," Saturday night parties, or Sunday morning sermons, primarily to disclaim that our Monday-through-Friday involvement with mere things is adequate for *human* happiness.

America is, on the one hand, an idea. In this capacity it has served the immigrant and continues to structure American manners: the idea of freedom from yesterday, equality with one's peers of today, and opportunity for tomorrow. At times, the idea itself appears as the sole support upholding and nourishing Americans. Yet America is also the land of plenty. As such it attracts the immigrants and also justifies its way of life to the Americans themselves: an abundance of places, of nature, of consumer goods testify directly to America's superiority. As a pure idea, America stands in no need of plenty, and flaunts its independence of materiality. As the land of plenty, America has no need of ideas, and parades its courage to face reality squarely, without ideologies. The contradiction here pinpoints an inner tension of the American heritage.

Although visitors and residents alike frequently complain that America lacks life of the spirit (sustained effort as distinct from frenetic outbursts), the absence of sensitivity to material things locates the heart of the problem. For the usual complaints about the inadequacies of the prevalent life-style tend to recommend a peculiarly American "turning inward" which deprives us of the one focus so urgently needed for a spiritual attitude. Paradoxically, all fretting about spiritual life kills it.

201

So, too, the child who pulls up the young carrots to make sure they have developed proper roots.

In short, we must beware of the vulgar spirituality which, recoiling from the crass involvement with things as materials for public exploitation and as goods ensuring private happiness, cleanses itself by rejecting all relation with the elements. The grime of things does indeed contaminate those who indulge in commerce and consumption. But cleansing oneself of this contamination does not at all entail rejecting one's relation with the things which happen to locate the smut. Yet American spirituality generally moves in that direction. And the error stems not from ignorance, it stems from an insistence that the interpretation of things effected by commerce and consumerism is correct. The result of this insistence follows with logical inevitability, and the baby gets thrown out with the washwater.

Mobile's juxtaposition of religiosity and consumerism allows each force to unstring the other. The one brings to light what the other conceals. However, the virtue of comedy proves also to be its limitation. It presents directly the human construct obscuring the reality, not the underlying reality. In comedy we accept these constructs, for we see through them. But the energy of comedy expends itself on the task of forming a vision without evoking indignation, fear, scorn, or disgust. We laugh, or at least smile, and the fog begins to dissipate. Nevertheless, as visibility improves we move on to other modes of discourse.

Without needing to pursue the other comic listings in *Mobile*, we can gather that the American heritage, for all its formative power and influence, has not yet provided *effective* channels allowing us to remain true to abundance. A question then arises: Is adequation to abundance possible and genuinely urgent?

Since man *is* his relation with things, he cannot live without them. The relation may be ill conceived, weak, or perverse, in which cases we find ourselves unintelligible, feeble, or "mixed up" in the face of things. It can also be spiritual—not in any exotic or esoteric sense, but as exemplified in the man or woman who tends carefully to the vines in the vineyard or the furnishings of the home. Indeed, our very own thingliness "strikes" us. For we discover that vineyards and homes may or may not demand our attention, but our bodies recurrently and fatefully do: and here again we can "take care" in a spiritual way, neither neglecting nor idolizing but simply upholding and respecting. Each man or woman is the "middle," the way he or she comports himself or herself toward what is "other," what is in one's care while escaping one's control. The "middle" realizes itself, is true to itself, as spirit, but receives concrete definition by the things within it.

In a truly spiritual relation things draw us toward themselves. *We* move into the spotlight only insofar as our abilities are called into question: there is always more than we can really handle. The relation goes askew precisely when we believe we have reduced things to our own command; for the relation then appears arbitrary and incidental, above all revocable by our own decree. Time has this significance, at least: tomorrow looms as the possibility that what we have conquered today will later on gain the upperhand, reducing us to ashes.

Acknowledging that there is always more, we experience things in the mode of abundance. This abundance takes us to things, and contrasts sharply with the accumulation of wealth which we must count and recount, like the miser in Balzac's novel *Eugénie Gandet*. Miserly abundance, the kind we think we possess, necessarily appears as a humanly measurable quantity. Genuine abundance, the kind we must face as marking the emergence of things in their thinghood, takes us to itself, summoning and surpassing our abilities.

Homer's *Iliad*, and to some extent the *Odyssey*, present man's relation to things in the mode of abundance, and so adumbrates in a tragic manner what *Mobile* presents in the mode of comedy. Not that Ancient Greece guaranteed a livelihood from the land; on the contrary, the lands sung by Homer were stingy and begot an extremely fragile life. Yet the earth is recurrently called "abundant" and "generous": *polyphorbos*, "providing fodder for many," as when Hera informs Aphrodite, "I am going visiting to the edges of the generous earth" (*Iliad*, XIV, 200). Often such epithets in the Homeric epics seem to function as mere fillers for the sake of the meter. But consider the following verses from Achilles' first angry rebuttal to Agamemnon, in which he announces his withdrawal from the "Trojan spearmen" (I, 154-6):

> For never in any way have they harried my cattle or horses,
> Nor ever in fertile generous Phthia
> Did they ravage the harvest. . . .

In the first of these verses the emphasis falls on Achilles' own property: since the Trojans have made no claims to his own possessions, his aid to the Achaian cause comes as a favor, if at all. In the second verse, however, the hero recalls his homeland per se: what *it* has to offer. As a "fertile" land (*eribolakos*, "very cloddy," a *sign* of fertility), it is "generous" (*botianeira*, "providing meals to men"). The third verse continues to explicate the significance of these epithets: the land yields a harvest, a tenuous gift which other men can easily destroy. Neither the land itself nor its vegetable produce belongs to men. These latter either accept the gifts of the earth with gratitude or destroy them in rage: they never *own* it absolutely.

Finally, toward the end of the *Odyssey* (XIX, 591-93) Penelope addresses the "beggar" who has not yet disclosed his identity; she would like to listen to his tales indefinitely:

> But in no way can men go forever
> Without sleep. For in each matter the immortals have given
> A share to mortals upon the grain-giving earth.

While we all know that sleep lays a claim upon us, Penelope's reason specifies a thoughtful interpretation of the human condition generally. In *all* things we are given a share, a *moira*. In *all* things (sleep being only one example among others), our share marks not only what we have, but what we *owe*. The waking hours of alert responsibility send us back to the slumbering hours when we are defenseless. Sleep is the brother of Death (*Iliad*, XIV, 231): in slumbering we return to our origins. But even here, after we are addressed as mortals, the poet adds a location: "upon the grain-giving earth" (*epi zeidoron arouran*). Man's *moira*, exemplified in sleep and in death, takes him into things as these appear in abundance. Yet perhaps only when we respond wholly to the claim laid upon us, and entailed by our share, do things appear as genuinely abundant.

4. SELFHOOD IN AMERICA: THE TRAGEDY OF *MOBILE*

America is without a doubt the land of the reborn self. Whereas a Chinese might spend an entire day performing rites in honor or his ancestors, asking himself incessantly whether his current actions and dispositions square with the expectations of family tradition, an American generally believes that he can be a new self each day, that he must jettison himself repeatedly out of the

204

mainstream of the past, beyond the claims and ideals of his ancestors.

Indeed, man fails most miserably, and reflects this misery quite melodramatically, when be becomes a mere deputy of the dead. Americans visiting Europe often recoil in horror from the civil society they encounter off the beaten tourist tracks. Office workers, whether clerks, secretaries, or petty officials, in business or in government, seldom meet any situation as unique selves up against a new day: each sinks back into the common fund of selfhood, which generations of bosses and underlings have formed on the tedious stairway of their petty successes; and each insists that the contents of the new day fit into the categories of yesterday. Thus, for Americans, Old World institutions manifestly enshrine the dangers of allowing traditions to gain the upperhand, while Eastern European bureaucracies and Oriental collectivities lurk as the monsters of total failure.

Concretely, a reborn self is a *free* self. In America we are unfree to the extent that we are locked into the patterns of action and thought already established by our predecessors. We become free, then, by realizing a distance from both the traditions of the past and the present society embodying these traditions. To be sure, our freedom expresses itself variously. We are free to establish ourselves in commerce, to run for political office, and to contest a given application of the law. But the one freedom most centrally located within the American mind is negative: we are free *not to participate* at all in ancestral institutions. Thus an American can retain his citizenship in good standing without ever casting a vote in an election. In some Western countries, on the other hand, one is fined for such neglect of participation.

The American attitude steers us toward rebirth and away from old births. It conceives of life as a linearly temporal affair. Yet one wonders whether this attitude is adequate to selfhood and freedom, since it seems to leave us helpless in the face of old selves. What do we do with the backwash of ancestral efforts? What happens to the *old* births? Do the now dead selves rest in peace, do they leave *us* in peace?

The first finial of *Mobile*, introducing Alabama, reads in its entirety: "pitch dark in CORDOVA, ALABAMA, the Deep South." This lapidary entry tells us very little. Cordova is the American transcription of Córdoba, the city in Spain built over three transparent layers of history: the Roman Empire with its

205

commercial interest (200 B.C.), the intervening Moorish culture (flourished in the 900's), and the victorious Christian faith (established in the 1200's). The "American Europeans" often bestowed upon their settlements in the New World names hearkening back to origins in the Old World. This disposition assumes sometimes comical proportions, as in Maine, where a plethora of Old World names mushroom within a rural setting: Naples, York, Belfast, Norway, Athens, Denmark, Poland, Moscow, and so on. Throughout *Mobile* the pattern introduced in "Alabama" repeats itself. It becomes thematic in "Iowa," where a series of finials explicitly comment on the disposition (*F*, 98-9; *E*, 95-96):

> They did not try to know this country, they had no desire to settle here. They were content with temporary habitations. They wanted only to survive and grow rich in order to be able to return... / Meanwhile, until this triumphal return took place, why not reconstitute a new Europe, effacing as much as possible this continent that received but alarmed us? New France, New England, Nova Scotia, New Brunswick, New York, New Holland, New Sweden, New Orleans, New Hampshire, New Jersey, New Amsterdam, New London on a New Thames.

Of course, historically speaking, the "they" here represents but a segment. Perhaps the rebirth characteristic of the New World does not revert absolutely back to the Old. Perhaps the reversion indicates merely a formal tie, for the sake of reminiscence at leisurely moments. However, an unwillingness to forsake the old, if not an inability to sink roots sufficient unto names of their own, does begin to crystallize.

The second finial, introducing "Alaska," connects with the first by the common name of Cordova (as though there were but a finite number of names and a consequent necessity of repeating them from State to State). And now we receive our first real "view":

> pitch dark in
> CORDOVA, ALASKA, the Far North, closest to the dreadful, the abominable, the unimaginable country where it is already Monday when it is still Sunday here, the fascinating, sinister country with unexpected satelite shots, ...

The references to the International Date Line, and to the launching of satelites (Sputnik I, October 1957), brings Alaska into focus against another gnawing country altogether, Russia:

206

dreadful, abominable, unimaginable, fascinating, sinister. Yet the passage talks not about the Soviet Union, but about the land purchased from Russia in 1867. Still, other than its separation from the "lower 48" by five hundred miles of Canada, Alaska is peculiar in its proximity to Asia, the very antithesis of everything American. By invoking this antithesis, the "view" describes what "infiltrates" the Alaskan/American mind:

> ... the country of bad dreams that pursue you all night and insinuate, among your daylight thoughts, despite all your efforts, so many tiny ruinous whisperings like the leak in the ceiling of an old room, the monstrous country of bears,— ...

The nightmares come *from* the land of Monday, but they encroach upon the land of Sunday. The encroachment clearly protrudes—as a leak in the roof reminds us unmistakably of its existence—, yet we refuse to acknowledge, let alone "fix" it. Is this selection of "contents" for Alaska arbitrary? Or does the reference contain a profound significance?

We may recall that the state of Alaska extends over an area one-third as large as the entire United States below. We like to think of the land as rich in natural resources (fish, oil, gold, sand and gravel), and in general as the last frontier where mountain peaks and grizzly bears retain their pristine self-assertion, a continuous challenge for those who wish to match their wit and brawn against the dangerous call of the wild. The history of the country takes us back to the gold rushes of 1896 (in the Yukon, Canada, but accessible via Alaska) and 1899-1903, and to the successful experiments in agriculture commencing during the Depression of the 1930's.

If we turn from Alaska's material and opportunity, toward the traditional human responses, another story rings in our ears. Fittingly, the new lands in "the Far North" rapidly became a mere means to the well-being of the "lower 48." For nearly two decades the country was governed by the War Department, then the Treasury Department, and finally the Navy Department. After the gold frenzy the population of the State actually dropped; in 1920 the census counted fewer people than in 1910. In essence, no human interest connected the residents to the land. Even the drive to extirpate the heathen in the name of God failed to gather momentum. Alaska has remained simply the land of the pure reborn self, with notable opposition only from the natural elements in their brutality. In short, it has been the

207

country of the *empty* self, the self which has nothing to live *with*.

At the same time, Alaska marks the end of linear westward movement. At this point on the globe we collide with what we thought we left behind. Already in 1914, F. J. Turner commented in detail on the *unsettled questions* raised by this "natural" but strangely unexpected event:

Alaska already beckons on the north, and pointing to her wealth of natural resources asks the question on what new terms the new age will deal with her. Across the Pacific looms Asia, no longer a remote vision and a symbol of the unchanging, but borne as by a mirage close to our shores and raising grave questions of the common destiny of the people of the ocean.... the long march of westward civilization [is about to] complete its circle.... The age of the Pacific Ocean begins, mysterious and unfathomable in its meaning for our own future.

One would assume that, with the end of linear movement, the human condition would elicit centripetal responses, that selfhood would emerge by a "turning inward"—not into an imaginary ghost within the individual, but into the domain of shared human effort. But such public responsibility makes sense only within a respect for old births, for the often hidden intent of the institutions established ancestrally.

By forming the Alaska finial as *haunting*, *Mobile* concentrates us perfectly on the significance of this State. As the last outpost of the pure reborn self, it introduces the tragic element of Butor's work, and so of America too.

The popular mind considers anything which is both a failure and somehow sad a "tragedy." Strictly, however, a tragedy is a human drama in which an individual first constructs a context of life, then discovers the construct coming back upon him, and finally affirms the primacy of the issues arising within but not reducible to the exigencies of the construct. A tragedy reveals selfhood as responsibility in the face of configurations of its own making, a selfhood responsive to what emerges within the context and therefore responsible for the context itself. The failure to continue what one is doing marks a profounder "success," and the sadness associated with the failure is subtilized if not obliterated.

Tragedy creates individuality of self by participation, not by separation. Thus in *a* tragedy, in an art work embodying the tragic emergence of selfhood, an individual struggles with circumstances of common concern. Modern collectivities defy tragedy because individuality is there taboo; in Christian com-

208

munities, a transcendently based martyrdom displaces tragedy; and the man who simply rejects society, and moves into virtual isolation, cannot become a tragic figure, since he participates in no context.

Noting the difficulty if not the rarity of this art form, we may well wonder in what way *Mobile* can incorporate it. No individuated narrator conducts the work, and no individual in the book constructs a framework, acknowledging its return and affirming the issues arising within it. Yet various finials of the mobile represent diffusely the essential moments of tragedy. Instead of an individual who carries, acknowledges, and pierces the entire construct, voices from our heritage represent this possibility among others. Instead of a climactic return of the construct upon a unique center of responsibility, we witness an insinuated return upon a multiplicity of centers. Instead of an embodied, an intimated affirmation of issues weaves through the configuration.

Thomas Jefferson's is the most prominent tragic voice in *Mobile*. In "Georgia," in association with the "Madisons" of three different States (specifically in Virginia, the home of this Founding Father), we read (*F*, 41; *E*, 39):

Thomas Jefferson, born April 2, 1743, Old Style, author of the Declaration of Independence:

"... We hold these truths to be self-evident: that all men are created equal... "

The subsequent pages of *Mobile* display over twenty excerpts from *Notes on the State of Virginia* (1782), his *Autobiography* (1821), and his letters (see "Kentucky," "Tennessee," and "Virginia"). The first of these reads (*F*, 43; *E*, 41):

"... It will probably be asked, Why not retain and incorporate the blacks into the State, and thus save the expense of supplying by importation of white settlers, the vacancies they will leave? Deep-rooted prejudices entertained by the whites; ten thousand recollections, by the blacks, of the injuries they have sustained; new provocations; the real distinctions nature has made; and many other circumstances, will divide us into parties, and produce convulsions, which will probably never end but in the extermination of the one or the other race... "

Later finials from Jefferson's *Notes* argue in favor of judging the Negroes as "inferior to the whites in endowments both of body and mind" (*F*, 313-14; *E*, 300). Still others from his *Autobio-*

209

graphy and letters yearn for Old World achitecture and music; in 1778 he writes (*F*, 122; *E*, 117): "fortune has cast my lot in a country where it is in a state of deplorable barbarism."

On the one side, the voice states the ideal; on the other side, it acknowledges what it takes to be fact. Whereas the hasty critic sees either self-contradiction in the opinions of this famous voice or hypocrisy in their public expression, *Mobile* integrates both the statement and the acknowledgement into a complex of moving finials. The work thereby plants the idea back into the land. The equality lauded in the Declaration of Independence is a *doctrine*, not a firm reality. It states that at each moment any man or woman can and even must prove himself or herself—as a reborn self. In *this* enterprise all men are equal. Precisely by dictating a task, the doctrine does not name a fact, but a contravention.

Jefferson's life does not assume tragic proportions; at least he himself never conceives of it as such in his extant writings. Nor does *Mobile* re-present him as a tragic figure. Rather, Jefferson comes to the fore as a tragic voice embedded within a multiplicity of other voices and apparitions. *Mobile* is not *a* tragedy, but it contains the American *strain* of tragedy interwoven with other strains.

Why the tragic voice and not a tragic figure? The poetic option must vindicate itself in reference to the materials of the American heritage. How do these materials, especially the doctrine of equality, give rise to tragedy? What is the shortcoming, the *hamartia*? Two testimonies suggest an answer.

At the end of his life Whitman, himself no tragedian, writes that his *Leaves of Grass* does not celebrate an established or even budding American spirit, but rather resists "the leveling tendencies of Democracy". He then continues:

Welcome as are equality's and fraternity's doctrines and popular education, a certain liability accompanies them all, as we see. That primal and interior something in man, in his soul's abysms, coloring all, and, by exceptional fruitions, giving the last majesty to them—something continually touched upon and attained by the old poems and ballads of feudalism, and often the principle foundation of them—modern science and democracy appear to be endangering, perhaps eliminating.

The very materials of our heritage detract, at least in the first instance, from the power and responsibility of individuals, the precise centers of human being which the American spirit sup-

posedly cherishes and promotes. Whitman pursues this contravening thought ruthlessly. The specified doctrines (and their
embodiment in popular education) endanger, perhaps eliminate
the efficacy of "exceptional fruitions" to give "majesty" to the
"soul's abysms" and to "all" things encountered in the course
of the soul's sojourn. Previously, the "old poems and ballads of
feudalism" had a place in society and had proven their salutary
effects. Nowadays, however, not only these instances of poetry,
but poetry itself, in every form, may vanish. Why? Because the
doctrine of the reborn self initially refuses to affirm the need for
recouping and recovering the established context of life. Yet this
is precisely the office of poetry; even Whitman, in singing the
reborn self, does so by reviving the tradition. We run the risk of
growing incapable of taking poetry seriously. In *Mobile* Jefferson's laments acknowledge this shortcoming: music and architecture must be imported from the Old World, they have no
native ground in the soil of the New.

We might reply that America is the land of concrete labor
and, while the fine arts may suffer, the manual vocations
flourish. Yet in the domain of the trades and occupations the
doctrines of equality and fraternity have led to some of the most
pernicious and strikingly dismal effects: workers generally do
not take their work seriously. Frances Trollope, a moralist if not
a feudalist, notices, already in 1830, that household servants
must be rechristened as "help," and that they lose, in the process, any sense of commitment to their tasks or loyalty to their
employers. In Chapter VI of her book she writes:

I cannot imagine it possible that such a state of things can be desirable,
or beneficial to any of the parties concerned. I might occupy a hundred
pages on the subject, and yet fail to give an adequate idea of the sore,
angry, ever wakeful pride that seemed to torment these poor wretches.
... One of these was a pretty girl, whose natural disposition must have
been gentle and kind; but her good feelings were soured, and her
gentleness turned to morbid sensitiveness, by having heard a thousand
and a thousand times that she was as good as any other lady, that all
men were equal, and women too, and that it was a sin and a shame for
a free born American to be treated like a servant./When she found she
was to dine in the kitchen, she turned up her pretty lip, and said, "I
guess that's 'cause you don't think I'm good enough to eat with
you...." I gave her very high wages, and she staid till she obtained
several expensive articles of dress, and then, *un beau matin*, she came to
me full dressed, and said, "I must go."... Her sister was also living
with me, but her wardrobe was not yet completed, and she remained
some weeks longer, till it was.

Exceptions abound, of course. But any man or woman who stakes his or her life out on manual tasks and personal commitments, formed through temporal durations of yesterday, steps *through* the doctrine of the reborn self, onto a plane vaguely contravening the doctrine. Karl Marx may have argued that society should be so structured that "help" could affirm themselves in their work, but to American employers and employees alike Marx's writings seem to advocate simply a better wardrobe for the workers. The American heritage nearly forbids us to consider the argument that human nature finds its fulfilment *in* labor—not through or after but within it.

Interestingly, Jefferson himself was extremely uneasy in the face of the prospects of what Trollope later recorded as fact. He set a high premium on the role of labor in the human condition. "Those who labor in the earth are the chosen people of God," he remarks, and goes on to insist that "cultivators of the earth are the most virtuous and independent citizens" (*Notes*, Queries XIX and XXII). In fact, he chiefly objects to the institution of slavery on the grounds that it has vile effects on the mentality of the whites (Query XVIII):

For in a warm climate, no man will labor for himself who can make another labor for him. This is so true, that of the proprietors of slaves a very small proportion indeed are ever seen to labor. And can the liberties of a nation be thought secure when we have removed their *only* basis, a conviction in the minds of the people that these liberties are the *gift* of God?   (italics added)

Extracting the material conditions of our existence from the labor of others not only reduces us to a subtle slavery, as Hegel and Marx remarked, but prevents us from considering the availability of these conditions as a gift. We may wonder today whether the nearly doctrinal refusal to take work seriously, as distinct from engaging in enterprise to achieve wealth, does not stem from a belief that labor belongs to the province of the slave, even if the species is extinct. Thus the reborn self runs the risk of finding itself neither in work nor in art, of asserting itself only spuriously in distraction and entertainment (see Chapter Two, especially "The Question"). And can we call the distracted or entertained self *free*?

Mobile gives voice to these two entailments of the American heritage: the germinal refusal of both poetry and labor, of the arduous recovery of the past and the dedicated engagement in the present. The voices issue from our history and yet carry into our contemporary world. Already in "Alaska" we hear the ominous words: "the country of bad dreams that pursue you all night and insinuate, among your daylight thoughts, despite all your efforts, so many tiny ruinous whisperings.... ." At first, "bad dreams" seem to characterize Alaska only, and to be caused simply by the proximity of the Old World and perhaps by the monstrous bears. However, these "bad dreams" during the night and "ruinous whisperings" during the day recur throughout the America of *Mobile*. A series of finials from "Kentucky" reads (*F.* 119-20; *E*, 114-15):

> He dreams he's driving... /Faster than his father drove... /That the trees, the lakes, the cities rush by... /That he has reached the shining mountains... /That he sees gold, and Indians around the gold, all befeathered, and that he kills them, kills them... /That there are no more Indians, no more gold, that he is covered with blood, that he has turned black...

Here the American Dream turns into a nightmare. In "Missouri," a sequence of *wakeful* whisperings climaxes in a single finial embodying the American sentiment of the reborn self in conflict with the conservative complacence and downright intolerance which typifies the decline of the American spirit. This dreamer who tries to go to sleep is incapable of giving himself up to it (*F*, 157, *E*, 151):

> If only it were possible to start everything over from the beginning, if only the frontier were still open and we could escape this new Europe and found new cities in a different way... I'll have to keep quiet before my colleagues and my bosses. They'd think that... They'd suppose that... I have a wife and children; they're asleep, dreaming; I see that she's smiling, things are all right in her dream, it's a good night; if only I could sleep; if only...

But the man can neither sleep nor "start everything over from the beginning." He cannot state his secret thoughts to his wife, in the presence of his peers, or his employers, he cannot even imagine clearly their precise objections to his views (so American, after all!). In a previous finial he does remark, however, about his own spouse: "She'd think I'm not normal, she'd tell me to go see a psychoanalyst."

Besides the nightmares and the soliloquies at twilight, defensive and offensive whisperings occur in broad daylight. In "Tennessee" a series of finials catches fragments of a Souther-

213

ner's efforts to explain to Northerners the seething Negro spirit (see *F*, 264 ff.; *E*, 253 ff.):

> We don't make the mistake of thinking these Negroes are weak, we don't think they are going to disappear, blend like a stream in the ocean of whiteness... /... But at least for a while they keep in the shadow, they know their hour is not yet come, they no longer strut around in the same way, for a little while, a very little while; they feed on this shadow...

In the next State, "Texas," the whispering issues from a Negro who is seducing a cooperative white girl on the beach (*F*, 291; *E*, 279):

> The sea,
>   your tears are salty like the sea,
> don't be afraid,
>   nothing will happen to you,
> I'm going to give you a little of my blackness,
>   a little sand will be left in your hair.

The people uttering the words in these instances of overheard speech matter very little. *Mobile* incorporates the utterances as whisperings *heard*. They saturate the American land- and mind-scape as heard, not as spoken. Far from lying in the revelation of what the minority does or says, their truth protrudes in how the majority responds. The present-day condescending efforts and counter-prejudices to promote and to placate "minority groups" suggest the impotence of the American mind to live up to its doctrines, to cope with the fact, and to acknowledge the deep-rooted failure merely apparent in social tensions but most fundamentally grounded in forgetfulness of the inherent risks and shortcomings in the doctrine itself. *Mobile* articulates this fundamental oblivion.

The finials from Jefferson's writings show the aspirations at their point of emergence, when they were known as ideas correlative to contravening facts. The dream and whispering finials echo the leftovers of this tradition in the mode of haunted oblivion. Jefferson's haunting voice thereby mingles with a haunted Everyman's voice. The effect of this technique is deliberate: the tragedy can only be *ours*. Since the voices are in effect our own, no separate tragic figure can come forward.

Discrepancy between idea and fact does not constitute failure. An idea functions as leading the way, as outstripping the fact. Failure consists in forgetting the task, and manifests itself in a general confusion as to the difference between the two. The seeds of any remarkable failure are sown in the original effort. In the case of America, the germinal failure sprouts already from the abandonment of old selves. This heritage denies the necessity to retain heritage. The failure is obviously internal, and any observable defects are merely partial, no doubt temporarily corrigible manifestations.

Tragedy, however, does not consist in failure alone; if such were the case we would all be tragic figures without the mediation of art works. Rather, it lies in a developed willingness to affirm circumstances emergent *through* the constructs of our efforts. Thus the difference within tragedy is not one between ideals and facts, the latter having to conform to the former, but one between configuration and emergence, the constructs of the former having to converge on the circumstances of the latter. *Mobile* fragments and intersperses both tragic and haunted voices among other finials reflecting *places*. Thus these voices can bring *things* to light, not by their own intention as historical or sociological phenomena, but by their arrangement in the work.

The ultimate affirmation is possible only when the original aspiration comes back to haunt. For only then can we acknowledge the difference between configuration (what now haunts in the way of doctrines and deeds) and emergence (our actual circumstances, the place where we live). Thus in *Mobile* the haunting never ceases, and it assumes multiple forms. Unlike the ghost in Shakespeare's *Hamlet*, the ghosts of *Mobile* are catholic, recurrent, and ours.

In Butor's work we hear the voice of wealth and its problems, the voices of religious freedom and religious persecution, and the voice of Eastern prejudice against the West. The voices recalling the American Indians exemplify especially well the tragic strain developed in *Mobile*. We have already remarked (in the section on the "Style of Address") on the ironic entry of the theme of the Indians, from the standpoint of today's reservations. But our distant forefathers also addressed themselves directly to the Original Americans. For instance, we hear William Penn speaking to the Deleware Indians (see "Indiana," *F*, 73 ff.; *E*, 70 ff.; and *F*, 133; *E*, 127):

"... And when the Great God brings me among you, I intend to order all things in such a manner that we may all live in Love and Peace with one another... "/"... I have already taken care that

215

none of my people wrong you, by good Laws I believe I have provided for that purpose... "

Penn's melancholy text dates back to 1682. Over one hundred years later President Thomas Jefferson stands in for the same voice when addressing the Cherokee Indians (*F*, 315; *E*, 302):

"... Tell all your chiefs, your men, women and children, that I take them by the hand and hold it fast. That I am their father, wish their happiness and well-being, and am always ready to promote their good. My children, I thank you for your visit and pray to the Great Spirit who made us all and planted us all in this land to live together like brothers that he will conduct you safely to your homes, and grant you to find your families and your friends in good health."

Amongst these well-meaning words from our heritage, *Mobile* integrates finial after finial recalling the gradual extermination of the Indians, yet also what these Original Americans did with the land apart from the intrusions of "the white invader." Once again, the history is repeated, the heritage retrieved in the form of a ghost demanding its due.

The unsettled significance of the Indians for our own relation to the land surfaces already in "North Carolina" and "Arizona," as discussed above. In its entirety *Mobile* constructs an America which appears as a floating configuration conspicuously lacking any roots in the earth: the Howard Johnson ice creams, the delapidated automobiles speeding along the highways, the historical ideas sadly out of tune with the voices of the present. Now, the Indians appearing in the work contrast strikingly with all other elements in the land- and mind-scape. They have, or had, roots. Their hunting habits and burial rites show them belonging to the country; they respected the land, thought of themselves as products and custodians of the earth. We read (*F*, 229-30; *E*, 219-20):

In 1855, the Indian chief Seattle, who gave his name to the largest city in Washington, ... declared to the European negotiators: "Every bit of this land is sacred ... Every hill, valley or plain, every woods has been sanctified by some glorious or horrible event in the past. Even the rocks that seem mute and dead when they bake in the sun, tremble with extraordinary events linked to the life of my people ... When the children of your children will suppose themselves alone in the fields, the shops, on the roads or in the silent forests, they will not be alone at all ... At night, when all sound has died away in the streets of your villages, and when you think they are empty, they will swarm with the host of those who once lived there, faithful to that sublime site. The white man will never be alone."

Yet the white man arrived determined to build an empire on strictly human terms, perhaps with reference to a divine plan, but with no genuine relation to the earth. Not that human construction can devise such a relation. On the contrary, the construction must issue from prior roots in the earth, and no amount of revision after the fact can institute what has been missing from the start. At a later date, ownership is the only relation with the land one can inaugurate: property bounded by surveyor's marks if not actually fenced in. In his letter of 1806 to the Cherokees, Jefferson urges the Indians to cease hunting, an occupation assuming that the land is a gift, to engage in farming and thereafter to institute laws protecting property. In general the white man espoused this policy, at least as a political gambit. As property owners, the Indians would fit into his society. However, this dream could only materialize if the Indians formed an agrarian society based on the laws of private property. Yet these precepts alienate man from the earth and violate the one principle defining the Original Americans. A number of finals in *Mobile* recall the threat to this principle; for instance (*F*, 53; *E*, 51):

> ... "You ask me to work the soil; I would have to cut off my mother's breast. When I die, she will no longer take me in.... To cut the grass to make hay. How would I dare cut my mother's hair?" And to the white men who seized his land: "I want my people to remain here with me. The dead will return, their spirits will be reincarnated. We must stay, for here was the abode of our fathers; we must prepare to meet them again in the breast of our mother the earth."

Whereas the white man knew property as the only possible relation to the land, this was an unknown category for the Indians. The Indian wars were waged over *whether* the land was to be owned, not over who would own it. Western Canada, for instance, was spared much of such hostility because the white man's relation to the land was dictated in a wholesale manner by the Hudson's Bay Company and by the English Crown; here property was not so conspicuously private and therefore not nearly as contentious an issue as south of the border.

Juxtaposing these elements from the American heritage, *Mobile* elicits the tragic strain of our history. On the one hand, the white man in the United States *had* to exterminate the Indians. His own ideas about property fired him on in this, not the Indians. Yet the Indians represented perhaps the *only* possibility of rootedness in the new land. In murdering the Indians, the white man cut off the one link he might have had with the earth. We can only surmise what America would be like today, had our forefathers miraculously renounced their idea of property and, as Jefferson had hoped, affirmed that white man and Indian alike were "planted... in this land to live together like brothers"—but partly on the basis of Indian autochthony rather than strictly on the white man's terms.

But does *Mobile* simply aim at exposing the scandals in American history? Would the constructive task not be to elucidate the positive features in America, and to point the way toward a more healthy response to circumstances? Does not the work, and our critique of it, run the risk of impotent and ill-tempered indignation?

Mobile is an art work. Its materials, the American heritage, haunt us and all mankind. It incorporates haunting and haunted voices in the faith that readers who participate in an artful representation of the materials can finally respond to their source. *Through* these materials, especially the voices, we might heed the demands laid upon us—for ourselves, our ancestors, and our posterity. Initially we interpret these demands in terms of a doctrine, the idea of the reborn self. Ultimately, we must understand them in reference to the land and the people—in short, the "things themselves" rather than our ideas about them.

Juxtaposing haunting and haunted voices with the givens of the land and the people, *Mobile* prevents the negativity of the scandal from negating America as a whole. For the technique here distinguishes between the oblivious *constructs* overlaying America and the "things themselves" of America. This special configuration may momentarily pain us, and precisely because the materials are drawn directly from historical documents. But simultaneously the pain merely marks the passage toward the emergence of America to which we must ultimately respond. And this final response is essentially affirmation.

Cruel fate becomes joyful destiny if only we turn around and head into our heritage. Paradoxically, our native insistence on "looking to the brighter side" stems from an ever growing denial of the factual dimensions of the situation in which we live. Refusing to bear the burdens of the past we deny everything definite in the present: here we witness a deplorable caricature of the reborn self knowing only the future, i.e., staking everything out in a never-never land. It is, then, not in our successes that we must find rebirth, but in our failures.

To alleviate the tragic tension, *Mobile* often yields to comic relief. Not only the comedy of abundance flows through the book, also numerous other comedies usurp momentarily the very materials presented in the manner of tragedy. Comedy makes light of the oblivion which tragedy shows in the painful process of dissolution.

Through a night tour of Washington, D.C., "Maryland" introduces most conspicuously one of the several comedies touching directly on the tragic dimension of the American heritage. Here the "guide" addresses us as an anthropologist explaining the American society, with its monuments resembling those of Imperial Rome, as one more specimen along with weird tribes of Africa and South America—and our own Indians. On the seven pages (*F*, 131 ff.; *E*, 125 ff.) there are about thirty major finials. Three of these may serve as examples:

> The most important religious practice of the American Europeans is the pilgrimage to the sacred city of Washington, where the principle temples and the essential government organizations are located.
> . . .

> The three divinities Washington, Jefferson and Lincoln are the most important in the American pantheon; hence it is not surprising to find them carved in colossal proportions on Mount Rushmore, South Dakota. The American Europeans consider the artisan who executed this work to have given evidence of the greatest piety.
> . . .

> The ceremonies and sacred objects of the American Europeans are perhaps less finished than those of the Hopi or Zuni Indians, but they represent nonetheless a totality of the same order that succeeds in connecting not hundreds but millions of individuals.

No doubt these finials mock us. But the underlying accuracy of their depictions belies the hasty judgement that they are meant as satirical distortion. Furthermore, since *Mobile* as a whole articulates a movement *into* heritage, the tone of these finials is not one of indignant sarcasm. Wherein, then, lies the humor?

First of all, of course, the "guide" does not expound the subject in the language to which we have been conditioned. We

219

are addressed with a familiar content, but the form is that of a Martian surveying "objectively" the various cultures of the world. A court jester commonly employs such comical objectivity to pierce the established views of kings and courtiers, stating immediately *what* is viewed and also reflecting the pretensions and rigidities which have led to a generalized oblivion of the issues. Americans do indeed make pilgrimages to their "historical sites" in Washington, D.C.—just as the Christian pilgrims would travel to Lourdes or Rome. They *do* deify historical personages in the hope of reviving the American spirit. And the ceremonies and monuments *are* less refined than aboriginal ones, and a bit awkward.

More deeply, however, the humor derives from the American mind's yearning for support from history, and this after its insistence upon independent rebirth of selfhood and the concomitant need to abandon the old. We may call it pride in the principles of freedom, but to a Martian or a court jester it would be a curious faith in the efficacy of the dead. We thus discern the logical inconsistency of the caricature into which the doctrine of the reborn self easily and factually falls. The caricature is comical rather than tragic because the need for tradition here appears innocuous rather than pernicious. While truly reflecting the oblivion into which American principles can fall, the caricature reveals so wholesomely and effectively the inadequacy of this answer to the craving for tradition that the need is not even vitiated, but reasserts itself untouched and unperverted.

Other prominent comedies of a tragic vein in *Mobile* include the sequence of extracts from the prospectus for the "Chapel Lake Indian Ceremonials" (commencing on *F*, 82; *E*, 79); for instance:

> "Michigan's Thrilling—New—Outdoor Live Indian Drama! Giant Cast of Real North American Indians!..."
>
> . . .
>
> "The throbbing drums of the Red Man beat again! His ceremonial fires burn bright! The voice of the Great Spirit calls! The eagle—the Thunder Bird—flies again!... "

Also, the bizarre extracts from press releases, testimonials, and the official prospectus for "Freedomland" (starting on *F*, 182; *E*, 175, and spreading over some seventy-five pages):

220

"Freedomland ranks as the world's largest outdoor family entertainment center; situated in a 205-acre arena, the U.S.-shaped park
spans 85 acres, with the remainder devoted to parking and service
facilities. Previous world's largest—in California—covered 65
acres... "

. . .

"Now you and your family live the fun, the adventure, the drama of
America's past, present and future! Now for the first time anywhere,
journey across a continent—across 200 years—to enjoy the entertainment thrill as big as America itself!... "

And finally, of course, there is the literature made available by
the chain of cafeterias known as "Clifton's," where one can
participate simultaneously in Modern Plastic and Ancient
Christian culture (see *F*, 234 ff.; *E*, 223 ff.):

... A red forest scene made of 10,000 miniature pieces lights up
while a recording of "Parable of the Redwoods" plays...
. . .

"... Comments of visitors are varied. They reveal an inward hunger
not to be satisfied by 'bread alone.'..."

In all these cases claiming to represent heritage (Indian life, free
institutions, and Christian faith, respectively), *Mobile* portrays
as hilarious the discrepancy between the reality and the pretension.

Perhaps *Mobile* concentrates heavily on the comical sides of
the tragedy because Americans themselves are not yet accus-
tomed to the pain which must be endured in any acknowledgement of failure where a self must emerge and assume direct
responsibility for the situation that remains. Before one can
assume such responsibility, one must accept the oblivion. While
comedy allows and encourages this acceptance, it also silently
suggests the next step. Failure teaches us something of our
mortality. And acknowledging our own essential mortality, we
are able to affirm what we face.

5. SOME CONCLUDING THOUGHTS

We have ranged far and wide in this and in the previous Chapters. At times our explorations have forged beyond the confines of the works under consideration, and even beyond the province of art itself. Yet the materials gathered on such occasions have been the ones integrated into the works, by way of presentation or response. Such is the function of art itself: to fetch the forces and issues arising in the human sojourn and to configure them into a convergence inviting renewed response.

Our own critique has emphasized the multiple kinds and myriad shapes of forces and issues. We may ask, then, whether there is *one* matter which appears central to the material of art works—at least in the works to which we have devoted our critical attention and which we hold to be particularly powerful in their address.

It has been implicit from the start that we today live within the purview of formalism. Rimbaud's and Mallarmé's poems are already responding to the developments within the human condition which now appear steadfast and localized in Butor's *Mobile*.

Formalism affirms movement without origins. Thus it *denies* the need of ongoing human construction to acknowledge roots in either selfhood or thinghood. Since art does adumbrate such origins, and since all true art works work with the forces of their age, artists and poets now have to make transparent materials which not only resist but also deny and, left to themselves, essentially destroy the origins which must reappear in their work. To understand the task of art today, we should not underestimate the prevalence of formalism.

Very early in our history, most obviously with the influential works of Bacon and Descartes but also sooner, the Western mind saw in conceptual systems a sort of salvation for man, for herein he could take his stand and through them he could contemplate and manipulate his circumstances. The situation of man here appears like unto a balloon: whatever is important to the human condition must enter completely into the sphere of human control; what remains outside can at most serve as material for the insides. Although philosophers fought for this view against the resistance of the Christian-classical tradition during the 17th and 18th centuries, the seeds were sown at the very beginning, in the land of our origins. For already Socrates' sense of the human condition recommends that the individual overcome his initial concerns for what happens to him and learn to take his stand in a mode of activity: only then (as Plato developed the point, and after him Aristotle), could a man see into things as they are in themselves and adjust his sight to them. If, on the other hand, man tries to have things as he would like to be affected by them, he becomes essentially passive, pathetic, and impotent, even if frenzied. The Stoics, however, abandoned the reference to the things themselves which grounded the insight, and rooted the activity in man himself; they envisioned the human condition purely in terms of the activity of the soul, with express indifference to circumstances.

The Western ambition takes a most telling form in Hegel's works. These accept explicitly the modern presumption that "anything true must be taken up and put forth not only as *substance*, but equally so as *subject*" (*Phenomenology*, Preface). That is, anything affirmable by man must ultimately *be* man, drawing its meaning and function from the conceptual framework. However, Hegel endeavored to show, in addition, that every single concept requires us ultimately to stand not safely within, but on the edge of the system, with one foot beyond: "anything true ... is an uncanny overstep of the inner into the outer" (*Philosophy of Right*, §270), i.e., for anything to be meaningful to us we must "step out" of the balloon which at any given moment seems to protect us from the givens of that moment. Hegel's notorious remark that "the true is the whole" states the task: without the "overstep" any given conceptual framework collapses. Only man-on-the-edge, man as "spirit finding itself in absolute torn-apartness," man as carrying a whole while "facing the negative"—only this spirit "wins its truth" (*Phenomenology*, Preface). Yet Hegel's statement of his project blatantly contrasts with the reception of his work in the English-speaking world: his followers and critics understand it as a justification of simple idealism, of the absolute as a balloon already containing all the essentials.

Now that the original ambition asserts itself as firmly established, we witness formalism in the precepts of nearly any academic discipline. Nowadays average intellectual work has become an empty, even if sometimes useful exercise. Not that competence has declined. Rather, the defining tasks expressly deny roots. Our not too distant forefathers in the sciences, in philosophy, and in the liberal professions endeavored to bring

223

into view, through research, example, and speech, the possibility and the urgency of a "higher" order of things knowable, a "deeper" insight into the world, a "greater" understanding of the human condition. The quoted qualifications took their meaning from a concern for *purpose*. The contemporary intellectual who "fits in" with his times and colleagues never "researches" purposes. These must be supplied by each individual on an *ad hoc* basis—as a "subjective" even if collective matter. Without always knowing it, present-day intellectuals are living out the decrees of Bacon, Descartes, and Spinoza who saw clearly that, in order to promote the construction of efficacious conceptual frameworks, we must strive to exclude all consideration of purpose (Leibniz and Kant indirectly cooperated in this project by reinstating such consideration on the strictly moral plane, thus securing it within the balloon).

First of all in America, but now also in Europe, Western man has committed himself to a political and economic system which needs and encourages the formalism currently predominant in intellectual work. For we believe that all legitimate structures of society merely provide channels for individual enterprise and avoid any stipulation of substantive goals. As the years go by, legislation becomes more and more stripped down to the regulation of commerce and industry; laws enacted against pollution and in favor of strictly individual well-being are justified in terms of long-range forecasts of energy needs and health costs. Formal goals, like full-employment, reduction of poverty, control of inflation, simply project *means* allowing for greater mobility within the social context of the individual's life. Purposes, including moral rectitude (in relation to such questions as concern abortion, use of drugs, pornography) belong to the realm of personal preference: otherwise they mushroom into encroachments upon the freedom of others. When the Declaration of Independence included, besides the then familiar rights to life and liberty, the hitherto unheard-of right to the pursuit of happiness, it stated an ideology to end all ideologies: the individual must make his *own* way toward purposes, the State and all publicly funded effort must merely provide structures essentially devoid of direction. In Britain and America mainstream philosophy has completely espoused this anti-ideology: witness any variety of the linguistic, analytic, or neo-positivistic movements—the research of means for searching out means, a metaposition absolutely clean of any purpose of its own and so perfectly adaptable to any purpose whatsoever.

Formalism as an historical ambition and as an intellectual exercise debouches into modern consumerism: frenetic ingestion of social products, movement without real reference and entailing, among other debasements, principled loss of discrimination. Consumerism is not merely a human disposition toward dissipation and distraction through self-deluded, frenzied, and purposeless movement—always thought to characterize the rabble, the masses, the crowd (to use terms interestingly out of favor among intellectuals nowadays). Rather, it is a structured faith that this disposition locates the heart of human nature and therefore deserves unending attention and assiduous development. Our forefathers were told to rise above the disposition, we are told to enhance, perhaps even slightly to redirect it.

If consumerism were merely a human disposition and not, in addition, a structured faith justified daily on the intellectual level, then its denial of the need for transparency to origins other than ongoing construction would have no force except inertia, and only human lethargy would stand accused. The lameness of efforts to compensate for the ills of the consumer society derives from the fact that the attitude behind such efforts is the very one causing the trouble in the first place. For instance, legislation aiming to control noise-pollution is justified in reference to decibels, toleration of the human nervous system, health costs, efficiency at work, etc.—categories which essentially bypass the simplest concrete instance of disturbance and cannot at all account for an environment in which peace has a time and place of its own. According to the dictates of enlightened egoism, we can cut back this or that activity entailing ill side-effects, but we cannot proceed directly to create a peaceful environment.

How does *art* stand with regard to formalism as historical ambition, intellectual creed, and contemporary plight? Artistic *talent* is certainly not lacking today. Commercial design on the one hand, and the ever growing entertainment industry on the other, demand and discover technical skill which leads to many technically perfect productions, particularly for television. However, in these productions the point of focus lies distressingly outside the work. By artificially moulding human needs and evoking groundless sentiment, such talent remains in the service of what it might otherwise overcome.

225

Art works, on the other hand, fulfil their destiny not when they fit into their age, and neither when they simply go beyond it. They are great when they gather up the forces within their age and create something from what is otherwise without origins— without any reality of self or thing. The works we have considered are essentially significant because they respond to, while neither endorsing nor abandoning, the forces of formalism.

SELECTED AND ANNOTATED BIBLIOGRAPHIES

A. *Works cited in the text.* (N.B.: editions are those on hand, not necessarily first editions.)

Anderson, John M. *The Individual and the New World.* State College, 1955.
Aristotle. *Works.* The Loeb Classical Library. London, 1926-1975.
Augustine. *The Confessions.* New York, 1960.
Balzac, Honoré de. *La Comédie humaine.* Edition de la Pléiade. Paris, 1976.
Bacon, Francis. *New Organon.* New York, 1960.
Baudelaire, Charles. *Oeuvres complètes.* Edition de la Pléiade. Paris, 1961.
Bible: An American Translation. Chicago, 1939.
Bible: The Greek New Testament. New York, 1966.
Brown, Dee. *Bury my Heart at Wounded Knee.* New York, 1971.
Buber, Martin. *Ich und Du.* Heidelberg, 1958.
Bugbee, Henry. *The Inward Morning.* State College, 1958.
Butor, Michel. *Mobile. Etude pour une représentation des Etats-Unis.* Paris, 1962.
————. *Mobile. Study for a Representation of the United States.* New York, 1963.
Charbonnier, Georges. *Entretiens avec Michel Butor.* Paris, 1967.
Collingwood, R. G. *The Principles of Art.* New York, 1958.
Conrad, Joseph. *Lord Jim.* New York, 1966.
Dewey, John. *Art as Experience.* New York, 1958.
Diels, Hermann. *Fragmente der Vorsokratiker.* Zurich, 1966.
Faulkner, William. *Go Down Moses.* New York, 1973.
Goethe, Johann Wolfgang von, *Faust, eine Tragodie* (I & II). Boston, 1954-5.
Hegel, G. W. F. *Ästhetik.* Berlin, 1955.
————. *Grundlinien der Philosophie des Rechts.* Hamburg, 1955.
————. *Phänomenologie des Geistes.* Hamburg, 1952.
Henri, Robert. *The Art Spirit.* New York, 1960.
Homer. *Iliad.* Tr. Lattimore. Chicago, 1951.
————. *Odyssey.* Tr. Lattimore. Chicago, 1968.
Jefferson, Thomas. *The Life and Selected Writings of Thomas Jefferson.* New York, 1944.
Kant, Immanuel. *Kritik der reinen Vernunft.* Hamburg, 1960.
————. *Prolegomena zu einer jeden kunftigen Metaphysik.* Hamburg, 1957.
Lao Tzu. *Tao Teh Ching.* New York, 1961.
Mallarmé, Stéphane. *Oeuvres complètes.* Edition de la Pléiade. Paris, 1963.
Marcel, Gabriel. *Positions et approches concrètes du mystère de l'être.* Paris, 1967.
Marx, Karl. *Kapital.* Frankfurt am Main, 1961.
Melville, Herman. *Moby Dick.* New York, 1963.

Nietzsche, Friedrich. *Fröhliche Wissenschaft.* Stuttgart, 1965.

Pindar. *The Odes.* Tr. Lattimore. Chicago, 1959.

Plato. *Works.* The Loeb Classical Library. London, 1926-1970.

Proust, Marcel. *A la Recherche du temps perdu.* Edition de la Pléiade. Paris, 1954.

Rimbaud, Arthur. *Oeuvres complètes.* Edition de la Pléiade, Paris, 1963.

Robinson, Joan. *An Essay on Marxian Economics.* London, 1972.

Santayana, George. *Philosophical Opinion in America.* The Third Annual Philosophical Lecture (Henriette Hertz Trust) delivered January 30, 1918.

Shakespeare, William. *The Tragedy of Hamlet, Prince of Denmark.* New York, 1958.

Sophocles. *Oedipus the King.* The Loeb Classical Library. London, 1968.

St. Aubyn, F. C. "A propos de Mobile: Deuxième entretien avec Michel Butor." *French Review,* XXXVIII (1956).

Tocqueville, Alexis de. *Democracy in America.* New York, 1847.

Troloppe, Frances. *Domestic Manners of the Americans.* New York, 1949.

Turner, F. J. *The Frontier in American History.* New York, 1940.

Weber, Max. *The Protestant Ethic and the Spirit of Capitalism.* New York, 1958.

Welch, Cyril and Liliane. *Emergence: Baudelaire, Mallarmé, Rimbaud.* State College, 1973.

Whitman, Walt. *Leaves of Grass.* New York, 1968.

B. *Works in philosophy and literary criticism which speak to the concerns and issues of the present work.*

Adams, Henry. *Mont-Saint-Michel and Chartres.* Boston, 1913.

———. *The Education of Henry Adams.* Boston, 1918.

This pair displays the puzzling predicament of our age by means of a remarkable contrast. As the author himself says in the second of these works: "Eight or ten years of study had led Adams to think he might use the century 1150-1250, expressed in Amiens Cathedral and the Works of Thomas Aquinas, as a unit from which he might measure motion down to his own time.... Setting himself the task, he began a volume which he mentally knew as 'Mont-Saint-Michel and Chartres: a Study of Thirteenth-Century Unity.' From that point he proposed to fix a position for himself, which he could label: 'The Education of Henry Adams: a Study of Twentieth-Century Multiplicity'."

Anderson, John M. *The Realm of Art.* University Park, 1967.

A demonstration of the finitude of man taking concrete shape in art works. Analyzes examples from the various arts to show the momentary emergence of selfhood and thinghood.

Arendt, Hannah. *The Human Condition.* Chicago, 1958.

Basically a treatise in political philosophy, the book analyzes the differences among, and historical evolution of, the notions of labor, work and action to bring into relief the contemporary crises of urban life, finite concern, and the lack of autochthony.

Auerbach, Erich. *Mimesis: The Representation of Realty in Western Literature*. Tr. W. Trask. Garden City, 1953.
An exemplary study of detail, showing how relatively short passages from great works already display *within* themselves the sense of reality typical throughout the work of a given author.

Barthes, Roland. *Essais critiques*. Paris, 1964.
Contains the essay "La Littérature et le discontinu," the first positive evaluation of Butor's *Mobile*; stresses the stylistic as well as the semantic innovations of the work.

———. *Le Degré zéro de l'écriture*. Paris, 1953.
Argues that, besides style, language, and content, the "écriture" determines the force and direction of literature and therefore enters into the full reading of a text: this dimension is the text's insertion into history, a free act of historical solidarity. Barthes is of course here responding affirmatively and yet critically to Sartre's *Qu'est-ce que la littérature?*

Blanchot, Maurice. *La Part du Feu*. Paris, 1949.
Series of studies focusing on Kafka, Mallarmé, Rimbaud, Nietzsche and terminating with the long essay "La Littérature et le droit à la mort." The theme linking many essays is that of the death of God, which is posited as the condition for the possibility of modern literature.

———. *L'Espace littéraire*. Paris, 1955.
Tries to fathom the literary and artistic experience by questioning the works of Mallarmé, Hölderlin, Rilke and Kafka. The themes of solitude, communication and reading are broached as Blanchot discusses the future of art in contemporary society.

———. *Le Livre à venir*. Paris, 1959.
A reworking of some essays which appeared previously in the N.R.F. under the title of "Recherches." Focusing once again on such extreme literary figures as Artaud, Mallarmé, Broch, Beckett, Proust, the author moves in close to the themes of death, ennui, sterility, self-reflection and impersonality of the self which find expression in the language of contemporary art works.

Butor, Michel. *Le Génie du lieu*. Paris, 1958.
Poetic perceptions cast into prose form, this book is the first testimony of Butor's fascination with the special ethos of geographical places. What is blown out fully for the U.S. in *Mobile*, finds its roots here in the prose essays on Egypt, Cordoba, Istanbul, Salonika, Delphi, Malia, Mantua, and Ferrara.

———. *Répertoires I - IV*. Paris, 1960-1974.
A general collection of Butor's theoretical essays. Contains studies on the novel ("Le roman comme recherche", "Le roman et la poésie", "L'espace du roman", "Le livre comme objet"), on the preoccupation of major poets (Baudelaire, Breton, Proust, Appolinaire, Faulkner, Joyce, etc.), on music and painting (Boulez, Picasso, Mondrian, Rothko, Monet, Holbein).

Derrida, Jacques. *L'Écriture et la différence*. Paris, 1967.
The author takes issue with the entire Western philosophic tradition's preoccupation with metaphysics. He also probes into anthropology (Levi-Strauss, Rousseau), psychoanalysis (Freud), literature (Artaud, Genet, Jabès Leiris, Mallarmé, Valéry, Sollers), linguistics (Saussure, Benveniste, Austin) to fathom their antimetaphysical aspects.

———. *La Dissémination*. Paris, 1972.
Contains the author's most complete statement of his theory of "text." The author's "de-structuring" analysis of Mallarmé's *Coup de Dés* argues that all texts point to previous texts and are not grounded in any pre-textual experience. Derrida also claims that literary language does not hold a special position as Heidegger, for example, maintains.

Friedrich, Hugo. *Die Struktur der modernen Lyrik, von Baudelaire bis zur Gegenwart*. Reinbek bei Hamburg, 1956.
Traces the symptoms of Modernity from Baudelaire, Rimbaud, Mallarmé up to the contemporary poets of the Latin, Anglo-Saxon and Germanic countries. Underlines the destruction of classical harmony, dissonance, ruptures within style, and the correspondences of poetry with music, sculpture and painting.

Gadamer, Hans Georg. *Wahrheit und Methode—Grundzüge einer philosophischen Hermeneutik*. Tübingen, 1960.
Provides a sound philosophical argument showing the peculiarities of reading tradition-bearing texts and demonstrating the necessity of participation, if not radical creativity.

Heidegger, Martin. *Erlauterungen zu Hölderlins Dichtung*. Frankfurt am Main, 1951.
Especially memorable series of four essays interpreting individual poems of Hölderlin. The essay "Hölderlin und das Wesen der Dichtung" enlarges the inquiry into a general discussion of the historical role of poetry and of the nature of language. Perhaps the most incisive contemporary statement of the function of poetry in the human condition.

———. *Holzwege*. Frankfurt am Main, 1957.
Especially noteworthy for our concerns. The essay "Der Ursprung des Kunstwekes" grounds the work of art in the difference between world and earth and interprets truth to be the manifest articulation of this difference.

———. *Sein und Zeit*. Tübingen, 1927.
The most original analysis of the human condition and interpretation of human possibilities since Kant's *Critique of Pure Reason*. Provides the foundation for many of the most incisive works of literary interpretation since World War II.

———. *Unterwegs zur Sprache*. Pfullingen, 1959.
Studying the poetry of Trakl, George and Hölderlin, Heidegger shows how poetry uncovers the hidden nature of language and how "language is the house of Being." An unequivocal endorsement of poetic language as original language, ordinary language being "fallen."

Jauss, H. R. *Literatur als Provokation*. Frankfurt am Main, 1970.
————. *Ästhetische Erfahrung und literarische Hermeneutik*. Munich, 1977.
  The author works out a new critical stance for the historian of literature: reception, discrimination and productive reinterpretation.

Merleau-Ponty, Maurice. *Phénoménologie de la perception*. Paris, 1945.
  A phenomenological analysis of man's being in the world. Especially helpful for understanding the spatiality and temporality of the human condition and the task of philosophy and poetry.

Natanson, Maurice. *Literature, Philosophy, and the Social Sciences*. The Hague, 1962.
  A collection of essays in which the author relates a number of issues, many arising in and about poetic works, to the philosophical principles of Husserl and Sartre. Of special interest in this regard are "Phenomenology and the Theory of Literature" and "Existentialism and the Theory of Literature," which raise the question, both methodological and substantive, What happens when we read a work of literature?

Piguet, Jean-Claude. *La Connaissance de l'individuel et la logique du réalisme*. Neuchatel, 1975.
  An extensive work, at the heart of which lies the distinction between "internal" and "external" totalities, the basis of which requires that we learn what the author calls the "semantic reversal."

Poulet, Georges. *Etudes sur le temps humain*. Paris, 1950.
————. *La Distance intérieure*. Paris, 1952.
————. *Les Métamorphoses du cercle*. Paris, 1961.
  All three provide phenomenological studies of time and space in a number of French authors more or less representative of their period. The second and third each contain an essay on Mallarmé.
————. *La Conscience critique*. Paris, 1971.
  A series of essays studying the critical positions of poets (such as Baudelaire and Proust) and of the most prominent contemporary critics (Richard, Bachelard, Blanchot, Starobinski, Sartre, Blin, Barthes). Contains also an illuminating exegesis of the dialectics of reading in the penultimate essay entitled "Phénoménologie de la conscience critique."

Richard, Jean-Pierre, *Poésie et profondeur*. Paris, 1955.
  Aspires to capture the literary creation at its birth, seeing how consciousness faces the world and defines itself in the works of Nerval, Baudelaire, Rimbaud and Verlaine. Shows how the various images arise from sensorial awareness and betray differing obsessions for depth in the four poets studied.
————. *L'Univers imaginaire de Mallarmé*. Paris, 1961.
  The most complete exegesis of Mallarmé's entire work. Preceded by a lengthy introductory essay on Richard's methodology which illustrates his theories with poetic virtuosity.

231

Sartre, Jean-Paul. *Qu'est-ce que la littérature?* Paris, 1948.
  Discusses dialectically the nature and function of writing. Sees
  prose writing in terms of its audience and the role of the writer as
  positing his own freedom while also bringing about social
  changes. Gives a sweeping history of the writer's role in French
  society from the Middle Ages up through World War II.

Sennet, Richard. *The Fall of Public Man.* New York, 1977.
  The book thoughtfully traces the retreat into impotent privacy
  (narcissism) through the last two centuries, with special attention
  given to the developments of the theater in London and Paris. In
  effect, the book responds to the question: How is it that we refuse
  to live where we obviously are—in the cities?

Starobinski, Jean. *L'Oeil vivant.* Paris, 1961.
  Provides a phenomenology of "the eye" and "the glance"
  and shows their literary importance in Corneille, Racine, Rousseau and Stendhal. The Introduction elicits the paradoxes of
  reading and writing. Asks the questions whether behind the surface of reality and literature true Being looms, whether man can
  grasp Being, and whether appearances cover not merely Nothingness.
———. *La Relation critique. L'Oeil vivant II.* Paris, 1970.
  The excellent first essay continues to delve into the peculiar
  relationship between the critic and the work of literature while
  stressing the forever shifting optics of the production-reception
  process keeping literary works alive. Contains also an essay on
  the contributions of the German critic Leo Spitzer and a section
  delineating the rapport between literature and psychoanalysis.

Staiger, Emil. *Grundbegriffe der Poetik.* Zurich, 1946.
  An instructive attempt to explicate a new basis for the generic
  terms of poetics. In the categories of the lyric, the epic, and the
  dramatic the author sees fundamental possibilities of human
  destiny. Thus literary theory contributes to reflection on the
  human condition itself.

Taylor, Charles. *Hegel.* Cambridge, 1975.
  The first and final chapters state in great detail the plight of
  modern man living his "public" life according to the dated dictates
  of the Enlightenment and his "private" life in accord with a
  frustrated Romanticism. In reference to Hegel, the author argues
  that we today must develop a way of thinking (ideation) affirming
  man's freedom as *situated* freedom (while dropping the Hegelian
  claim to absolute and therefore situationless insight). In effect, an
  introduction to contemporary reflection as a whole (as has been
  unfolding in Europe since World War I).

Welch, Cyril. *The Sense of Language.* The Hague, 1973.
  Revolves around the premonition that speaking and listening,
  reading and writing owe their sense to the configuration of
  meanings converging upon a moment.

INDEX

233